ALSO BY MAURENE GOO

Since You Asked
The Way You Make Me Feel

I BELIEVE

IN A

THING

CALLED

LOVE

I BELIEVE
IN A
THING
CALLED
LOVE

Maurene Goo

SQUARE
FISH

MARGARET FERGUSON BOOKS

FARRAR STRAUS GIROUX
New York

SQUARE
FISH

An imprint of Macmillan Publishing Group, LLC
175 Fifth Avenue, New York, NY 10010
fiercereads.com

Square Fish and the Square Fish logo are trademarks of Macmillan and
are used by Farrar Straus Giroux under license from Macmillan.

Our books may be purchased in bulk for promotional, educational, or business use.
Please contact your local bookseller or the Macmillan Corporate and Premium
Sales Department at (800) 221-7945 ext. 5442 or by e-mail at
MacmillanSpecialMarkets@macmillan.com.

Library of Congress Cataloging-in-Publication Data

Names: Goo, Maurene, author.
Title: I believe in a thing called love / Maurene Goo.
New York : Farrar Straus Giroux, 2017. | "Margaret Ferguson Books." | Summary:
   A disaster in romance, high school senior Desi Lee decides to tackle her flirting
   failures by watching Korean television dramas, where the hapless heroine always
   seems to end up in the arms of her true love by episode ten.
Identifiers: LCCN 2016035865 (print) | LCCN 2017009716 (ebook) | ISBN
   978-1-250-15841-3 (paperback)   ISBN 978-0-374-30407-2 (ebook)
Subjects: | CYAC: Dating (Social customs)—Fiction. | Love—Fiction. | High
   schools—Fiction. | Schools—Fiction. | Korean Americans—Fiction.
Classification: LCC PZ7.G596 lah 2017 (print) | LCC PZ7.G596 (ebook) | DDC
   [Fic]—dc23
LC record available at https://lccn.loc.gov/2016035865

Originally published in the United States by Farrar Straus Giroux
First Square Fish edition, 2018
Book designed by Elizabeth H. Clark
Square Fish logo designed by Filomena Tuosto

5   7   9   10   8   6

LEXILE: HL690L

To anyone who has fallen in love
with love through K dramas

I BELIEVE

IN A

THING

CALLED

LOVE

PROLOGUE

When I was seven, I thought I moved a pencil with my mind.

I heard this story about a man who taught himself how to see through objects so that he could cheat at card games. The idea was that if he reached a state of complete concentration and focus, he could do things with his mind that normal humans were incapable of, like levitate, walk on coals, and move objects. All of which he learned to do. The very first thing he tried, however, was staring at an object for hours to make it move.

So, late one afternoon, I cleared off my desk and placed a rabbit-patterned pink mechanical pencil on the pristine, flat surface.

I shut my bedroom door and closed all my curtains, shrouding the room in darkness as the sun started to set. I sat at my desk and stared at the pencil. Willing it to move.

I stared and stared. For what felt like hours. When my dad knocked on my door I shrieked, *"I need privacy!"* and kept my eyes on the pencil. He grumbled from the other side but eventually shuffled away.

When it was dinnertime, he pounded on the door and said that I needed to eat. "Privacy pause!" he hollered.

My mouth was parched and I was starving, but I kept my eyes fixed on the rabbit patterns on that pencil and told my dad to leave the food outside my door.

Instead, he opened the door and popped his head in. "Desi?" he called out.

"Appa, I am trying to do something very important here," I said.

A normal dad would probably have demanded an explanation from his seven-year-old daughter. Showed some mild curiosity as to why she was holed up in her bedroom staring at a pencil for hours.

But this was *my* dad. And his daughter happened to be *me*. So he shrugged and went to make me a tray of fish, rice, and beef radish soup, which he carried to my desk. Careful not to disturb the pencil.

I smelled the food and felt faint. But I wouldn't let myself move my eyes from the pencil.

"Um, Appa . . . ?"

Without a word, my dad scooped up some rice, dipped it into the soup, and brought the spoon to my mouth. I ate it in one big bite. Next, he took the chopsticks and fed me some of the fish. I nibbled it. He brought a glass of water to my lips and I gulped it gratefully.

When I had finished most of the food, my dad patted my back and made his way out with tray in hand. Before closing the door behind him he said, "Don't stay up too late."

Refueled, and my brain feeling stronger than ever, I continued to stare at that pencil.

So what then? Well, I swear on my life, to this very day, that this thing happened: That pencil moved. It was the slightest of movements—probably not discernible to anyone except me, but the second I saw that pink pencil roll *ever so slightly* toward me and then come to a stop, I shrieked. I jumped out of my seat and pulled at my hair in disbelief. I ran around in circles and did a little dance. And then I face-planted into my bed and fell asleep.

I tried the trick with a few other objects—an eraser that smelled like a strawberry, a ballerina cake topper, a single pine nut. But no dice. Despite that, for years after, I believed I could move things with my mind. I secretly knew that I existed in this very special little sphere where magical things happened. Stuff that doesn't happen to normal humans, but rather to a select group of exceptional people.

This childhood belief in my powerful brain faded over time. I wasn't necessarily shaken out of it, or doused with the frigidity of the cold, hard truth of how unmagical real life was. I just eased out of that stage of my life.

But I never lost the belief that you could *will* something just by sticking to it, by being unwavering. By keeping your eyes on the prize. And by doing that, there was nothing you couldn't control about your own life.

This was a crazy-powerful tool to have at your disposal when you were seven years old and had just lost your mother. My memories of the time right after my mom's death have grown hazy, but they always involve a version of my dad that only existed in those months. A shadow of himself—someone who put me to bed, made dinner, and gave me the same amount of attention. But when he thought I wasn't looking, he was someone who sat in a chair for hours in the dark. Someone who watered my mom's geraniums at three a.m., who kept her alarm set at six a.m. even though he didn't have to be awake until an hour later. Someone who stared at an empty bowl for five minutes every morning—waiting for my mom's patented simultaneous-cereal-and-milk pouring. She always timed it exactly right so that the cornflakes and milk finished filling up the bowl at exactly the same time.

Then one day I overheard my aunt speaking in hushed tones to my uncle in our kitchen. "Time will heal all wounds."

And so I decided to speed up the process.

I broke my dad's alarm clock and tearfully showed him the pieces. It took him weeks to replace it, and when he did, he had it only set to seven a.m. Every morning I made sure his cereal was ready for him before he could sit and just stare at an empty bowl. And while he ate, I watered the geraniums.

Then my old dad returned. He put my mom's wedding band in a small porcelain dish and lovingly dusted all the photos of her around the house—and we moved on. The shadows under my dad's eyes faded and the geraniums flourished, climbing across our garage door.

Time, schmime. Desi Lee heals all wounds.

You just needed a plan, to take action. It's how I convinced my dad to let me raise geese in our backyard, how I saved our underfunded middle school library from closure, how I overcame a fear of heights by bungee jumping on my sixteenth birthday (with only a little pee escaping me), and how I became number one in my class year after year. I believed, and still believe, that you can build your dreams brick by brick. That you can accomplish anything with persistence.

Even falling in love.

CHAPTER 1

If you thought of life as a series of nostalgic images arranged in a slo-mo montage, you'd miss a lot of the tedious bits. In between the fuzzy images of blowing out birthday candles and first kisses would be a whole lot of sitting on your sofa watching TV. Or doing homework. Or learning how to create the perfect beach wave for your hair with a flatiron.

Or in my case, overseeing yet another school event. Like the fall carnival.

Add to that, some vomit.

I gingerly tapped Andy Mason's back as he hurled into a recycling bin. This was definitely one of those poignant scenes that would *not* make it into my life montage.

"All good?" I asked the six-feet-four tennis team captain as he straightened up. He wiped his mouth gingerly and nodded.

"Thanks, Des," he said sheepishly.

"No problem, but maybe don't go on the Brain Melter three times in a row?"

It was a Saturday night in late November and the Monte Vista High School fall carnival was in full swing on our campus—a sprawling state-of-the-art modern architectural wonder built on an Orange County seaside bluff.

Andy staggered off, passing by my best friend, Fiona Mendoza. She steered clear of him, wrinkling her nose. "A barfer?" she asked, wearing slouchy sweatpants, a crisp men's shirt, hiking sandals, and a lightning-bolt-patterned scarf. Her heavily lined amber eyes were staring at me, blinking slowly and deliberately. She would have looked like a Mexican American Disney princess if it weren't for the fact that she dressed like a hobo with a mean makeup collection.

"It's always the *huge* guys that have delicate little stomachs," I said.

"Lucky you." She winked.

I snorted. "Yeah, you *love* huge guys." Fiona, in fact, loved tiny girls.

My snort morphed into a hacking cough, and I bent over from the sheer force of it. When I straightened up Fiona was holding a thermos. "Your dad asked me to bring this to you," she said.

There were two cold-and-flu pills taped to the lid and I smiled when I saw the Post-it attached. My dad's scrawled handwriting read: *Eat a lot even if you feel like shitty!* There were black smudges on everything, the signature of a car mechanic.

I opened the thermos and the aroma of salty seaweed soup wafted out. "Mm, thanks Fi."

"You're welcome but why the hell are you here? Don't you have, like, the black lung?" she asked as we walked over to a bench and sat down.

"Because, hello, I'm in charge of it. Also, black lung is now commonly known as pneumonia. So no, I don't have that."

"You're in charge of *everything*. No offense, Desi, but this is just the lame-ass school carnival." Fiona draped herself across the bench. "Couldn't some underling in the student government have handled this?"

"Who? My hapless veep, Jordan?" Jordan was my vice president and was voted in primarily because of his hair. "He would have shown up tomorrow. No way. I didn't spend weeks planning this so that someone could mess up the Monte Vista carnival rep."

Fiona stared at me, letting the dorkiness of that statement settle between us. When I had been duly punished, she spoke. "Des, you need to chill. It's senior year, calm down already." Fiona's entire body punctuated that point—sitting cross-legged on the bench, one arm propped up on the armrest, her chin resting on it.

I took a sip of my soup before responding. "Have I been accepted into Stanford yet?"

Fiona straightened up then, pointing a long, glittery fingernail at me. "No! *No.* Once you turn that application in, I don't want to hear that word for the rest of the year." She paused dramatically. "Actually, never again for my entire life."

"Well, too bad!" I popped the pills into my mouth and downed some water.

She stared at me again, her gaze unnerving and a little scary. "Des, you're like a sure thing. If a nerd-Mother-Teresa-Miss-Teen-America like you doesn't get into that school, who will?"

I coughed again, a phlegmy rattle that harkened the end of days. Fiona visibly recoiled from me.

I pounded my chest before speaking. "Do you know how many kids look just like me on paper? A 4.25 GPA, student body president, varsity sports, perfect SAT score, one billion hours of community service?"

Fiona's expression slackened at this familiar refrain. "Well, isn't that why you requested an interview?" Her voice was on the edge of boredom as she eyed a group of girls walking by us. My best friend since second grade, Fiona had had the Desi Lee Stanford dream ballad memorized since I started belting it at the age of ten.

"Yeah, but the interview's in February, a month after I turn in my application. It's making me nervous now that the early action application deadline's actually passed," I muttered.

"Des, we've talked about this a million times. You *wanted* to do regular decision, better odds and all that?"

I poked at my soup. "Yeah, I know."

"So don't sweat it, okay?" Fiona patted my arm.

After I finished my soup Fiona bailed to go find our friend Wes Mansour. I roamed the carnival again—making sure the boys' junior varsity baseball team wasn't giving away all the plushie prizes to cute girls and keeping people from rioting while in the never-ending line for the soft-serve ice cream truck. I was headed toward the restrooms when I ran into a few juniors whom I recognized—a well-groomed boyish bunch with impeccable T-shirts and expensive kicks.

"Hey, boss. How's it going?" one of them asked me, all sparkly eyes and charm. The kind of guy *born* with a fedora jauntily perched on his head.

I felt their eyes on me and my cheeks flushed. "Um, good. Have fun!" I waved at them with awkward jazz hands before walking away. For God's sake. *Have fun!* Who was I—their *mom*? I was mentally kicking myself when someone grabbed me from behind.

"Yeah, what's up, *boss*?" The teasing voice was inches from my ear. Wes. Thick black hair set back into a kind of modern, perfectly mussed pompadour, the most immaculately smooth brown skin, and sleepy eyes always weighed down by his outrageous eyelashes. Girls loved him. Yes, my two best friends were these sexy people who reminded me of my own unsexiness on a daily basis.

I spun around and smacked his arm.

Wes clutched it and winced. "Use your words!" he barked. Fiona was behind him, holding a giant plastic bag full of pink cotton candy. I scowled at both of them but before I could respond, another coughing fit struck.

"Ew, Des," Wes said, covering his nose with his T-shirt collar. "I've got a huge game next week and if I get sick, I'll kill you." Like me, Wes was also a nerd jock. His sport of choice was basketball, his science of choice physics, his geekery of choice comics and Settlers of Catan. He once held the number one ranking online for three months until he got beaten by an eight-year-old girl from Brazil.

"It's good to get exposed to germs, you know," I said, and cleared my throat violently. Both Wes and Fiona made faces.

"Spare us, Dr. Desi," Wes grumbled.

"Oh, I'm just getting started. Shall I start my lecture on the future of fecal transplants?"

Wes closed his eyes dramatically. "I'd like to go one week without having to hear about the merits of freaking gut bacteria."

I shrugged. "Fine. But you guys will all be thanking me later when I'm a doctor curing seasonal allergies with fecal transplants."

"God!" Fiona tossed the rest of her cotton candy into a trash can.

I waited for more complaints but instead I got silence. And strange expressions. Fiona and Wes were looking behind me. I turned around and stared into a very large chest.

"What are fecal transplants?" a low voice asked.

I looked up. Oh, Lord.

Max Peralta. Six feet two inches of hot, hot . . . freshman. Then I heard snickering behind me. When Fi and Wes had found out that my first-week-of-school crush had turned out to be a ninth grader—well, it was the best day *ever*.

"Oh, uh nothing. Hey, hi!" I said, my voice already at a weird level of dog-hearing-only pitch. *Desi, do NOT speak until you can freaking control your voice.*

He smiled, teeth white against tan, sun-kissed skin. Howww in God's name was *this* a freshman?

"Hey, so good job with the carnival, Desi."

I blushed, deeply. "Thanks, Max." *All right, you've got this. Just keep your expression cool, relax your shoulders, keep your natural eager-beaver instinct in check!*

He looked down at his feet for a second, then cocked his head up with a smile. *Dang.*

"Um, I was wondering . . . Are you busy after this?" he asked.

My voice caught in my throat. I cleared it. *NO squeaky voice!* "After . . . the carnival?"

"Yeah, do you have to, I don't know, clean up or something?"

My ears started to burn, and I could feel the friend eyeballs on me. "Nope, no cleaning. I'm free." Wait, was I encouraging this? He was cute, no doubt . . . but still a freshman.

It was like he read my mind. Keeping his eyes on mine, he asked, "I know you probably don't date freshmen . . . ?"

Ha-ha-ha: "date."

But he was right. He was a freshman. I was a senior. So I tried to muster a kind rejection. But instead, I felt a cough coming on. I put my hand to my chest and shut my mouth tight—*no, this was NOT the time.*

But there are just some things that have a force of their own. So I coughed. Really hard.

And that phlegm that had been rattling in my chest all day? Landed right on the front of his crisp, striped shirt.

CHAPTER 2

Wanting to kill myself was too mild a description.

I felt a familiar paralysis set in and covered my mouth with my hands, staring at the glob on the navy and red stripes. Those stripes would be forever burned into my memory. Thick blue stripes with thin red ones in between. A pretty nice shirt, really.

"Ugh . . . is that?" I heard Max, but I still couldn't bring myself to look at his face. Only saw him stretch his shirt out and make a disgusted sound.

Finally, I let out a feeble, "Sorry, I'm sick."

"It's . . . okay. Um, okay I'm just going to . . ." And then he scurried off into the crowd.

I threw the hood of my jacket over my head and turned to Fiona, screaming into her shoulder.

She petted my head awkwardly. "Wow, that was an epic flailure, even for you. I mean, wow," she said. Wes was too busy laugh-crying to say anything.

Flailure. The clever word Wes had come up with for when I failed at flirting. Get it? Flirt + failure = *flailure.* Birthed during freshman year, when the shy and sweet Harry Chen, whom I had tutored in English exhaustively for a year because I was in love with him, confessed that he had a crush on our English teacher. Our male English teacher.

But even before that incident, I had always flailed. Every time I tried talking to a guy. Every time a guy talked to me or showed any inkling of interest. *It always went wrong.* It didn't make sense; in all other parts of my life I was the Together Girl. Stanford-Bound Girl. It was the one thing that I couldn't ever seem to get a handle on.

How utterly clichéd—excelling at all parts of life but love. *Wah-wah.*

I looked up at Fiona with bleary eyes. "Thanks. Always a beacon of comfort. Bosom buddy. Buddy ol' pal. Pal gal. Gal . . . pal."

Fiona shook her head grimly. If one was seeking comfort and a cozy embrace from a friend, Fiona Mendoza was not open for business. She was more of the slap-you-silly, back-to-reality type.

She shrugged. "At least he's just a freshman." The word *freshman* made me wail harder into her shoulder. I had let my crush on Max die a swift death when I found out he was in ninth grade, but he was still hot. A hot guy who had been about to ask me out.

My two best friends, for all their good intentions, could never understand why being in a relationship was almost mythical to me. These two came out of the womb with built-in fan clubs.

Wes held up his phone and took a photo of me.

"Give me that!" I screeched, snatching it out of his hands and swiftly deleting the picture.

He whined, "Come on, I'm just adding it to my Famous Desi Flail moments."

"Do you want to die?" I threatened Wes with death on a daily basis.

My flailures had become so expected, so reliable, that I was even making a joke about them in my college application essay to Stanford. You know, to show actual human flaws. Because even flaws could be spun into something positive. I hoped that my winning combination of humility and humiliation would get me in. That, or my SAT score.

And for the most part, I could laugh about it. I had so much on my plate that it was probably for the best that boys didn't take up my time, in addition to everything else. There were so many other things that I needed to focus my attention on.

Plus the idea of letting another human see your pores that up close was frightening to me.

The next week at school, I was on the soccer field battling it out against Eastridge Academy.

I loved soccer; it was like chess and a hundred-yard dash all mixed into one. On a good day, it was like I could see into the future: each pass part of a master plan that ended with a ball in the back of the net.

And today was one of those good days.

It was deep into injury time and we were tied 1–1. *Now or never, Des.* My teammate Leah Hill and I made split-second eye contact before she passed the ball to me. I leaped above the matching gleaming braids of Eastridge's defense and powered the ball down into the corner of the net.

The whistle blew and I wheeled away to celebrate our win as the Eastridge players collapsed in a heap of tears and instant recriminations.

After a round of high fives, I said bye to my teammates and headed toward the parking lot.

"Rest up, Lee!" Coach Singh called to me as I reached my dad's car. I waved limply in the direction of her voice because I was still battling that stupid cold. Now that the adrenaline rush of the game had subsided, I was exhausted.

A lumbering baby-blue American-auto masterpiece was waiting for me. Even though my dad was a mechanic who could fix up any classic car to perfection, he drove a very unsexy 1980 Buick LeSabre the size of a houseboat. I swore my dad's eccentricities grew exponentially every year.

And yes, my *father* was picking me up from school. Last year, I had crashed my birthday present from my dad—a restored hunter-green Saab convertible which I'd had all of twenty minutes—into a street lamp ten feet away from our house. A rabbit had jumped out in front of me and instead of braking, my immediate reaction was to steer the car wildly away from it.

After that, my dad was convinced that I couldn't be trusted to have my own car, but he did let me drive his uncrushable boat short distances and I never asked him to replace the Saab. At the top of my life goals was to never worry my dad.

He was reading a newspaper in the driver's seat when I walked up and heaved the car door open.

"Oh! There she is!" he said with a wide smile, folding the newspaper and tossing it on the dash. His smile lit up his broad, round face. Laugh lines crinkled the corners of his eyes and his tan skin. He still had a shock of thick black hair, his only vanity. My dad spent every morning carefully combing and fluffing that head of hair, only to pull on a grease-stained shirt and cargo shorts afterward.

"Hi, Appa." I tossed my backpack and duffel into the backseat and then dropped into the passenger seat with a relieved groan, every part of me aching.

My dad's rough palm was immediately on my forehead and he tsked disapprovingly. "Oh my gah. You have a fever!" *Oh my gah* killed me every time.

I leaned back and closed my eyes. "I'm fine, I just need some *juk* and a superhot shower." *Juk* was Korean porridge, and my dad made a mean one, with mushrooms and shredded bits of salty seaweed.

"*Ch*, who you think you're kidding? You shouldn't go to school tomorrow. No homework tonight, only fun things," my dad said as we drove home.

"No, no fun things!" I said with a laugh, only half joking. I had to drop off some of the senior class's donated canned goods at a nearby church and finish up an AP English lit paper.

"Hey! If Appa says fun things, then only fun things!"

My dad always referred to himself in the third person, and it was always Appa, the Korean word for Dad. It would be embarrassing if it wasn't, you know, endearing. My dad's kinda bad English had the most perfect comedic touch, and sometimes I wondered if he wasn't just faking it to crack me up. We spoke both Korean and English at home, more often than not a wonky fusion of my bad Korean and his bad English.

When we got home I took a quick shower, slathered lotion onto my tan face (*Country skin, like me!* my dad proudly claimed all the time), then ran downstairs to the pantry. I was counting the canned goods in the pile when I heard the familiar sound of Korean people yelling from the next room.

"*APPA!* In the name of all that is holy, turn the volume down!" I hollered. The volume went down a minuscule notch, and I dragged the box of cans into the living room, where my dad was sitting in his favorite recliner watching his beloved Korean dramas. Only the top of his head was visible above the worn-out forest-green upholstery.

He paused the show on a classic Korean drama moment: a

hotheaded stud carrying a very drunk mousy girl home on his back.

"Haven't you watched this one already?" I teased. Wait for it . . .

My dad straightened up and bellowed, "*This is different one. They're not all the same!*"

I cackled. I loved making fun of my dad's obsession with K dramas. He spent every single evening watching them, come rain or shine. (The only other TV love of his life was *I Love Lucy*. Yup, I was named after Desi Arnaz. Don't ask.) Nothing got between my dad and his dramas.

One time I had called them Korean soap operas and my face almost melted off from his fury—"They are *not* the same as that junk!" I had to give him that much. For one thing, they were in a miniseries format, so they had a predetermined number of episodes rather than endless decades of the same couples dealing with evil twins and such. Also, unlike soaps, they were wildly varied in genre, like movies—romantic comedy, fantasy, suspense, or your classic romantic melodrama. And my dad loved every single one of them. I watched bits and pieces with him on occasion, but they were never really my thing.

I pointed at the screen. "Let me guess. That drunk girl is an orphan."

My dad paused the TV and turned his nose up haughtily. "Not orphan. But very poor."

"And that guy is the son of a department store CEO."

"*Ya!*"

"*Ya* yourself. Have fun. Can I borrow your car to drop off these cans?"

He looked at me with concern. "Are you sure you don't want Appa to drive you? You're sick."

"I'm fine, the church is only five minutes away. Thank you, though."

He got up and walked me to the door, handing me his keys. "Okay, but come right back. The *juk* will be ready and you need to rest."

"Okay, Appa, see you in a bit."

I pulled on my shoes and was loading the box of cans into the car when I heard my dad yell from the doorway, "*Ya! Desi! Put on socks! You always get sick because you don't wear socks!*"

Oh my God, my dad and socks. Seriously. I hollered back, "It's a common misconception that people get sick from being cold! *Go back to your dramas!*"

But I still ran inside and pulled on a pair before leaving the house again.

CHAPTER 3

"Discuss why Geoffrey Chaucer's *Canterbury Tales* was social criticism for its time. And lay off the fart jokes! We all know how bawdy the wanker was."

Ah, Ms. Lyman, an actual *English* English teacher being forced to teach Chaucer to a bunch of California brats. It was Friday and I was sitting in AP English when we started shifting desks around to get into our discussion groups. Mine was made up of the usual brainiacs—Shelly Wang, Michael Diaz, and Wes.

"Okay, so maybe we could start by discussing what problems ailed society during Chaucer's time?" Michael said, already writing furiously in his notebook. He always had to be first.

Not to be outdone, Shelly piped up, "Well, the oppressive Catholic Church for starters?"

Wes nodded in agreement. "Yeah, dude was ahead of his time with that observation."

I furrowed my brow and racked my brain for other fourteenth-century societal ills in England. While deep in thought, I doodled absentmindedly in the margins of my notebook. I was sketching out a dress I'd been Internet-creeping on for the past few weeks—short, strapless, dove gray with a sweetheart neckline and floral embroidery on the bottom. Maybe for prom, which felt like a million years away.

"Holy shit."

I looked up at Shelly, aghast. Miss Cardigans and Glitter Pens never cursed. Then I followed her gaze. Half the classroom's gaze, actually.

Standing in the doorway was some guy. Scratch that—some insanely perfect specimen of a guy.

Tall but not lanky, he had messy black hair partially tucked into a gray beanie, and was wearing dark jeans and a long-sleeved shirt under a puffy navy-blue vest. And good gracious, his face. Olive skin, angular jaw that could cut through glass, dark eyes framed by a pair of serious eyebrows, and a wide mouth that was smiling tentatively as he peered into the classroom.

My pencil fell out of my hand, clattering onto the floor.

"And you are?" Ms. Lyman asked.

"Luca Drakos. I'm new."

Luca. Who the hell was *actually* named Luca? At the sound of his low, quiet voice there was audible twittering from the female portion of the class.

"Well, Luca, we're in the middle of discussion groups about

The Canterbury Tales. Why don't you go join that group over there," she said, pointing to us. "Guys? Fill him in, please."

I scrambled to pick my pencil off the ground and when I looked up, everything moved in slow-motion as Luca made his way over to us. I swear a breeze whipped through the classroom just to lift the thick mop of hair away from his eyes so that he stared directly into mine. *Hooooly cuh-rap.*

"Hey," he said when he finally reached us.

I felt Shelly flutter next to me. She squeaked out, "Hi!," then got up quickly to pull an empty desk over. "Have a seat!"

He smiled at her. "Thanks." Luca sat down a mere three feet away from me. I lost the ability to speak while everyone else politely introduced themselves. He finally looked at me expectantly.

"I'm Desi," I said, but it came out raspy and quiet. I cleared my throat. "Desi," I repeated stupidly. Why oh why did I choose today of all days to wear my "fashion" sweatpants.

"Hey," he said, his voice all handsome. He had a handsome voice.

"Where are you from?" Shelly asked him.

"Ojai," he answered. "It's about an hour east of Santa Barbara."

Shelly nodded vigorously. "Oh yeah, I know where that is, my mom goes there on yoga retreats. So, um, we're discussing social criticism in *The Canterbury Tales*," Shelly said, holding up the book. "Have you read it?"

Luca shook his head. "Nope." His disinterest was palpable.

I frowned. *Way to make an impression, new kid.* Shelly, however, didn't seem deterred, batting her eyelashes and staring openly at him. I rolled my eyes. Good luck there, Shells. I continued to doodle, knowing to stay far, far away from anyone this ridiculous looking. I didn't feel like repeating Phlegmgate. The pain was still fresh.

But I snuck a glance at him anyway.

Someone kicked my chair and I looked up to see Wes shaking his head. I glared at him and mouthed, *Die.* He laughed and waggled his eyebrows suggestively at Luca. I kicked his chair back, and he lowered his head, hiding his laughter.

Then, suddenly, as everyone else was mired in some discussion about Chaucer's disdain for chivalry, Luca was scooting his desk closer to me. I froze. Why was he getting closer?! Noooooo.

A mental checklist of everything that could be gross about me popped up like a Tom Cruise–movie hologram: Dry, chapped lips. Check. That one weird long eyebrow hair I kept forgetting to trim. Check. Potential eye crust leftover from this morning. Check. Joyous new upper-lip hair growth. Check. Smattering of small yet offensive zits on my forehead. Check. Not to mention my *sweatpants.* No, this was not the day to talk to a new cute boy.

I looked at Wes in panic, and he pressed his lips together regretfully, knowing that I was headed to Flailureville.

Mere inches away, Luca gave my notebook a sidelong glance.

"Nice drawing." He kept his eyes straight ahead, his voice so low that I wondered if he had actually said what I thought he said.

My eyes flew down to the bad doodle of my dress. "Um, thanks, it's just . . . a doodle." I casually moved my arm over it.

"Do you take AP art?"

I let out a snort of laughter and immediately flushed. *Gather thyself.* "Um, no," I finally managed to respond. "Are you taking it?"

He nodded, then whispered, "So, hey. Tell me the truth. Somehow I've landed in a subgroup of nerds where you guys are the alpha-nerds. Am I right?"

I resisted the urge to laugh lest another snort be released. Instead I bit back a smile. "What gave it away? Our zeal for Middle English?"

He laughed then. Whoa, I just made a cute guy laugh. Okay, I needed to stop while I was ahead. Yet . . .

"We, like, *thrive* on fourteenth-century fart jokes," I said before I could even stop myself. O-M-G whyyyy.

But again, Luca laughed. And it made me laugh—a snortless one.

I could feel the heat of Wes's eyeballs on me. He was now sending me dire telepathic messages to stop talking.

I was about to lean over and make a crack about Chaucer's proclivity for lusty milkmaids when I noticed that Luca's hand was casually trailing over to my desk. Inching closer to mine. What the—?

All signals in my body were going berserk—red lights, honking horns, wailing sirens. I thought maybe I was dying. My heart flew out of my chest with a final, triumphant *Adios, muchachos!*

But I didn't die. Instead I watched as Luca gently took my pencil from me. I was so startled that my hand just stayed in that awkward pencil-holding position, empty and curled around nothing. Then, ever-so-slightly, Luca tilted my notebook toward himself and slid it down my desk so that it was within his reach.

Without ever looking at me, he started to trace over my drawing. With swift, assured strokes. His lines moved on top, over, around my own. Until the dress was transformed from a childish shape into layers and layers of dark lace. Fit snugly over a slim yet curved body. The front of the dress was short but there was a long bustled skirt covered with feathers cascading down the back, puddled at the bottom. Then he made the imaginary girl a pair of truly killer heels, strappy and towering. She wore black lace gloves that ended at her wrists, and her hair was a long tangled mass pulled to one side. The other side exposed a delicate ear pierced to oblivion with geometric studs and long chains and jewels that reached past her shoulders.

Discussions of Chaucer turned into white noise in the background as I watched the drawing come to life. Luca paused for a moment and I glanced up at him, impatient, wanting to see what was next. His face was bent close to the paper, brow furrowed in concentration, but I could have sworn he was smiling.

He filled in her face. Thick, straight eyebrows. Dark, wide-set eyes with long lashes. Broad cheekbones and a small mouth with a bigger upper lip than bottom. The hint of an overbite.

Me.

I stared at it, physically unable to look at Luca. My cheeks were hot and my heart was pounding in my ears—so loud that I couldn't believe it wasn't being heard by everyone on planet Earth. When I finally looked up, I stared directly into his eyes and a zap of electricity shot between us.

Before I could react, before I could say one thing, the bell rang.

Everyone moved their desks back to their original positions, metal scraping across the floor. Luca left my notebook and pencil on my desk before moving his desk back, too, grabbing his things without a word to me.

I opened my mouth and closed it again. I picked up my pencil gingerly. I swear it was still warm from his touch.

"If you need help finding your classes and stuff, I can walk with you," I heard Shelly purr to Luca.

A small smile hovered over Luca's lips. "Uh, thanks, but I've got it." He swung his backpack around to his chest, and it looked like he was *pretending* to fish something out.

Wes thumped my arm with his bag. "Hey, you ready?"

I blinked. "Oh yeah, uh-huh." We headed out of class together, and I glanced backward at Luca one last time. Was he going to say *anything*? Apparently not, he was so engrossed in the thrills of backpack rummaging.

"So what were you giggling about with John Stamos over there?" Wes asked as we stepped outside.

"Ha-ha. I wasn't *giggling*." I started giggling as I said it.

Wes raised his eyebrows at me. "Shiiiit."

"Shut up," I said with another involuntary giggle. But when I turned around, Luca was walking toward me, backpack on correctly now. I froze. And apparently, whenever Luca walked toward me, the world moved in slow-motion. He pushed the beanie out of his eyes with glacial speed. By the time he finally reached me, we had already dated, married, and sent our two daughters off to college tearfully. Giggles immediately dissipated.

"So I know you said you're not in AP art, but are you in Art Club?" he asked. The flirty vibe from earlier was gone, and I couldn't tell if that was because Wes was with me. But he was being friendly enough, so . . .

I tried to remain composed. "Ha, no way."

He laughed—a honking laugh that made me break out in a huge grin. What an undignified laugh for such a hot specimen. *Oh my God, stop being excited. You know where excitement leads, Desi. Stop!* But I never made guys laugh. At this point in any of my interactions with guys, I had already done something spectacularly stupid. For the first time in forever, I felt a flicker of hope.

Wes subtly walked up ahead of us.

"Too bad," Luca said, with an inscrutable expression. My heart thumped.

Then. I felt it—a familiar loss of control, all competence taken over by nervous insecurity. *No, no, no.* "Too bad I'm not in Art Club?" I asked, my voice already reaching a strange pitch.

"Yeah."

I shook my head. "I would never waste my time pursuing something at which I'm only mediocre." Oh sweet Jesus, I was doing the know-it-all, strangely colonial-era talking. *Stop, stop now and just be aloof and cool. ALOOF AND COOL. Check your posture.*

I watched his smile fade. The gleam in his eyes dulled. *Okay, aloof-and-cool moment is officially gone.* I knew I should stop now, but maybe I could save this. A surge of ballsiness coursed through me. Just *explain* yourself. *Communication is key.* "It's just that I'm really busy." His face froze—paralyzed, if you will. I powered through. "I have a lot riding on my shoulders. I'm school president, on varsity soccer and tennis, in five different clubs, and am pretty much slated to be valedictorian."

An all-too-familiar expression of politeness-disguising-panic took over Luca's face. "Wow. Busy bee. All right, see you around then."

I blinked and shook my head, feeling my wits return to me as he walked off.

"Wait, Luca!"

He turned around, reluctantly, if one were to judge reluctance on the literal dragging of feet.

Now what? Why the hell did I just do that?!

I nervously pulled at the drawstrings on my sweats. "Um, when does Art Club meet?" *All is not lost. Just try to flirt. Be cute. PLAY UP CUTE.* I bit my lower lip for added effect.

Luca's eyes darted around, as if looking for a way to escape this. "Um, I'm not sure yet, but I think it's on the website . . ." His voice trailed off.

And then.

My fashion sweatpants fell off. In a puddle at my feet.

I looked down. Luca looked down. I looked up. Luca was still looking down.

And I heard Wes yelp, "Are you *kidding*?"

I pulled them up and ran. Like the wind.

CHAPTER 4

My phone was buzzing all that evening—Wes and Fiona were trying to cheer me up about the sweatpants incident but I ignored them. My last text to them had been: **Consider me dead. Bye.**

When my dad came home from work, he found me in full-on pity-party mode: wearing my pajamas, I was watching a reality show about young women competing for their very own cupcake shop and was inhaling my binge-eating snack of choice—pickle spears. My dad stood in the entryway and tsked. "That many pickles?! Right now? Appa won't make dinner for you."

He grumbled all the way into the kitchen, where he unloaded groceries. Normally, that was my job, but today I let myself luxuriate in my terrible mood. With my long history of flailures, you'd think the latest would just be a drop in the bucket. And in the past, after a couple of hours, the inevitable next urgent Desi Lee thing had distracted me—science fair, soccer game, etc.

But I just couldn't shake it off today. And something about the Luca flailure was sending me spiraling into some seriously embarrassing flashbacks.

Jefferson Mahoney. First grade. I kicked my first crush, Jefferson, in the nuts during tae kwon do class, and he had to be taken to the ER.

I stuck my hand into the jar for another pickle. My dad walked into the living room and shook his head at me. "Okay, whatchu going on?"

Normally, *whatchu going on* got a giggle from me. I smiled halfheartedly. "Nothing."

Diego Valdez. Fourth grade. He asked me if I wanted to look at his "special" books and I told him I wasn't allowed to look at pornography. Turned out to be comic books and he didn't even know how babies were made yet. I was a fourth-grade perv.

"Those are the special pickles I get from Persian market. Give to me, they're Appa's favorites."

I hugged the jar close to me and turned my back to him. "No!"

Oliver Sprague. Seventh grade. We were at the Halloween dance and he leaned in to give me my first kiss but I started laughing until I cried.

My dad pursed his lips. "Okay, stop. This isn't funny anymore. Appa has to watch the show and you are being very annoying."

"Rude."

He plopped down next to me so forcefully that I bounced and some pickle juice splattered on me. Then he wrestled the jar from me. "No dinner for both of us, then." He took a bite before picking up the remote.

"Let's watch something else." I had never been able to sit through an entire K drama and I was in the mood for something way more sinister and miserable.

My dad ignored me as he deftly navigated the smart-TV options to the Internet and launched his K drama streaming site. He could barely e-mail but he could launch that website in his sleep. I tried to grab the remote from him and he bonked me over the head with it.

"What's the matter with you? I work all day, what did you do, pickle monster? No, you watch what Appa watches."

I rubbed my head and glared at him. "I don't *wanna*."

Nyma Amiri. Sophmore year. I sent Nyma secret-admirer notes for a few weeks, only to discover that he knew it was me from the beginning. Because I accidentally signed the first one.

Another bonk. "*Ya*, stop complaining. Also, we *are* watching because this is the *last* episode of the show and Appa been *soooo* excited to see this one."

As the title credits rolled over the theme music I had heard in the background all week, I felt something snap. "How are you even remotely excited about this? *They all end the same.* These people"—I pointed to the screen, at the wide-eyed nymph and the Bieber-coiffed cad—"there's no way in hell they should be together. But miracle of miracles, they end up happily ever after. It's complete bullshit."

Max Peralta: Phlegm rocket.

Luca Drakos: Pantsed myself.

My dad shoved my head. "Watch your mouth, Miss Complaining USA. Don't you know that if it's true love, even bad beginnings end happy?"

True love. I wanted to scoff at that, but the lurch in my chest when I saw Luca's drawing was something I had never felt before. The light-headed buzz in his proximity was new. I had crushed hard in the past, but I had the nagging feeling that this was something different.

I sat back out of sheer laziness and watched the start of the episode. My dad helpfully turned on the English subtitles so I could follow along with my remedial Korean skills.

The scene opened on a busy city intersection—the two main characters standing on opposite sides of the street, staring at each other in the rain. Music was swelling as the cars sped by them.

My dad gleefully clapped. "Oh, *finally!*" he said. "*Finally* they see each other after so many bad things! This is where they'll kiss!" He glanced at me. "Maybe this is adult stuff."

I scoffed. "Appa, seriously? We watched *Brokeback Mountain* together."

Just as the light was about to turn green for the two lovers to meet, there was a flashback: The girl is sitting in a supply closet at work, her skirt hiked up, mending her torn stocking with clear nail polish. The guy accidentally walks in on her, and she startles and throws her arms up in the air—tossing the nail polish bottle at his eye. He howls and when the girl scrambles up to help him, he yells at her and shoves her aside. The girl's mood changes instantly and she kicks him and he falls face-forward into a bucket.

I snorted. "Yeah, so super-believable that they go from this to kissing passionately in the rain."

My dad shoved me again. "Be quiet, Desi. Just watch, they show *everything* that happened in all the other episodes."

In the next flashback, the girl stumbles into a cabin from a snowstorm. The guy rushes over to her, yelling; he's furious that she put herself in danger. Then he notices she's limping and injured. He sits her down on a stool and wraps her ankle gently in a bandage, and as his eyes skim from her bare ankle up to her face, they lock eyes awkwardly. He shoves her away and she falls off the stool.

I smiled. Okay, admittedly that was pretty cute despite the slightly violent element.

The next flashback: The girl's at dinner with some other bland-looking dude, and the guy rushes in angrily, taking long strides across the fancy restaurant to grab her wrist and pull her away. She shouts at him and starts pounding his chest with her little fists, furious, but he kisses her roughly and she melts against him.

Hmm . . . that was kind of . . . hot. I straightened up and

leaned forward. The last flashback: The two are at work, and the girl is getting yelled at by her boss. He throws a folder at her, papers flying everywhere. The guy is watching her, his face contorted with emotion. She makes meaningful eye contact with him and walks out of the room with her head held up high.

My dad elbowed me. "That was when she took blame for something he did wrong."

We flashed back to present day, the couple staring longingly at each other after so much misunderstanding and suffering. The light turns green and the two walk toward each other in slow motion. Just as they were about to meet in the middle of the street, I grabbed the remote and paused it.

"*Desi!*" my dad yelled.

I looked at him, and even though you don't usually *feel* your eyes gleaming, I felt my eyes gleaming. I had always assumed that when relationships went bad, that was the end. But the entire premise of K dramas was that *they always ended happily*. And that if you looked closely, there was a *formula* for making a guy fall in love with you. One that often began with a heavy dose of humiliation for the girl. And why had all my flailures, my humiliations come to nothing? It was because I never had a *plan*. There had never been any *steps* to follow.

But the steps were right in front of my eyes all along. Just slightly blocked by my dad's big head. I sprang up from the sofa. "It's like a freaking equation! Why didn't I ever see it?" I yelped. "We're starting from the first episode!"

My dad's jaw dropped and he threw his arms up helplessly at the screen, where the two were about to kiss, eyes closed, leaning in. There would be about thirty more excruciating seconds of them squinting their eyes to lean in for this kiss, moving a millimeter per second.

Like *everything else*, Luca could be won over with some good old-fashioned planning. This renewed sense of order propelled me up the stairs to grab a notebook. I might be a flailure in love, but I was the motherf-ing *boss* of studying. And until Luca, the motivation to study and plan my way out of humiliation had just never come to me.

Two days later, on Monday morning, it was done.

I turned off the TV and leaned back into the crinkly leather sofa. My mouth was parched. My contacts were stickers on my eyeballs. I glanced over at my dad, who, when he wasn't working, had joined me for the marathon on and off during the weekend. Then, last night, he had conked out next to me on the couch while I stayed up all night. He was sleeping with his mouth open, white-sock-clad feet tangled up in the plaid comforter I had brought for him.

I looked down at my notebook. I had done it—I had watched three entire K drama series over the course of the weekend, including the one that we had started on Friday night. When my dad had asked why I was on this sudden K drama kick, I said it was for a school research project. Part of that wasn't a lie.

The dramas I watched were all of the romantic comedy variety, because that was clearly the genre that best fit my current life scenario. I hadn't left my house, showered, or seen another human aside from my dad in that entire time. I had ignored texts from Fiona and Wes.

It was funny, K dramas had been the white noise of my life. They were always on in the background as I washed the dishes, did homework, or hung out with friends upstairs in my room. But I had never sat there with my dad and fully given myself up to the K drama drug.

Over the course of an entire weekend, I had become a convert. I had graduated from K Drama Rom-Com School.

I had laughed, cried, felt the entire spectrum of K drama emotions. When I started the first episode, it took me a while to take the general aesthetic of the show seriously. First of all, the hairstyles on the male actors—OMG, so distracting and outrageous. Then, somehow, they evolved from ridonk to cute and dreamy! And while the posh sets of "rich people" made my eyes roll violently, they were offset by the cozy and romantic snapshots of Seoul—midnight drinks and hot snacks in *pojangmachas* (pop-up tents), adorable coffee shops playing American Top 40 music, city avenues lined with cherry trees in bloom, the iconic Han River at night. Seoul just seemed so *pleasant* and *alive*.

And although I'm Korean American, there was a bit of culture shock. Like, how a hug was a momentous relationship marker (in American shows the leads would barely blink twice before jumping into bed). Or how *huge* obstacles were brought on by class differences, and how it was considered kind of okay for a rich mom to start hitting a *grown* woman for daring to date her son despite being poor. And the grown woman would just sit there and take it because the rich mom was her elder!

Then there were the *emotions*. My God, I have never witnessed this level of emotion from human beings, on-screen or off. So. Many. Tears. So much *yelling*. I now understood why my dad spoke in all-caps, why everything was laced with incredulity. Not to mention all the fierce hugs, sweeping across rooms and grabbing girls, and close-ups of quivering mouths and clenched jaws. Hello, Hollywood casting directors who think there aren't any Asians with star power? You need to go to Korea.

Yeah, the stories could be formulaic, downright clichéd at times, but with the strong characters, it all worked. Characters that you rooted for, that you hated with the heat of a thousand suns, that you crushed on hard-core, that you envied, that you *cared* about. They were more real than anything the Oscars served up.

K dramas bottled up swoony true love in addictive ten-to-twenty-hour packages. My reactions to chaste first kisses were akin to heart attacks. I bawled with abandon when couples had to break up, when one of them was suffering. I sighed happily with glazed eyes when my characters finally got their happy endings.

And now I had to go to boring school. In America. But I was armed with something that I truly believed would work.

"*Appa . . . Appa!* Wake up!" I nudged him until he finally stirred. It was like waking up a giant four-year-old, but I managed to get him upstairs to shower. When he closed his bathroom door, I glanced down at my phone. I had a good twenty minutes before Fiona showed up.

~~CHAPTER~~ STEP 5:
Have a Secret Dream That Brings You Closer to the Guy

Fiona was late and it was cold. Waiting for her in my driveway, I hugged my thermos of coffee, which was barely saving me on zero hours of sleep. A quick glance at my phone's weather app showed that it was fifty-two degrees. Freaking glacial for Orange County, even if it *was* December. I was about to rage-text Fiona when I heard a loud clattering noise just before her copper-colored death-on-wheels, lovingly called Penny, turned the corner. I could sense all my uptight neighbors flicking their venetian blinds aside to stare out at the loud hooligan car.

Fiona's music was blasting, too, but I couldn't hear *that* over the clattering until she was pulled up right in front of me. I hopped in and immediately turned the volume down on the Swedish reggae. "God, you're going to go deaf. Either from terrible music or your trash-can car. You do realize Penny has an exhaust leak?" Always the mechanic's daughter, I could identify a car by the sound of its exhaust in my sleep.

"I ran over a neighbor's skateboard the other day, maybe it was that." Fiona pondered for a second before glaring at me. "Were you in hibernation because of the sweatpants flailure?"

"In part."

She tapped her long lavender nails on the steering wheel. "Well, I'm glad to see you're not dead. If it wasn't for your cryptic post on Instagram last night I would have sent the cops over."

"I know, sorry. I was just super—caught up in something this weekend."

She glanced over at me again. "Look at you today. All sharp."

I was wearing dark jeans, black flats, and a gray peacoat over a heart-patterned sweater. "Fi. I'm just wearing normal clothes."

Fiona, on the other hand, was wearing shorts overalls over tights, a long-sleeved thermal, and a giant tweed men's coat over the entire ensemble. Her lips crimson, her faux-red hair tied in a high, messy knot. Bow down.

I nervously snuck a peek at myself in the visor mirror. I had managed to execute my favorite hairstyle—worn down with soft waves framing my face. I saw a flash of Luca's drawing of me, the long hair swept to one side.

"I have something to tell you."

A beat of silence. "Okaaay, I'm listening."

"Well, it's always been kind of lame that despite how well I do in so many things, I can't seem to get a boyfriend because of my flailures, right? Clearly, there's that magic something I'm missing, that all you overdeveloped lovers seem to have."

"Thanks."

"You're welcome. So . . . you know how my dad's always watching those Korean dramas?"

"Yes, adorable." My dad melted even the coolest of hearts.

I went on. "Well, so after a hot guy saw my green-striped underwear on Friday, I actually watched a bunch of K dramas. Like, three of them."

"Three episodes?"

"No, shows. Like entire series!"

Fiona turned onto the main road, then looked over at me incredulously. "You watched *three series* of shows in *one weekend*?! Aren't they, like, one hundred episodes each?"

"No! They're all different, running from, like, ten to twenty."

"*What!* Are you on *speed*?"

"I was propelled by epic flailure, Fi. And call me crazy but I think Luca and I had a serious moment."

"You mean before your pants fell off?"

"*Fi!*"

We got to school and she turned off the ignition and stared at me. "Okay, in all seriousness. A *moment*? Didn't you know him for a total of thirty minutes before . . . you know?"

A mental flash of Luca staring down at the gray puddle of sweats at my feet. I shook my head to erase it like an Etch A Sketch. "Yeah, but . . . I can't explain it."

"I can. He's hot." Fiona shook her head.

"It's not just that! I mean, yes, my God. He's hot. But he also . . ." I looked away from her and into my lap where I was nervously wringing my hands, embarrassed to go into details. "He did this thing—he took my pencil from me and freaking *drew a picture of me*. It was . . . so. *Romantic*. It was the most special thing any guy has ever done for me."

Fiona was silent for a second. "You are such a dork."

I swatted Fiona's arm. "Don't make fun of me, I'm serious! Sorry I'm not an experienced seductress who like, has men drinking champagne from her high heels."

"*What!* That alone, Des, makes me really worry about you. What you know about romance is, like, weird clichéd crap. From 1980s champagne commercials."

We sat in the car, the air growing chilly with the heater turned off. "Well, that's the whole point, right? Something is clearly wrong with *me*. I'm stunted or just . . . lacking something when it comes to relationship stuff. It's not natural for me. But. When do I excel at stuff?"

Fiona threw up her hands. "I dunno, you excel at most things."

"Yes! And do you know why? Most things have *rules*, steps, and methods for getting better."

Fiona looked at me, hard. "What are you getting at?"

I pulled out my notebook and held it up with a grin. "I discovered the steps to conquering flailure." I handed the notebook to Fiona. Her face remained impassive while she read.

THE K DRAMA STEPS TO TRUE LOVE

1. You Are the Living Embodiment of All That Is Pure and Good

2. Have a Sad-Sack Family Story

3. Meet the World's Most Unattainable Guy

4. Let the Guy Get to You Whether It's from Annoyance or Obsession

5. Have a Secret Dream That Brings You Closer to the Guy

6. Doggedly Pursue Your Dream, No Matter the Cost to Your Well-Being

7. Mystery Surrounds the Guy but Find Out More

8. Be Caught in an Obviously Lopsided Love Triangle

9. Get into a Predicament That Forces Both the Guy and You into an Intimate Bonding Moment

10. Find Out the Guy's Big Secret, Preferably through Excruciatingly Repetitive Flashbacks

11. Prove That You Are Different from All Other Women — IN THE ENTIRE WORLD

12. Life-Threatening Event Makes Him/You Realize How Real Your Love Is

13. Reveal Your Vulnerabilities in a Heartbreaking Manner

14. Lock That Baby-In With a Kiss! Finally. 💋

15. Fall Deeply-into Cringe-Inducing Mushy Love 💗

16. Pick Your Very Own Love Ballad to Blast Jarringly Over and Over Again! 🎵♪

17. Worlds Have to Collide for Some Comic Relief 😄

18. Meet His Family and Win Them Over 🏆

19. You Must Make the Ultimate Sacrifice to Prove Your Love

20. You Are Not Allowed to Be Happy Until the Very Last Possible Minute

21. Betrayal Time—One of You Kinda-Not-Really Betrays the Other

22. At Your Lowest Point, Your Life Is Only Made Up of Flashback Montages of Good Times

23. Take Drastic Measures for Your Happy Ending

24. Get Your Happy Ending 💗💗

When her eyeballs finally stilled I waited expectantly for her response.

Her electric-blue-lined eyes shifted over to mine.

"Are you . . . out of your damn mind?"

I released a tortured breath. "Hear me out—"

"No way, Des. This is the most deranged thing I have ever seen, even for *you*. Some of these things . . . I mean . . . who the hell . . ."

"Fi, I'm not going to take it all *literally*. Some of the real wacko stuff you're reading is part of these formulas but not necessarily things I need to do. It's a rough . . . inspirational blueprint if you will. But it essentially lays out, step-by-step, all the ways to get into predicaments that will endear me to Luca and then ultimately get us closer together."

"Oh God, you're getting that annoying look on your face."

I nodded. "Yeah, that look that always gets stuff *done*." I flipped to the blank pages after the list. "So here I'll be writing little notes on my progress and my actual tactics."

While her expression was still dubious, the deep creases in her forehead unfurrowed slightly. "Okay, so what was step 1 again?" Fiona reached for the notebook and flipped to the list. "*You Are the Living Embodiment of All That Is Pure and Good.*" She looked at me, then cracked up.

I crossed my arms. "That one . . . well, some I'll have to kind of gloss over."

"Please. Desi, you collect cans for the needy, hug trees, and tutor idiots. You've got the goody-two-shoes thing down."

Sometimes the line between compliment and insult was so very fine. "Thanks, friend. Moving on . . . see, number 2, *Have a Sad-Sack Family Story*? Check."

Fiona shot me a quick, cautious look. "Well, I mean, this *kinda* applies to you?"

I shrugged. "I'm not a sad sack, obviously. But on the surface, to strangers, the dead-mom thing is always, like, the *ultimate*. Fairy-tale-princess-level tragedy."

Fiona nodded. "Okay, fine. And number 3. *Meet the World's Most Unattainable Guy*. Hm. I don't know if he's the *world's most* unattainable, but okay, you've met him. Step number 4, *Let the Guy Get to You—Whether It's from Annoyance or Obsession*."

We were both silent for a second and then Fiona smacked me over the head with the notebook. "You are *beyond* obsessed."

"Ouch!" I rubbed my head. "Anyway, yeah, obsession level pretty much reached. So where does that leave us now? Step number 5."

Fiona glanced down at the notebook. "*Have a Secret Dream That Brings You Closer to the Guy*. What's your secret dream? Do you *have* one?"

"Well, my *actual* dream isn't a secret at all: Stanford, then med school. But for this to work, it has to be a secret dream that brings me closer to Luca."

Rolling down her window, Fiona let a cold gust of air into the car and took a deep breath. "This plan is making every feminist hair on me stand on end."

"Whatever, Fi. Feminism isn't just one thing. Me taking control of my love life is totally feminist."

"If you say so. And did you think of a secret dream?"

I popped up my coat collar and burrowed my face into it to shield myself against the cool air. "Yup," I said in a muffled voice.

"I'm afraid to hear it."

"Art."

She choked. I pounded her back.

STEP 6:
Doggedly Pursue Your Dream, No Matter the Cost to Your Well-Being

My outfit was totally wasted that day because I didn't see Luca at all. As soon as the bell rang for the start of AP English, Shelly blurted out, "Where's Luca?"

Ms. Lyman looked up from her desk and rolled her eyes. "Clerical error. Sorry, ladies. He wasn't supposed to be in AP English."

I knew it was too good to be true. Between classes, I looked for him in the hallways but he was nowhere to be found. I was a little disappointed but also somewhat relieved. Now I had a bit more time to figure out how to salvage my pride when I saw him again after the sweatpants incident. Which would be at my first Art Club meeting tomorrow.

That evening, I guzzled down a couple mugs of coffee to stay awake until dinner. I also needed to hype myself up for the K drama antics ahead, so I started another drama with my dad while cooking.

"Appa, how does a character in these dramas save face after

they do something really embarrassing?" I asked as I stirred the giant batch of spaghetti sauce I was making. Our kitchen and family room were part of an open floor plan, so I could easily watch *Flower Boy Ramen Shop* while cooking. And I use the word *cooking* generously—spaghetti was one of three meals that I could confidently cook without my dad politely pulling out Korean side dishes to compensate.

From his position on the recliner, my dad took a thoughtful sip of beer before responding. "Okay, well, usually they just have to be brave and not be so embarrassed. Many drama girls are very strong and that is why the boys like them even if they aren't the prettiest ones."

Well, that was reassuring. I added some garlic powder to the bubbling marinara. "So, they just kind of deal with it?"

"*Ya*. Deal with it."

Afterward, still buzzing from the caffeine, I Googled the K dramas I'd watched and read up on every bit of fun info on the casts. And *then* I discovered the wonderful world of hilarious K drama blogs and Tumblr gifs; the fandom that existed for these shows was *huge*.

I fell asleep with my phone inches away from my face, streaming *Flower Boy Ramen Shop*.

The next day after school, on to step 6 of doggedly pursuing my dream, I headed to my first Art Club meeting. I had spoken to

Mr. Rosso, the Art Club adviser, yesterday and he said I'd just need to bring a sketch pad and pencils for today because this meeting happened to be a field trip to the zoo. Like, first-grade style. The K drama steps notebook, nestled with my brand-new art supplies, was in my backpack to fortify my resolve.

But the second I got on the school bus, I suddenly wanted to turn around like the Road Runner and book it the hell out of there. Meep-meep! Brave K drama heroine be damned. I was familiar with most of the student body but this was the "artsy" crowd—a group of hipster types who made me feel two inches tall for blasting Taylor Swift and reading *Twilight*. Not that I've ever done that. At the same time.

And I was fully aware this move was kinda lame since Luca knew I wasn't in Art Club and would suspect I'd joined because of him.

"Desi?" a girl with a bleached-blond pixie cut called out dubiously. It was Cassidy from my soccer team. I scurried over to her, relieved to see a familiar face.

"Hey," I said, sitting down next to her and attempting to smile, like this was all totally normal.

Cassidy smiled back quizzically. "What are you doing here?"

My eyes darted around the bus, looking for Luca, but no sign of him yet. "Um, well, I'm joining Art Club?"

"Wow, really? Never would have guessed . . ." Cassidy's voice trailed off. Before I could respond with some flimsy excuse to substantiate my presence, I looked out the window and saw Luca walking toward the bus with some girl—all long limbs and combat boots. Her mirrored Ray-Bans glinted in the sun, and she tossed her lavender-tipped black hair over her shoulder. The two of them lowered their heads together and laughed as they walked to the bus.

What in the bloody f-ing EFF was *this*. Did he have a girlfriend *already*? *Three days into a new school?*

When they stepped onto the bus, Luca stopped to say hi to someone sitting in the front and I turned my back to the aisle so he couldn't see me. This was the worst plan ever, what in the world was I thinking—

"Desi Lee? Wow, knew you were an extracurricular hoarder, but stooping so low as to join *Art Club*?"

The question was aimed at my back, so all I saw was Cassidy's reaction. Her jaw dropped and her green eyes bulged out. *"Violet!"* she exclaimed.

I turned around and looked at said Violet. She of the waist-long hair, ripped black jeans, and worn-out white V-neck. Complete with ironic fanny pack.

I stared at her. "I'm sorry, do I *know* you?"

"I'm shocked you don't know me, my *word*. Me being a constituent of yours and all. Violet. Violet Choi," she practically drawled.

Choi. Korean. Hm, I couldn't place her and I was totally unprepared for this sudden open animosity.

"So what's your problem?" I snapped.

"My *problem*"—Violet's voice was high-pitched, as if to imitate me—"is that as the most annoying overachiever at Monte Vista, you're *everywhere*. And Art Club is the one place where I could get away from you because you're *not an artist*."

I was so shocked that I couldn't even register that Luca was probably witnessing all of this. No one had ever spoken to me like that before. I may be the textbook definition of high school popular but I wasn't the type to have any enemies because of it. I liked to think that I was well liked because I was *friendly*. This wasn't some clichéd high school full of evil queen bees and long-suffering bullied types. Or so I thought. I didn't know how to respond.

What does a K drama heroine do when faced with blatant bitchiness? Suddenly I remembered when Eun-Sol from *Protect the Boss* got an ice cream cone shoved onto her *butt* from that drama's queen bitch. Her reaction was to remain calm and stay sweet even in the face of blatant animosity.

Luca was now standing next to Violet in the middle of the aisle. So even though my eyes went prickly—that mortifying feeling before they filled up with tears—I kept my mouth shut. His brow furrowed when I made split-second eye contact with him.

That small hint of concern landed a face-punch of swoon into my heart. And immediately, I forgot that this was the first time he was talking to me after the sweatpants disaster.

He glanced over at Violet and asked, "Do you guys know each other?"

His eyes stayed cool as he looked between the two of us.

I was quiet, still trying to wrangle the crazy mix of rage, humiliation, and hormonal butterflies hurtling through me.

Cassidy spoke up even though he hadn't directed the question at her. "Um, yeah, Desi and I are on the soccer team. Do *you guys* know each other?" she asked, her eyebrows raised.

I glanced at Luca, who shrugged and answered, "Kind of. I know she prefers briefs over thongs." He looked straight at me with a shit-eating grin.

Oh. My. Gaaaaaah.

Cassidy's mouth dropped ever so slightly and Violet's head swiveled toward me at demon speed. Before I could react, Mr. Rosso walked onto the bus and bellowed, "All right, my little Renoirs, let's get seated!" He patted his belly with relish, his Hawaiian shirt lifting a little at the bottom. "Everyone ready for the zoo?" He was met with some very deliberate silence.

Mr. Rosso chose that moment to look over at us and say, "Oh yes, first things first. We have two new members—everyone give a warm welcome to Desi Lee and Luca Drakos." Someone clapped slowly and deliberately in the background and laughter erupted.

Mr. Rosso glared at the clapper. "*Anyway*, Desi and Luca, we've been spending the last couple of weeks working on our pieces for a charity art show. All proceeds will be benefiting the California State Parks fund. But today we're taking a little break for some drawing at the zoo."

I nodded—smiling on the outside, crying on the inside. "Sounds really great," I chirped quickly.

More laughter, and I heard Violet squeal, "Yeah, *really* great!"

Mr. Rosso sat down with a last look behind him. "The rest of you—*behave*, we should get there in about twenty."

Violet sat next to Luca a couple of rows in front of Cassidy and me. Hmph.

Cassidy shot me a questioning look. "So . . . Luca knows what kind of underwear—"

I waved a hand to silence her. "It's not what you think. He's joking."

Cassidy looked like she wanted to keep digging but pressed her lips together instead. After a few seconds she said, "Sorry about Violet, she's not usually such a . . ." Her hushed voice trailed off.

"Warm, welcoming presence?" I finished drily.

She snorted. "Yeah, exactly. I don't know, she's just super-passionate about art and has some strong opinions on people that she thinks are . . . poseurs." Her voice got a little sheepish.

I sniffed indignantly even though I *was* technically a poseur. I glanced over to Violet and Luca. "So, um, are those two to-gether or something?" I hoped my hair toss made the question believably easy-breezy.

Cassidy's brow furrowed. "Huh? Luca and Violet?" *Could her voice be any louder?!*

I smiled through gritted teeth. "Yeah?"

"No, no way. He hasn't even been here for a week, girl would have to move *fast*." She smiled devilishly. "Not that she *won't*, believe me. She's had her sights set on him since art class on Friday."

Over my dead body. "Hm," I replied calmly.

Cassidy leaned in closer. "But I think it's a hopeless case." I briefly had a Harry Chen flashback. Did Luca . . . not like girls?! But Cassidy continued. "Some girl asked him out in class, the *first day*, and I actually overheard him say he doesn't want a girlfriend."

It was my turn to furrow *my* brow. "Why not?"

She shrugged. "Who knows. I figured it was because he's this major serious artist and I know he's going after this big scholarship to help pay for RISD if he gets in." She glanced at me. "Rhode Island—"

"School of Design. Yeah, I know the name of every college in North America." I immediately regretted saying it. I smiled apologetically. "Sorry, I'm a freak."

Cassidy laughed. "Noted."

I looked at her curiously. "How do you know so much about him already?"

Cassidy blushed. "He was talking in class about RISD and the scholarship and . . . um, you know, you just hear things." A few seconds passed and her shoulders slumped. "Also, I looked him up online."

Couldn't blame the girl.

I settled deeply in my seat, staring at the back of Luca's beanie-bedecked head. I was relieved that he and that terrible human being weren't together, but the whole mysterious no-girlfriend thing was a major obstacle I hadn't anticipated.

Good thing there was nothing that motivated me more than hearing that I couldn't do something.

Well, the verdict was in: I cannot draw. I erased my unintentionally Cubist giraffe furiously.

Cassidy glanced over at my sketchbook and tried to keep a straight face. "Honestly, if you were good at this, too, I might have to kill you."

While that was flattering, it drove me crazy to hear that. I stared at my shitty giraffe mutinously.

We were sitting on a bench across from the giraffe pen. Everyone had paired off as soon as we got there, and before I could even attempt to talk to Luca, Violet had linked her arm through his and whisked him away. Hm, I wasn't the only one without shame.

So here I was with Cassidy, trying to draw animals. This was not going according to plan.

"Hey, have you seen Luca?"

My head snapped up to see a furious Violet stalking over to Cassidy.

"No, did he ditch you?" Cassidy teased.

Hands on bony hips, Violet scowled. "*Not* funny." God, what a gem. "I've been looking for him for the past twenty minutes. He said he was headed off to the bathroom and then, like, completely disappeared."

"Maybe you should call the lost and found," I muttered.

She glanced at me with her upper lip curled. "I'm sorry, was I talking to you?"

You know what? In *Protect the Boss*, Eun-Sol eventually shoved an ice cream cone onto the bitch's butt, too. *Have backbone on occasion.*

I lifted my chin, looked back at Violet, and said, "I'm sorry, did I ask you to block my view of these magnificent creatures?"

Without her Ray-Bans on, Violet was able to fix her steely eyes directly on mine. "Stop pretending to draw."

Cassidy threw up her arms. "Enough, Violet! Geez, let's go find him." She looked at me apologetically. "Sorry, Desi, do you mind?"

I did not mind. At all. I smiled and waved them off. "No, go find him, good luck!" Violet made a face, then grabbed Cassidy roughly to her feet.

When they were out of sight, I jumped up and gathered my things. This was my chance. Somewhere Luca was alone.

I saw Art Club kids sketching in various areas of the zoo: The sea lion pool. The bear den. The reptile tanks. But no sign of that gray beanie. I took the path toward the entrance of the zoo, but still nothing. I was about to head back to the giraffes when something caught my eye by the entrance. Hidden behind a few eucalyptus-tree branches was an old-fashioned brass plaque welded onto a gate. It looked so out of place in the pristine and remodeled zoo that I walked over to read what it said.

Historical site of the original South Orange County Zoo. Built in 1932, this beautiful park was hailed around the nation as one of America's first modern zoos. It suffered a fire in 1994 and was fully rebuilt and remodeled in 2001. The only remaining group of original buildings and animal pens is located near the south exit, down the trail by the giant rainbow eucalyptus tree. Please take care not to disturb any of the fragile structures or the surrounding plant life.

Hm. If I were an artist type, where would I go to find something more interesting than the bored, sedentary animals that everyone else was drawing?

I peered down at my zoo map and headed for the south exit. Glancing at my phone, I realized I only had an hour before the bus would head out. I set an alarm on my phone just in case. You better be there, art boy.

You couldn't miss the eucalyptus tree—about sixty feet tall with really cool rainbow-striped bark. It's also the only eucalyptus species found naturally in the northern hemisphere. (Yes,

I am the treasurer for the Arbor Society's Monte Vista chapter.)
I spotted a trail right at its base.

I walked down the path, between thick groves of live oak and
sycamore trees, their dropped leaves crunching under my feet.
It was beautiful here, but no hot guy to be seen. Then I spotted
what looked like ruins in the distance and sped up.

"Whoa," I breathed.

Surrounding me in a big clearing were rock caves and rusty
cages covered in thick and stringy moss. The plants surrounding them were overgrown and had a junglelike quality, only bits
of filtered sunlight making it through. There was a paved path
that wound through everything.

I pushed aside branches to climb into one of the open cages.
The walls inside were rusty and mossy like everything else, but
they were also covered in graffiti. I wrinkled my nose. I was
headed toward one of the caves when I heard a hissing noise. I
froze. Holy crap, was that a snake? Were there now wild animals
roaming this postapocalyptic-looking zoo? The hissing paused,
then started again. I tilted my head—no, it didn't sound like an
animal.

"Hello?" I called out tentatively.

The hissing immediately stopped. Then—crunching leaves.
Someone . . . *something* was moving through the trees. Oh God,
why oh why did I decide to do this? Stupid idiot K drama steps!

"Desi?"

A familiar, very low, very boy voice.

Luca walked out from between a couple of run-down Spanish-style buildings. "What are you doing here?" he asked.

I clutched my chest, waiting for my heartbeat to slow down. "I saw a sign for the ruins of the old zoo and got curious." Hm, lay it on thick, Des. "Also . . . I was a little embarrassed to draw with the others. I thought I'd try out buildings instead of animals." I saw a flash of genuine pity cross Luca's face. Okay, he bought it, then. "What are *you* doing here?"

He adjusted his backpack. "Got bored, wanted to look around." We stared at each other for a second.

"Well—" I started.

"So why are you so embarrassed to draw? You're not that bad."

"Pff. Yeah, not bad for a kindergartner."

He walked over to me and held out his hand. "Let me see."

"See what?"

"Your drawings."

My instinct was a giant *no freaking way*, but I knew that would kill any momentum I was gaining. So I reluctantly pulled my sketchbook out of my backpack and handed it to him.

He flipped through it, and I felt the seconds pass like years. When it was almost too unbearable to stand anymore, Luca finally stopped on one of my horrid giraffe drawings. "Okay, this one, it's not bad. But can I teach you a trick?"

The patient and considerate tone in his voice melted all self-consciousness into a puddle at my feet. (Um, like a pair of sweatpants.)

"Mm-hm, sure," I squeaked.

Luca dropped his backpack and sat down cross-legged on an area overgrown with flowering sage bushes and tall grasses, patting the ground next to him. I sat down, carefully scooting my butt closer to him an inch at a time until I felt like I was sitting at an acceptable distance.

"So you're getting caught up in the details, which are hard for anyone to draw, you know?" He pointed at all the spots I had painstakingly sketched and then eventually given up on, creating a scribbly mess.

"When you look at something, anything, you should first see it as a bunch of shapes that create an object," he said, gesturing with his hands. He had nice hands. Long fingers, short clean nails, and the right amount of veins and boniness.

He was looking expectantly at me. "Got that?" he asked. Uh . . . what?

My confusion was obvious, so he turned to a new page in my sketchbook and handed me a pencil that had been tucked behind his ear. "Okay, look at that pine tree over there," he said, pointing.

"Um, actually, that's a deodar cedar, they're often mistaken for pines."

Luca blinked. "Why do you know that?"

Drats, a slip of nerd. I shrugged, oh so casual. "Oh, just . . . I'm a member of the Arbor Society." *No need to mention I'm the treasurer.* I braced myself for derision or teasing.

But instead he looked me in the eyes a beat longer than

necessary. "Of course you are." My heart thumped. *Was that a good thing or a bad thing?!* He smiled with a little head shake. *Good thing.*

Then he glanced back at the tree. "All right, study that *deodar cedar* and draw the basic shapes that it's made up of."

I tried not to get too excited by the mere fact that this pencil had been resting on that precious skin, and squinted at the tree. Hm, okay. So I started sketching the tree from the top, every little line representing a needle. When I finished, it looked like a hairy blob.

"Er, let's try this." He reached over and placed his hand on mine, which started sweating immediately at his touch. He kept his hand on mine and drew a rough, large triangle and then a little rectangle below it.

"Um, that looks like a cartoon tree," I said.

His face was so close that I could feel his warm breath on my cheek when he sighed in exasperation. "Miss Literal, can you wait a second before jumping to conclusions?" I refrained from calling him Mr. Abstract.

"Do you see how it felt to make that nice loose shape? Warms up your hand, right?" Yeah, I would say my hand was warm. Real warm.

He continued to draw while holding my hand, making smaller triangles within the tree. "Then you can focus in more on each area, and get more detailed as you go." When he finished, he let go of my hand, and there was a tree on my page. And it was just a lot of loose shapes, but it was one hundred percent recogniz-able as a tree. Way more so than mine was with all its needles.

"Cool!" I grinned and looked up at Luca, who was grinning back at me.

Zap. Another bolt of that *something* shot through me.

And then my phone alarm went off, shrill and jarring. "Oh crap, the bus leaves in ten minutes!"

We quickly gathered our things and bolted down the trail. There was a bit of an incline before we hit the concrete path leading to the normal part of the zoo. When we reached the eucalyptus tree, I turned around to see Luca struggling to keep up. "Wait . . . I need . . . a sec."

I looked at him, amused. "We ran, like, twenty yards."

He waved his hand up at me, catching his breath. "I have no idea how to measure in yards. What a jock."

I laughed. "Well, clearly anyone who doesn't go into cardiac arrest when jogging for thirty seconds is a jock."

He finally caught his breath and straightened up—awfully close to me. He tilted his head to the side, scrutinizing me. "So what's a jock like you doing in Art Club anyway? I thought you weren't into it?"

I heard the slight tease in his voice—almost daring me to be honest and say that I joined because of him. I bit my lip. Here's where an Oscar-worthy performance needed to kick in. I tried to make my voice sound wistful. "Well, um, when you noticed my doodle, I just . . . I realized I'm always doodling." *Who doesn't, dummo?* "And that, um, it's just something I've always wanted to do. Draw." *Shameless, flat-out lie.*

He looked at me for so long that I was sure he was on to me. This was pure idiocy! But then something shifted in his expression. The corners of his mouth slowly lifted until a huge, gorgeous grin broke across that unbearable face. "Cool, glad to see you here. Let me know if you need more help with anything."

You know that feeling when it's been a crappy overcast day and then suddenly the sun peeks out, right onto your face? That's what Luca's smile was like. Like it was beaming straight from outer space onto my face specifically.

I turned my head so he wouldn't see me blush. "Thanks." When I felt my face cool off, I glanced over at him again, upright and so at ease in his own body. (Who could blame him, really?) "Hey, so why aren't you in AP English anymore?"

"Oh, that. With my grades, there's no way I should have been in that class."

My brow furrowed. "Why didn't you say anything?"

And again, that smile. *Zap.* "It was fun to see what you nerds were up to."

Confidence boosted, I decided to actually try flirting. *Lord, here I go.* I gently bumped my hip against his. He looked over at me lickety-split, surprised. I smiled. "I'm a nerd that can clearly outrun you. Can you handle the rest of the walk back to the bus or do you need me to carry you?"

He raised an eyebrow and I flushed—had I gone too far? Had

I offended his manhood? But then he threw his head back and laughed—this for-real laugh complete with signature honk. He grinned and replied, "Yeah, actually, *can* you?" I cracked a huge smile, not even thinking about whether I had food in my teeth or if I was at a flattering angle so that my cheeks wouldn't puff out too much.

It was only when we got to the bus that I realized I'd never asked him if he had drawn anything at the abandoned zoo. But at the exact same moment, Violet and Cassidy found us.

"Where have *you two* been?" Violet demanded, running her hand through her hair with agitation. Ah, subtle as always.

Luca glanced at me then, the quickest little intimate look.

"I just ran into him, calm down," I said while breezing by her. I didn't want Violet to know. The old zoo felt like a secret place, special to us.

Her glare burned a hole in my back as I walked up into the bus ahead of her.

Violet was your classic K drama bitch, but if ever there was a sure thing in dramas, it was that the good girl always won in the end.

STEP 7:
Mystery Surrounds the Guy but Find Out More

The next day, Wes, Fiona, and I were crammed into Penny, headed to Fiona's house to study for our calculus test. Even though Wes drove an SUV that could fit two entire families in it, our preferred mode of transportation was always Penny. I suspected it was because we got a secret thrill from nearly dying every time we got in it.

From the backseat, Wes leaned forward so that his head was two inches away from mine in the passenger seat. "I commend your effort, Des. I, too, think one should get laid before entering college."

"*Oh my God!*" I yelled, along with Fiona. He got a pummeling from both of us, Fiona using her right arm to reach behind her and smack him in the cheek.

"Hey, just being totally real here." He sat back in his seat. "But also, aren't you worried that you'll be caught? If he ever finds out you're using him as some sort of boyfriend experiment—"

"What the hell, Wes? I'm not doing this as an experiment!"
I exclaimed. I looked at my two friends, staring especially hard
at Fiona, who was suddenly unusually focused on her driving.
"Um, Fi, did you not fill him in on why I'm doing this?"

"Nooo, I mean . . . I didn't know how private our discussion
was?"

"Oh, but not *so* private that you didn't mention the plan to
Wes?"

Fiona just shrugged.

"So wait. Then why are you doing this?" Wes asked.

I sank back into my seat. "What do you mean?! I *like* him!"
I paused for a second. "I mean, somehow it feels like more than
a crush. There's something about the way he's so calm and confident about art—his patience and kindness when he was helping me at the zoo the other day . . ."

Wes scoffed. "Yeah, so hard showing off in front of a girl."

"It wasn't like that! He actually wanted to help me. It was
really nice." I glanced at Wes and Fiona nervously. "In fact, I'm
pretty sure I want him to be my first boyfriend."

Fiona cleared her throat. "Des, the leap from crush to boyfriend . . . maybe you should take it slow—"

Wes interrupted her abruptly. "Oh God, I don't wanna see
flailure heartbreak. I was hoping it was just you needing to round
out your high school years with a good old-fashioned devirgin-
izing."

"Gross. Also, geez, what kind of emotionless robot do you

think I am?" A conspicuous silence permeated Penny. I huffed. "You guys, there's something really interesting about this. This is my way out of flailure. When I know I have a blueprint for this, I remain normal Desi. I was able to hang out with him yesterday without any incidents! In fact, I think we *flirted*."

Fiona glanced over at me in the passenger seat. "So no flailure moments?"

"No! Like I said, when I have a plan—all's well." I shook my head, amazed yet again at how my past flailures could have been avoided.

Wes kicked the back of my seat. "Well, just don't let him find out. It's kind of creepy what you're doing."

"You're a creep!" I barked.

Fiona laughed. "Aren't you so glad you missed that Phoenix concert to help us study for calculus?"

"Yeah, super-happy about that decision!" I turned around and held a fist threateningly over Wes's head.

We pulled up to Fiona's house in a cul de sac that basically looked just like mine. In fact, our houses were the same layout. Monte Vista architecture was very cutting edge.

"Lita! We're home," Fiona announced when we stormed the house. I sniffed the air. Yesss, it was starting. Fiona's grandmother, who lived with her family, was making us pork mole poblano tacos as a study reward. As in, tacos with a chocolaty sauce. Served with pickled onions on fresh-made corn tortillas. Going to Fiona's to study over a concert was really a no-brainer.

A vision of elderly elegance appeared from the kitchen—wool trousers, silk rose-colored blouse, sleek white bob, and impeccable pearls. No lace shawl for this grandma. Fiona's Lita (short for Abuelita) looked like she ran a global makeup corporation.

Balancing a tray of iced teas, she lifted her cheek up for a kiss from Fiona, then stepped back to examine Fiona's tropical-print shorts-and-shirt combo with a floor-length crocheted sweater. She looked like a *Golden Girls*–themed human. Lita's delicate eyebrows lifted while she handed the tray to Fiona. She turned to Wes and me with a smile. "Hi you two, ready to study your little brains out?" She reached over and ruffled Wes's hair, something *no one else in the world* was allowed to do.

"Yes," we both answered obediently. Lita's mere presence commanded straightened spines and clear enunciation from everyone.

"Okay, tacos will be ready in three hours, so work hard until then." With an air-kiss she was off into the kitchen again.

We spread out in Fiona's living room with our drinks, pushing aside piles of toy trucks and picture books. Teddy and Nicky, Fiona's twin brothers, basically owned the house. Luckily they were at a play date, so we could actually get work done without them quizzing us on our favorite Avenger. Wes plopped down onto the sofa and Fiona sat on the floor at his feet, her back pushed up against the sofa. I lay belly-down on the living room rug with my calculus book opened. But after a few minutes of staring at the same equation, I slammed it shut.

"You know what, Wes? That's sexist crap. When a guy goes through obstacles to get a girl, it's considered 'romantic.' Think climbing through a girl's window unannounced to watch her sleep. However, when it's a *girl* making dramatic gestures for a guy, it's *creepy*. Double-standard bullshit!"

Wes laughed from the sofa. "Are you still thinking about Luca? Damn, you *are* crazy."

Fiona frowned and threw an ice cube from her iced tea at him. "Shut *up,* Wes. Why do you even hang out with a bunch of girls, anyway, you caveman douche?"

Wes threw an ice cube back at her, which she deftly knocked away. "I like being the only voice of reason surrounded by irrational females," he replied.

People often wondered why I didn't date Wes. Yes, he was cute and funny and charming as hell but he was also the most annoying brother I never had. Also, fully witnessing his player ways since middle school had made me lose all attraction to him.

Flipping Wes off with one hand, Fiona started swiping furiously on her iPad with the other, announcing, "Hey, before we start studying, let's do something more fun." The corners of her hot-pink lips curved into a smile and she held her iPad face-out for us to see.

It was a blown-up photo of Luca. I lurched over and tried to grab it from her but she held it away with a bratty, "Nuh-uh! Let's stalk him. Isn't that on your list somewhere?"

Hm. I pulled out my notebook where I kept the K drama list.

I was on step 7, *Mystery Surrounds the Guy but Find Out More.* "Well, I was going to do this on my own time, but why not now? But then we have to study, okay?" I said sternly.

Fiona rolled her eyes. "Okay, Mom. First, let's see what dirt we can get on this guy, make sure he's worthy of this K drama insanity."

"Whoa, he's got a lot of Internet action," Wes said as Fiona scrolled through the Google results.

Something caught my eye. "Luca Drakos *Official Fan Page*? What the heck is that? Click on it!"

"That can't be for *your* Luca, right?" Fiona asked skeptically while tapping on the link.

It led us to a website full of beautiful, strange drawings and paintings. Dark, exquisitely rendered figures entwined in ropy vines, being lifted or held down by nightmarish creatures. Elfin faces painted in painstaking detail with complex layers of milky paint washed over them, dotted with tiny insects. Though totally different in subject, they looked incredibly similar in style to that doodle in English class.

"This looks like Luca's stuff," I murmured.

We were quiet as we absorbed image after surreal image. Was this *all* Luca's work? What kind of teenager was this prolific? And why the hell was he going to *our* high school rather than some art school for talented mutants like him?

Fiona whistled. "Damn, girl. You picked a good one."

"No, she picked a *difficult* one. Des, end it now while you have your dignity," Wes said, settling deeper into the sofa, his skinny jeans squeaking against the leather.

I sputtered. "Excuse *you*."

I took Fiona's iPad from her and clicked on the "Bio" link on Luca's fan page. "Luca Drakos was born on August 16, 1999, in Santa Barbara, California. From a young age he loved art—according to his mother, his first word was *Impressionism*."

We laughed.

I continued reading. "He grew up in the Southern California spiritual enclave of Ojai, taking art classes at a young age, the star in every class."

"Bet everyone *loved* him," Fiona interjected.

I shushed her. "By the time he started high school at Santa Barbara School for the Arts, Luca was already notorious—not just for his groundbreaking neo-surrealist paintings, but for his reputation as a rule-breaker as well."

Fiona grabbed the iPad from me and continued to read from Luca's bio. "He has won numerous awards, including the National Young Artist and Bright Star to Watch awards. His personal Tumblr page, which skyrocketed him to fame, has over one million followers."

"*What?*" Wes sat up at that bit of geek info. "That's like . . . he's, like, Tumblr famous."

I held up my list dramatically, pointing at step 3. "So clearly he *is* the world's most unattainable guy. He's basically famous." My heart started to beat quicker, because even with the K drama steps as my magic feather, I had just now fully comprehended the monumental nature of the task at hand.

I looked up at my friends in despair. "I can barely speak to normal cute boys. How am I going to land *this* guy? This—this unattainable *artist*. Like, you know how people talk about leagues of hotness—he's so out of my league when you add this crazy talent to it all. My league is here, firmly planted in Orange freaking County. And Luca's league is somewhere floating in space, idly and sexily orbiting some distant planet."

A beat of silence and then Wes burst out laughing. "Jesus, Desi! Your inner monologues."

Fiona rolled her eyes. "And he's so *not* out of your league. You're freaking out of *his* league. Any guy would be so lucky." It was Fiona being fiercely protective, not empty best-friend buildup, but it was still nice to hear. She kept talking. "And yeah, he's hot, but whatever, you're hot, too. Do I need to start my 'Ode to Desi's Perfect Bubble Ass' rap?"

"Oh my God, please no." Wes groaned. "And Des, whatever, I was just kidding about ending it with your dignity still in place. So just chill. I've never known someone to have such *selective* low self-esteem. It's like, soccer? You're the best player to have ever lived and nobody better mess. But then with guys? You have this warped view of being some underdog."

I flushed—while my friends were being kind, I suddenly felt like I was fishing for compliments. "Well, I *am* the best soccer player to have ever lived," I said breezily. "Not counting Messi."

"So you're really gonna do this?" Wes asked with a wide, mischievous smile.

I nodded slowly, feeling my insecurities melt away as that ol' familiar can-do Desi Lee determination came back in full force. "Yes. The steps will guide the way." I paused. "But we have a minor setback."

Fiona fished an ice cube out of her glass and popped it into her mouth. "What?"

"Cassidy told me that he doesn't want a girlfriend. He actually *said* that."

"Please. That's easy, you'll just have to change his mind," Fiona said, one eyebrow raised like a Bond girl villain.

I pressed my lips together. "Right. First things first then. Can you teach me how to do that eyebrow thing?"

When I got home that evening, I opened my K drama steps notebook and carefully ripped out the pages with just the steps written on them. I folded them up and put them in my wallet. I knew it was silly, but having the list near me was reassuring. Its magical powers pulsing near my ID and cash at all times, always close, always watchful. And I needed all the help I could get.

A couple of days later, I was still scheming to find ways to get more Luca time beyond just Art Club, which only met once a week. So far in my K drama reconnaissance I had been able to find out that his group of friends seemed to be Violet, Cassidy, and a few other art kids. They either hung out on the grassy lawn in the courtyard or in the art room for lunch. He wasn't in any other extracurricular activities or sports as far as I could tell (surprise, surprise). He was also in remedial classes, except for art.

Another note: he ate a frozen burrito for lunch *every single day.* Gross.

My phone buzzed during physics but I ignored it because we were in the middle of a quiz. Then it buzzed two more times. I glanced up to see Miss Clark on her computer, completely oblivious. I quickly pulled it out of my denim-jacket pocket and glanced down at the texts. Fiona. Who was sitting a few rows ahead of me. What the heck? I unlocked my phone to read the texts.

Did you hear about Luca?

???

How he got arrested??!!

I quickly texted back: **No??!! Talk after class.**

I whizzed through the quiz, double-checked my answers, then watched the clock. I waited impatiently until the bell rang. When it did, I practically dragged Fiona outside, where everyone else around us was rushing to class.

"Well?!" I demanded.

Fiona raised her eyebrows at me. "So everyone's talking about it."

"Who's *everyone*? He's been at this school for, like, a week!" I exclaimed. "Is he okay?" I was instantly worried, over this guy I barely knew.

"Well, this kid, Spencer Something, was skating around the zoo last night and saw him get arrested."

"Wait, who's this Spencer Something?"

Fiona shrugged. "I don't know, one of those skater guys." She adjusted her backpack. "Anyway, I have to run, my coding class has a special guest lecturer today. But"—she looked at me meaningfully—"apparently this wasn't his first time." With that, she was off in a cloud of sultry men's cologne and a jangle of bangles.

Not the first time?! I did recall something about *rule-breaker* from our Google stalking, but nothing illegal . . . also, the zoo? What had he been doing when I ran into him at the abandoned zoo? I needed to find out more, but unfortunately Art Club wasn't until next Tuesday. Until then, Luca would have to remain a mystery.

The following Tuesday, I walked tentatively into the art studio after school. It was a large room with a low ceiling and a wall of windows to let in plenty of light. Whatever wall space was left was filled with student art projects and vintage posters from various museums. The back of the room was reserved for supplies, closed off partially by a dark green canvas curtain.

I looked around, feeling more like a fraud than ever. Pretending to draw animals at the zoo was one thing; spending an hour actually trying to create art was another.

Everyone was already knee-deep in their charity art show projects—some were paintings on canvas, others mixed media, some were even sculptures. I didn't see Luca. But there was Violet, front and center, her canvas set up on an easel as she sat on a stool with her long legs stretched out, wearing a pair of big, pretentious, clear-framed glasses as she concentrated on her masterpiece.

Ugh.

I spied Cassidy going through the green curtain that led to the supply area, so I followed her in. "Hey, Cassidy."

She glanced over at me as she grabbed a set of charcoals. "Hey, Desi!"

"Sorry to be annoying, but would you mind helping me pick out some supplies for the charity show project?" I asked, embarrassed.

"Sure! What kind of medium were you thinking? Acrylic, watercolor . . . ?"

"Well, that's where I need help. I'm not quite sure." I scanned the shelves of art supplies—they were arranged row after row, like library stacks. There were coffee tins full of paintbrushes, tubes and bottles of paint, plastic trays, which I assumed were palettes, bundles of pastels and charcoals, canvases and easels, etc. I was impressed—this was a great art department for a California public school.

Cassidy stood back and squinted while assessing the supplies. "Okay, well, I think oil would be kind of intense for a beginner and watercolor can be tricky, too. Let's go with something more forgiving—acrylic!" She grabbed a few bottles of primary colors. "You know the whole thing about mixing these colors to create all the other colors, right?"

Hm. Kind of. "Sure!" I answered brightly. A few minutes later I was armed with a sixteen-by-twenty-inch canvas, a few different paintbrushes, a plastic tray, and the bottles of paint.

When we left the supply area, I instantly spotted Luca. It was like every nerve ending in my body was attuned to his presence.

He was sitting next to Violet, feet propped up on a desk, laughing at something she was saying. Ugh, really? How funny could she be? I had never met anyone as humorless as that walking American Apparel ad. And I was immediately irked by how at ease he seemed to be in her presence.

I thought of my current K drama step: *Mystery Surrounds the Guy but Find Out More.* Break down the mysterious wall like a sassy jackhammer.

And the first thing I needed to figure out was whether or not Luca had actually gotten arrested. And if yes, for *what*?

"Let's go sit with those guys," I said cheerfully, steering Cassidy over to Luca and Violet.

She raised her eyebrows at me. "Really?"

"Yeah, why not?"

A quick, shrewd expression passed over Cassidy's face, but she didn't say anything. She was probably clued in to my Luca crush now. *Oh well.*

"Hey guys," I said, laying my supplies down on a desk. *Keep your voice cool, Des. Nix the enthusiasm.*

Luca glanced up, his eyes meeting mine for a second. "Oh, hey Desi."

Every part of me warmed up, including my cheeks. I dropped my head pretending to fish something out of my backpack so that he wouldn't notice the telltale blush.

"Why are you here? Didn't you have enough at the zoo?"

My head whipped up and I looked straight at Violet. "Same reason you are, Andy Warhol."

Luca cracked a huge smile and Cassidy coughed abruptly.

"I doubt it," Violet muttered, but she seemed to be bored by me already, and her body leaned toward her painting in concentration.

I get it, you're an *artiste.*

While I was setting up my paints, I couldn't help but glance over at Luca. Who was still in his reclined position, staring at his phone. This was going to be difficult. How could I bring up the arrest in front of everyone without putting him on the spot? And would he even give me a straight answer? No, I needed to take the more casual, natural route. And if there were any two words in the English language that defined me? Well, literally, the last two would be *casual* and *natural.*

"So what are *you* working on, then?" I asked. The breeziness of my question was offset by the sudden fart noise my bottle of acrylic paint made when I squeezed it. I froze, letting a second of silence pass. "Um, that was my paint."

Luca smirked. "Sure."

"Shut up." But I had already started giggling. And couldn't stop.

Deadly, poison-laced daggers were being stabbed into my face from Violet's eyeballs. I pursed my lips, willing the giggles to stop.

"My project's a secret. What's yours?" Luca asked.

Giggles stopped abruptly. I hesitated. I had decided on painting my favorite tree, the California sycamore. An idea that had seemed cool last night when I thought of it, but now in front of Violet and the other art kids I felt self-conscious. I stammered, "Um—well—I was thinking maybe . . ."

Then the voice inside me that usually told me to be cool around guys was saying something else: *be earnest*. Because K drama heroines were always earnest to a maddening degree. It was their most endearing trait. Other than their klutziness.

And let's be honest, sycamore trees *were* cool.

"I'm painting a California sycamore." As anticipated, I got a blank face from Luca. I powered ahead. "It's a fast-growing deciduous tree that tolerates heat, smog, and drought as well as moist conditions. A total badass."

Cassidy's mouth dropped open ever so slightly and Luca was still staring at me. I flushed but refused to back down. "So yeah, I'm painting a tree."

Violet cackled. "Are you *serious*?"

Before I could defend myself, Luca sat up, propped his elbows on his desk, and looked at me intently. "That's amazing."

Great. Now he was making fun of me. "No need to be *rude*," I sniffed.

He shook his head. "No! I'm serious! Will you be making some sort of statement about climate change and the need for drought-tolerant trees like this in city landscaping?"

Zap. Again. Usually it was the brush of his hand or some adorable thing he did with his mouth that gave me that little jolt. But this time, it was his *nerdy* reaction to *my* nerdiness.

"Yes?" My brain was scrambled eggs and it was the only thing I could muster with my rapidly beating heart. "So why is your project a secret?"

But before he could respond, Luca's phone buzzed. He glanced at whatever text message he had received, stood up, and slipped the phone into his back pocket. He smiled down at me, as dazzling and fleeting as a comet. "Because it's a secret." He headed toward the door with a "Later, guys." And then he was gone.

What the *heck*?

Violet looked over at me with narrowed eyes. "You ruin everything."

Ignoring her, I tried to feign interest in my blank canvas while frustrated by knowing that I'd probably done as much as I could with step 7. Luca was way too good at this mysterious-guy act.

STEP 8:
Be Caught in an Obviously Lopsided Love Triangle

I stared at Wes. He stared back at me. Then winked. I shuddered.

This was not going to work. "Don't be gross."

He took his right hand off the steering wheel and clasped mine. I pulled it away and slapped his hand. "Creeper, don't make me regret this. I am not above destroying everyone you love if you make this difficult for me."

He adjusted his hair and continued to grin. The grin that had slain a thousand hearts at Monte Vista High. "Hey, I'm doing you a favor right now. All in the name of K drama love."

It was true. We were headed to a party. Together, as a date. The other day, when I passed by Luca between classes for half a second, I asked if he was going to the party and he said, "Yeah, I guess I'll check out that sex party."

So Wes was chosen to be the Other Guy (aka second lead) for step 8: *Be Caught in an Obviously Lopsided Love Triangle.*

I still hadn't been able to find out anything about Luca's no-girlfriend deal, so I was hoping that some raging jealousy might make him rethink that whole thing.

Wes was a stellar candidate for the secondary love interest. Cute enough to be a viable threat to the hotness that was Luca, and a good actor, too. Which he had to be—we had to convince *everyone* at this party that we were interested in each other, not just Luca.

"Okay, so the rules for tonight—" I started.

"Chill, Des. You already told me the stupid rules."

"Weeeell, I am going to *repeat* them since you've already violated one," I said, staring pointedly at his hand. "Okay, so we're not *overtly* dating, and it will never be confirmed that we are. I just want there to be enough insinuation to keep Won Bin on his toes, to see if we can make him jealous." Won Bin was our code name for Luca. Also, Won Bin happens to be the hottest Korean actor alive.

I poked him. "So this means only heavy flirting. *No* sexy touching. Keep this PG, my friend."

He leaned over and reached for a strand of my hair. "Done and dunzo, my *friend*. I have the flirting-but-not-dating thing *down*." A little tug on my hair for added emphasis.

That earned him a K drama finger-flick to the forehead. "We'll only resort to PG-13 if we need to." Then I handed him the list of love triangle rules I had written and printed out.

He squinted down at it. "What's with all the colors?"

"Certain rules are highlighted to denote levels of importance. There's a legend at the top of—"

Wes crumpled up the piece of paper and tossed it into the backseat. My mouth dropped open. "Hey! I spent a lot of time on that!"

"I'm saving you from yourself. I know you're following these K drama steps and all that, and you think you've got it down to some science. But trust me—Wes Mansour doesn't need a list."

I wanted to argue, but it was true.

We arrived at Gwen Parker's house, a giant McMansion sitting on a beach with a beautiful view of the marina filled with boats and glittering lights strung along the pier. Gwen was the captain of the dance team and her dad was a movie producer. Every year she threw this raging holiday party that the entire school showed up to—it was "romance" themed. Aka fertile ground for hooking up. Aka why Luca called it a sex party. Wholesome holiday activities, high school style—there were rooms for spin the bottle and seven minutes in heaven, and everyone was required to wear red, either for holiday cheer or, you know, for general debauchery devil references. But not everyone went there to just hook up. There was also plenty of alcohol and bad dancing. I had never been before, but I'd heard all the gory details from Wes and Fiona.

Staring up at the front stairs covered in red confetti, I took a deep breath. *You can do this. You are NOT flailure girl tonight. You are a K drama heroine destined for love.*

89

I stopped Wes before we reached the front door. "Hey, hold on a sec." Then I held up a Santa hat.

"What's that for?"

I plopped it onto his head and adjusted it so that it fit properly. Then I held up a second one, my eyebrows raised, and put it on. "So that it's clear we're together," I said.

He grumbled, "This is really cramping my style."

Once inside, we hung up our jackets and then wove through groups of people drinking and dancing. I instinctively moved closer to Wes, feeling nervous. The hormone levels in here were ridiculous. Was *everyone* having sex but me? God.

And then. It hit me that if Luca was here, was he here to hook up?! And ew, what if he came with *Violet*? Did *that* not break the no-girlfriend rule? Hm, hooking up didn't necessarily entail dating . . .

I shook my head. I didn't want to contemplate Luca hooking up with anyone. Well, other than me. And just that thought alone sent mutant butterflies hurtling through my stomach.

"Hey lovers," a female voice growled behind me. I turned around to see Fiona and her girlfriend du jour, Leslie Colbert. Girls lined up for Fiona every year. Sometimes it was the classic bad-girl type and they'd make out rebelliously in the hallways at school. Other times it was a hot hipster in a band who would serenade her with a guitar solo onstage. This year it was the captain of the cheerleading squad, Leslie. An odd pairing until you saw the two of them together and it was like being blinded by the beauty of God's creations.

Fiona was in a slinky backless black top and high-waisted flowing black pants, her hair straightened tonight into a high, sleek ponytail. The touches of red were her hair and ruby lips. Leslie was wearing a red bikini top. Okay.

"I'm so overwhelmed. Do you think people are actually *doing it* in here?" I whispered to her.

Fiona waved her hand at me dismissively. "We've got bigger fish to fry. Guess who I just saw?"

I sucked in a breath. "Won Bin?"

"Yup."

I looked around, but couldn't see much in the dim lighting.

Fiona grabbed my arm. "Don't be so obvious, Des! He's loitering with a bunch of those art kids. Including that purple-headed dumb-ass." Fiona was never one to mince words.

I frowned. "I wonder if they came together."

I was trying to look around as subtly as possible when I spotted Luca. His hair was perfectly mussed under a red beanie. *Hot damn*. Always. That was always how I was going to feel when I looked at this guy.

I tugged Wes closer to me. "Psst, Won Bin's here," I said in a low voice. I saw his head snap up. "Stop! Don't look. Anyway, I think you know what this means."

He raised his eyebrows.

I held up my fist and said, *"Hwai-ting!"* Wes looked at me blankly.

"It's the Konglish misuse of *fighting*." His face remained blank. I rolled my eyes. "It's the Korean equivalent of *Let's do this!*"

He grinned and bumped my fist with his. "Got it. *Hwai-ting!*"

My eyes drifted over to Luca again, and I saw him heading upstairs with Violet and Cassidy.

"Won Bin's going upstairs, let's follow him." I grabbed Wes's arm and dragged him to the second floor where I saw Luca and company slip into a room with a sign that said SEVEN MINUTES IN HEAVEN, surrounded by angel wings. What in the world?! Why were they going in *there*? All three of them?

I stared at the door. Well, it was now or never. "Ready for seven minutes in heaven?" I asked Wes.

His eyebrows disappeared into his hair. "Whaaa—are you serious?"

"Yup. Here we go."

Holding his hand, I pulled him toward the door. He protested, "Desi, I don't want to, like, besmirch your reputation." I didn't respond. Instead I paused for just a second before swinging the door open.

It was a big bedroom (maybe the master?), filled with people and a trail of rose petals leading to double doors, with a sign that said HEAVEN. I saw a couple slip out and then another slip in.

Everyone else was casually milling about. As if it was normal to be that close to other people making out.

And there were Luca, Violet, and Cassidy. Just lounging around and acting normal. I had to find out why they were up there, but first it was time for my grand-entrance moment. Think Young-Shin in *Healer*, when she whips off her coat to show off her insanely hot red dress at that press conference. Healer the Hottie couldn't believe his eyes.

So when Luca turned and looked at us, I stood there for a few seconds, letting him eye my lacy red dress and black booties. I started to blush, though, so I headed over to them before I lost my resolve.

"Hey, what are you guys doing up here?" I asked, losing cool points *immediately* by asking that nosy question. I could hear Wes's sigh behind me.

Cassidy looked uncomfortable when she answered, "We wanted to see . . . um . . ."

"We wanted to see what kind of desperate hornballs came up here," Violet finished for her, grinning widely.

Wes threw his arm over my shoulders. "Well, take a good look, sister." With that he pulled me away toward the heaven doors. I was swiveled around so quickly that I couldn't even gauge Luca's reaction.

"What the hell, Wes?!" I hissed.

He clamped his hand on my upper arm. "I'm saving you, Des. Come on."

When we got to the door, the couple from earlier came out, laughing their asses off. "Have fun!" the girl cackled to me as she walked by us.

I pulled Wes in close and whispered, "Is he looking?"

Wes whispered back, "I don't know, I'm staring at you right now."

"Right," I whispered again. I was too nervous to look behind me, so I just opened the door and Wes and I stepped in. It was a giant walk-in closet, lit with candles, with Sade playing quietly in the background.

Wes started to laugh but I clapped my hand over his mouth. "We have to make this believable!" I whispered loudly.

"So what do we do? Just sit here?" he asked, settling down into some pillows strewn about the closet.

I pushed aside some suits and sat next to him. "Yeah, let's just chill."

I was eyeing the row of women's shoes in front of me when I got a weird feeling. I turned my head to see Wes staring at me. "What?" I asked.

He scooted closer to me. "Well, maybe we should take this opportunity to take our friendship one step further . . ."

I pushed him away with the palm of my hand on his forehead. He nodded quickly. "Yeah, just thought I'd try." So we pulled out our phones and stared into our screens.

A few minutes passed and then someone started knocking on the door. "Hey, lovebirds, get out of there! Your seven minutes are *up!*" Startled, I stood, but Wes stopped me before I could open the door. He placed his hands on my shoulders and scrutinized me. Then he started messing up my hair.

"Hey!" I reached up to fix it but he smacked my hands away.

"You wanna look properly made-out with or what?"

Oh, right. I rubbed my lip gloss off, too, for good measure. Wes nodded his head in approval. I took a deep breath and opened the door.

"Whoa. *You* guys?"

My student government secretary, a short and really buff junior named Eugene Adams, was staring at us, aghast. I brushed him aside as I looked around for Luca. No sign of him. *Damn it!*

"Let's get out of here," I muttered.

Wes followed, trying to comfort me. "Hey, maybe he saw us and in a fit of jealousy left the room."

"Yeah, right," I said sullenly, already feeling defeated. I just wanted to go home. But as we stood at the top of the stairs, I spotted Luca down in the foyer. Red beanie in the sea of bodies . . . and then his face tilted up, eyes making contact with mine.

My heart surged. Then Wes pulled me super-close and his lips hovered by my ear. "I see him. This is it, Des."

I startled. "What do you—" but before I could finish, I felt my heel slip on the edge of the top step I was standing on, and I lurched into Wes, our heads bumping. He lost his balance and my body leaned into his so much that he fell backward down the stairs—holding my hand.

As we tumbled down together, I felt myself float outside of my own body to watch the train wreck in real time from a safe distance, eating popcorn and shaking my head. But before we could full-on crash all the way down, Wes managed to grab the banister and stop the momentum, his other hand still clutching mine. I grasped it with both hands and used my boot to push against the wall so that we came to a full stop. For a split second, I was able to appreciate how badass we were for managing to do that, in awe of our combined upper- and lower-body strength.

But then the real world came into focus and I heard the gasps first, then the laughing. I cringed and looked at Wes.

"Oh my *God*," he sputtered, letting go of my hands and taking the Santa hat off his head. "How the hell did you manage to flail on a fake freaking date?" he hissed.

"It's a freaking *gift*," I hissed back.

Wes reached over to help me up, but before I could take his hand I felt someone grasp my other hand. I turned to see Luca. A laughing Luca.

"Thank you, that made this creepy party totally worth coming to." His voice could hardly contain his damn *mirth* as he helped pull me up and walk me down the rest of the stairs.

I pushed a strand of hair off my face and stiffly replied, "You're so welcome." His obvious joy at the accident made it clear that he was absolutely *not* jealous of *anything*. Plan failed.

"I'm going to fix . . . myself," I said to Wes, who nodded as a couple of girls fussed over him. I ignored Luca and stalked off down a hallway, fuming. I couldn't even be embarrassed, I was so irritated by the entire evening.

After I readjusted my hair (tossing the Santa hat in the trash) and splashed my face with cold water in a bathroom, I decided to take a minute to gather my wits, sitting down on a bench in the hallway next to a giant potted palm that kept poking my face. I swatted at it as I stared blankly at the giant gilded mirror across from me. I looked unhinged, and was haunted by Wes's words when I had first told him about the K drama steps: that what I was doing was downright creepy. Was it time to throw in the towel, was I edging into weirdo territory? Was this going to be my first disproved hypothesis? I shuddered at the thought.

"What are you looking at?"

My spine turned into jelly at hearing that voice.

Luca was standing in the hallway, his beanie pushed back a bit so that his thick hair was perfectly tousled and carefree. Like a little French child. Aw, Luca as a child. *Aw.*

"Are you high?" His voice exuded genuine curiosity.

I snapped out of it. "No! God, not everyone's hitting the janga during parties."

He looked at me for a second, mouth slightly agape. "Whaaa . . . What did you just say?"

I stood up and walked over to the mirror, adjusting my hair so I didn't have to be in the direct path of his disconcerting stare. In the reflection of the mirror, I was still able to see Luca's expression.

97

"Let me guess, Luca, you *love* the janga. So artistic and freeee," I said.

"Did you just—Did you just—" He was laughing between words.

A couple of girls trickled in and they stared at Luca, then at me. I threw my head back and laughed along with him, smiling and waving at them. After they slipped into the bathroom, I whispered, "Did I *what*?" I knew that somehow he was making fun of me.

Before he could answer, I felt two hands nip at my waist.

"What's up, Des?" a voice said close to my ear. Argh! Wes!

Luca pointed at me. "She . . . she just called weed *janga*." He let out another bark of laughter.

I turned around toward Wes in confusion, but one look at his face filled me with dread. A familiar dread.

Wes grinned. "Oh, yeah. *That*."

I punched his arm. "What do you mean, *that*?"

He bit his bottom lip. I punched his arm again, making him wince.

"Ouch! All right. Des, how do I say this? Fiona and I have let you say *janga* for years. The word you are actually trying to say, in all your drug-free virginity, is . . . *ganja*."

It took a moment for my mind to be blown into space and back. "*What!* And you just kept letting me say it?!"

He laughed. "Yeah."

"Freaking *janga*?!" I let out a snort of laughter despite myself.

98

Wes clasped his hands and said in a girlish voice, "Are you guys smoking the janga again? Ugh, boring, see you after you're done getting high on janga!"

We were both laughing so hard at this point that we were clutching each other. That's when I realized Luca was staring at us with an odd expression.

Wes seized the moment before I could. He tugged a strand of my hair and looked at me with intensity, a hint of meaningfulness. "You're so freaking cute, I can't stand it."

My cheeks flushed despite the grossness of Wes saying those words to me. I felt a momentary flash of pity for all the poor girls who had ever crushed on Wes. He was *good*. I mean, I knew this was all fake and yet I still felt a twinge of *Aw, I'm special!* Pathetic.

When I looked toward Luca, he was already turned around, walking back out into the party. "I'll leave you guys to it then. *Later*," he called out.

Oh my God. It worked. *He was jealous!*

"What are you waiting for?" Wes asked me, looking pointedly at Luca's retreating figure. "I didn't do *all this* nonsense"—he gestured at himself—"and fall down a freaking flight of stairs in front of our entire school, for nothing. What's the next step on your list?"

"Huh?"

"The K drama steps? You need to seize this opportunity!"

I snapped open my clutch and pulled out the list. "Um, it's

number 9: *Get into a Predicament That Forces Both the Guy and You into an Intimate Bonding Moment.*"

"Perfect! Go!" Wes gestured to where Luca had walked away.

I shoved the list back into my bag and shrieked, "Wait, *now*? I need at least a few days to set this up."

"You'll figure something out. It's the perfect opportunity, go do it *now*!" Wes pushed me toward the party. It had dispersed a bit; no doubt a lot more people were upstairs now. So I was able to spot that red beanie as it slipped out the back door. I followed Luca outside as he walked rapidly, disappearing into a small grove of trees on the edge of the property. I got nervous as I sped up. Where was he going? And what the heck was I going to say when I caught up with him?

I entered the trees and squinted in the dark, trying to find him. I shivered, rubbing my arms and thinking about hightailing it back to the party when I detected a movement out by the marina.

And then I heard a familiar hissing. Like the snake I thought I had heard at the zoo.

I walked straight ahead until I was out of the trees and facing an old shed attached to a closed bait shop. And standing there, tagging its wall with a can of spray paint, was Luca.

STEP 9:

Get into a Predicament That Forces Both the Guy and You into an Intimate Bonding Moment

I'd like to think my reaction was one of cool level-headedness.

"What are you doing?!" I screeched.

Luca started, his spray can making a giant splotch on the wall. "Shit!" he cursed, swiveling around to look at me.

I opened my mouth to continue my shrieking, but he strode over to me in two swift steps and placed a hand wearing a surgical glove over my mouth.

He brought his mask-covered mouth to my ear and said, "Will you please shut up for a second?"

I responded by biting his gloved hand. I tasted rubber.

He yelped and let go of me, yanking the mask off his face. "What's wrong with you?!" His lower lip pouted as he took off his glove and inspected his hand.

My chest heaved as I stepped back, injured by his reaction. "What's wrong with *me*? Am I the one freaking defacing public property right now? At a *mom-and-pop bait shop*?" The questions came out in sharp jabs and my hands balled up into fists as I continued to yell at him. "What's wrong with *you*? Is this how you get your kicks?"

He shook his head at me. "If you can just stay quiet for, I don't know, a *minute*, you'll find out."

I opened my mouth, but he sent me a warning glance, thick eyebrows shooting up into his hair, jaw setting. I shut my mouth and tried to calm my racing heart. So Luca was just some bored suburban kid rebelling by tagging stuff. The arrest was no longer so mysterious, and I was heavy with disappointment.

He walked over to the wall again, which already had some old tagging on it. Actually, on closer inspection it was some very elaborate graffiti—a lot of twisted cursive letters in a rainbow of colors that blended in seamless gradients, but it was impossible to read what they spelled out because delicate vines and thorns were drawn all over it with what looked like a black Sharpie.

"Did you bring all these to the *party*?" I asked as I lightly kicked one of his spray paint cans over. Luca put his glove back on and crouched down to pick one up. He lifted a finger to his lips to shush me and whispered, "I hid them here beforehand, okay, Nancy Drew?"

"Why? Did you know you'd get a hankering for some graffiti time at a *party*?" I whispered loudly.

He shook the can until the little metal ball bearings clinked around. "I've been to this marina before and I spotted this graffiti a while back. So I hid this stuff ahead of time." Then he started spraying directly onto the graffiti—meticulously painting around the graffiti, not touching it, but *extending* it. First, a light-as-air layer of indigo lines curling out of the letters. Then, as he stood closer to the wall, the lines grew darker, more solid, and the edges were crisp, like calligraphy.

He turned to me, and I scooted back. He raised an eyebrow and then picked up another spray can. He shook it, then sprayed tiny gold dots along some of the indigo lines. I watched silently as the nonsensical letters with vines turned into a small piece of a mural. A graphic, gorgeous piece of art.

After what seemed like years, he was finished. And it was beautiful. Shimmering, layered, and equal parts intense and light.

Luca stepped back and took a photo of it with his phone. Then he gathered the cans, gloves, and his mask into a trash bag, and tossed it all into a large Dumpster by a little café across the dirt road. He leaned against the café wall and looked at me. I felt unnerved by his challenging gaze. What was he thinking?

"I don't . . . I don't know how you want me to react?" I asked, keeping my voice calm, my arms crossed defensively.

He shrugged. "I don't expect anything. Especially from someone whose view of what's art and what's not is so narrow." My head throbbed. Why did I like this guy again?

"Well, that's too bad. Because I think what you just did is pretty cool." Despite hating the halting tones of my voice, I continued. "And, I mean, it's kind of gorgeous."

He tilted his head and continued to look at me—not

challenging this time, but that familiar expression I couldn't quite read. As if he was trying to register an emotion that he didn't quite understand himself. And when the butterflies hit again, it was pretty easy to remember why I *did* like him.

As I stood there burning, dying, under his gaze, his eyes suddenly darted past me and he straightened up and cursed.

I turned around to see two security guards coming out of the trees behind us. The kind that patrolled fancy neighborhoods like this and would love any excuse to badger us out of boredom. My blood froze when I saw one of them dangerously close to the graffiti, the paint still fresh. But before I could react, Luca grabbed my hand and whispered, *"Run!"*

I hesitated for about a second before I bolted down the road with him.

"No way."

I stared at the small yacht that Luca was trying to convince me to get on.

"If you don't hurry up, I'm going in on my own—those security guards aren't far behind," Luca said as he abruptly let go of my hand and hopped onto the boat, somewhat clumsily.

I was so frazzled that I couldn't even appreciate the fact that we had *held hands* as we ran away from the guards.

"We can't hide there! What if the owners—"

"This is my dad's boat. Just get on."

Why was I not surprised. I glanced at the name painted along the side. *Carpe Diem*. Are you for real.

Luca had a leg propped up on the edge, one hand holding onto the rail, the other held out to help me get on.

His hand was warm and strong when I grabbed it and stepped on. The boat swayed a bit and I lost my balance immediately, falling into him. His arms wrapped around me to prevent us from toppling over and my face pressed into his shoulder.

We stood like that for a second, him holding me, the breeze off the ocean whipping my hair around, raising goose bumps. I was terrified to look up at him, to ruin this tiny, perfect moment.

"Um, we should get inside so they don't see us." He cleared his throat and let go of me gingerly, making his way toward an entrance in the middle of the boat. "We won't stay long, just until those guys pass us." Wait. I needed to maximize this situation. But how?

Seconds later, I found my answer. As Luca headed below deck, I spotted something out of the corner of my eye—two ropes on the side of the boat tied tautly to the pier. They were the only things that seemed to be anchoring the boat as it bobbed gently in the water. Just two measly ropes.

I knew I was moving into nutjob territory. I thought of Nae-Il in *Cantabile Tomorrow*, and how she was so determined to get the guy that she even moved random things of hers into his house, slowly and over time, so that she eventually found herself living there. Wacko, but got the job done of being "intimate" . . .

I looked at the ropes again. The boat could easily float out beyond the marina, buying me some time before Luca noticed what was wrong and drove us back. As quickly as I could, I stepped over to the rail, untied the two knots on the ropes (thank you, Girl Scouts!), and dropped them over the edge of the boat.

Oh man. Before I could register the craziness of what I had just done, Luca popped his head out from the doorway. "Desi?" he called.

I dashed over. "I'm here! Sorry." And as I walked down the stairs, I felt the boat shift slightly. My heart roared in my ears.

He switched on some lights and immediately dimmed them to the lowest level so the cabin was barely lit, then pulled the curtains shut. "So the guards can't see the light if they're still looking for us," he explained.

When my eyes adjusted I looked at my surroundings. Everything was white leather and dark, gleaming wood—there was a sofa, a dining nook, a bar, and a couple of doors leading off to other rooms. Your typical fancy-boat fare as seen on TV shows about rich people.

Luca peered out between the closed curtains. "Shouldn't take long to lose them."

"Mm-hm," I said, my voice only squeaking a little. That's when I realized my feet were throbbing. I sat down on the sofa and kicked off my booties to look at my blistered toes. "Ugh." I poked at one of the blisters curiously.

Luca looked over at me. "What's up?"

"Just some gross blisters—I'm not used to wearing heeled stuff, let alone running in them."

Expression unchanging, he didn't respond but opened a door that led into a bathroom and rummaged around. After a few seconds he came out with some Band-Aids in hand.

"Here." He held them out in front of me, and I couldn't tell if he felt annoyed or guilty.

"Thanks," I muttered as I tore the packaging off one. This wasn't exactly him wrapping my ankle in a bandage but it would have to do.

He squinted down at me. "Did you also get hurt when you fell down those stairs?"

I shook my head. "No, Wes stopped us, luckily." Hm. "He's, like, so athletic, thank God, or it could have been a disaster." I held back a wince, knowing that pointing out Wes's athleticism was rudely highlighting Luca's lack of it.

Luca gave me a funny look. "So was Wes your date or something tonight?"

I bent my head, pretending to be preoccupied with the Band-Aid while smiling under my curtain of hair. *Heh-heh-heh.* "Yeah."

"Isn't he going to wonder where you are?" Irritation laced his words.

It took all my willpower to hide my smile. I already had an excuse handy, too. "Oh, I told him I needed some air and was taking a walk by the marina." I was relishing this obvious display of jealousy. I finished putting the Band-Aid on and glanced around the boat again. "So this is your dad's boat? The *Carpe Diem*?"

Luca hopped onto the bar counter. "Yeah, like, 'O Captain! My Captain!'" he said with a scoff. "He'd love to know I was hiding out here. If I got caught by those guards, it would, uh, further tarnish his reputation with the upstanding community of Monte Douche-sta." The boat moved suddenly and Luca glanced around in slight alarm, clutching the edge of the bar.

Nope, he can't know we've floated out to sea yet.

"Monte Douche-sta. Ha-ha. Wordsmith," I said with a hearty laugh, trying to distract him. "So why's your dad so worried about his reputation? What does he do?"

That seemed to work. Luca leaned forward, placing his elbows on his knees. "He invented some kind of machine that helps do something in ambulances. It's still used in every ambulance in the country."

"*What?* Really? That's *so* cool!" I quickly did a mental run-down of what emergency procedures were used by paramedics. "Wait, is it the external auto-resuscitator? Or is it the CPR device? Oh, wow, it can't be the—"

I stopped short when I noticed Luca's slack-jawed expression. He shook his head quickly like a little terrier. "*Why* do you even . . ."

"I want to be a doctor one day," I said matter-of-factly.

His expression turned to bemusement. "A lot of people want

to be doctors. Not all of them know the names of every piece of medical equipment."

I flushed. Why couldn't I keep my know-it-all mouth shut?

Luca shook his head. "*Anyway*. I don't even know what the thing's called. My goal in life is to never pay attention to anything related to my dad. It's bad enough I have to live with him in this crappy place." He glanced at me quickly. "No offense."

I rolled my eyes. He continued. "Besides, he didn't do it out of, like, the goodness of his heart and a desire to save people's lives." His feet kicked at the bar beneath him. "He did it because he knew he could make a lot of money. And despite being a terrible human, he could live out the rest of his life being able to come off as some genius Saint. While being obscenely rich."

Whoa. Daddy issues. I was careful with my next words. "So . . . he's not a big fan of your, uh, subversive artwork?"

"Yeah, that's one way of putting it," he said, his voice finally losing its edge, a hint of humor creeping back in. And when it did, I was surprised by how relieved I was to hear it, to have the Luca I liked back. Even if that Luca was an insufferable smartass when he wanted to be.

Then I remembered that day in Art Club, when he'd hinted that he had a secret project for the gallery show. "Wait, is this your project for the show?"

"Yup. I've really been into this idea of unwanted collaboration," he said, growing animated. "Basically, I find other people's graffiti, the ones I think are interesting, like the one at that bait shop, and imagine that they started something that I was meant to finish. But of course the artists didn't intend that. So it's unwanted, a kind of violation, you know? They violate buildings, and I violate their art."

Words were coming out of his mouth at record speed. He was energized in a way that I'd never seen him before. It reminded me of . . . me. When I was in full-on school mode, running for class president or explaining a particularly badass chemical reaction to my dad to help diagnose a car's troubles. "But how? I mean, you can't actually *show* it in a gallery . . ." My voice trailed off lamely. There I go again, thinking literally like some devoid-of-creativity square.

He held up his phone. "Photos. Anyway, I was doing that last week, to this completely weird tag I saw in one of those cages at the zoo. I went back that night and snuck in to finish it. But I got caught by some security guard there since there's obviously nothing else going on in this entire town. But I didn't get arrested like everyone thinks. The security guard just called my dad, who worked his super-bro strings to get me out of trouble."

"Was that the first time you got caught?" I asked, remembering Fiona's comment. *This wasn't his first time.*

He paused, taken aback for a second. "No, I was arrested once in Ojai." A deep exhale. "That's why I had to move here to live with my dad. To keep me out of trouble, since my hippie mom was clearly incapable of disciplining her 'wild artist son.' Quote unquote, by the way. As if I'm not *his* son, too."

"What did you do then to get arrested? More graf—uh, art experiments?"

"Kind of."

I tilted my head. "Hm, if he's so worried about you, how are you at this party?"

He flashed a smile at me. *Zap.* "He grounded me for a week, so duty done."

"A week? That's it?!"

He shrugged. "It wasn't fun being stuck in a house with him, don't worry. I was properly punished."

That coaxed a smile out of me. "So can I see the photos?"

He hopped off the bar and and was walking over to show me when the boat lurched again—making Luca fall right on top of me.

Mrrmm, okay. Laid back on the sofa, I was smushed under Luca, who was straight-up stretched out on the entire length of me. He raised himself up on his elbows and stared down at me. "Whoa, sorry." His legs shifted and one of them slipped between mine.

My mouth moved, but there were no words. This was it . . . I could feel The Kiss coming. It was ahead of the K drama schedule, but who cared?! His eyes were searching mine, a little line forming at his brow. Then the boat moved again and he scrambled off me, opening a curtain. "What the . . . *Where are we?*"

Mother! I sat up and looked out the window—the marina lights were in the distance now.

"What the hell, how did this happen?" he yelped, fleeing up the stairs. I heard his heavy footsteps above me. "Holy shit!"

I grabbed my shoes off the floor and made my way up to the deck. I saw Luca standing stock-still at the top of the stairs. And sure enough, we were out at sea . . .

Kind of. The marina wasn't that far, actually.

Straight ahead was a black sea meeting an inky-blue sky scattered with stars. Behind us were the twinkly dock lights and Gwen Parker's blazing mansion in the distance.

A perfect romantic moment setting if ever there was one.

"I can't believe this," Luca breathed.

"You know how to drive one of these, right?" I asked.

Luca shook his head, pulling his beanie down over his eyes. "N-o-o-o, man, I hate this stupid boat."

Aw, God. *Okay, don't panic.* "Let's go see if we can figure it out?" I asked hopefully.

After a couple of seconds of beanie hiding, Luca pushed the hat out of his eyes. "No," he said, pulling out his cell phone. "I'll call for help."

Oh *shit*. I just stood there while he made the call to who-knows-what and started to panic. This could *not* get to my dad.

When Luca hung up I stammered, "Who did you just call?" My voice was shrill and he looked at me with alarm.

"I called the coast guard," he replied.

Visions of emergency vehicles and local news vans made me cringe. "Really? Do you think that's necessary?"

He looked at me incredulously. "Are you joking? We're freaking lost at sea!"

"Lost at sea?! We're, like, two feet away from civilization!" I pointed toward the marina. "Do you think they'll call our parents?" I crossed my arms tightly.

"Probably?" He peered closely at me as I started to wring my hands. "Are you okay? Do you have super-strict parents or something?"

I raked a hand through my hair. "No, it's just . . . I can't have my dad get some kind of scary in-the-middle-of-the-night call. It would just upset him too much."

Luca glanced at his watch. "But it's only ten-thirty."

I barely heard him. Instead, I was suddenly seven years old again, refusing to eat the tiny marinated stir-fried anchovies my dad was forcing on me. "I don't like the crunch!" I yelped.

My dad pushed his chair back from our dining room table and stood up. "Desi, you have to at least try it. If you don't like it, then you don't have to eat it. I'm going to get you some water but Appa knows if you didn't eat because I memorized how many are in bowl."

I was marveling at my dad's ability to do that and staring into the bowl of dozens of tiny fish when the phone rang. Our house line, which no one but telemarketers ever called. He glanced at the caller ID and said, "Your mom's hospital?"

He picked it up with a cheery "Hello?" I was poking at the little bowl of sweet, crunchy anchovies with my mint-green wooden chopsticks when I heard a muffled cry coming from my dad. I dropped the chopsticks and turned around to see him clutching the kitchen counter, phone still up to his ear.

"Desi?"

And then I wasn't in my kitchen anymore. I was on a boat with Luca.

"Don't worry, I won't let them call your dad, okay?" he said, hand on my shoulder, head bowed down so that he was looking into my eyes.

I blinked and tried to smile. "Okay, thanks. I mean, you don't have to handle that, I'll make sure they don't."

With a jerky, very unsmooth movement, he pulled his hand away from my shoulder and shoved it into his pocket. "Um, okay," he said.

Before I could answer, lights flashed and sirens blared toward us.

Luca and I sat on the boat in silence, side by side, blankets draped over us. We were being towed to the dock, enveloped by the smell of the ocean and the sound of lapping water. And of course the emergency coast guard crew. I had convinced them to let me call my dad myself, so I fake-dialed from my silenced phone and gave a very persuasive performance of being chastised by my strict Korean father. Satisfied, the crew had left us alone for the rest of the ride back.

Luca broke the silence by clearing his throat. "So . . . uh, what's the story with Wes?"

Again? This was what he was thinking about? All tension dissipated and I started to laugh.

"What?" he asked defensively.

I couldn't believe it—all this craziness, and yeah, the love-triangle step had *really* worked. I took a breath and responded, "I don't know what our story is yet. We've been friends for a long time. Why?"

Luca's shoulders stiffened visibly. "Do you *normally* go to a sex party with your friend?"

Heh-heh.

I pulled the thin blanket around my shoulders tightly. "It *wasn't* a sex party, geez. And yeah, he was my date tonight, but . . . I don't know. We're just friends for now." *For now.* I let that hang in the air for a moment. "What about you? Do you have a girl-friend?"

He didn't answer right away and I was suddenly aware of how ridiculous this entire conversation was—how everything was wrapped up in so much damn subtext. Why couldn't we just say what we were feeling?

I squirmed as I waited for his response, wanting to hurl myself off the boat into the water with every second that passed.

"Nope, not anymore," he said, eyes staring off into the dark water.

"Oh, okay." Not *anymore*?

He looked down. "I'm not into the whole dating thing."

My heart deflated with a slow squeak. I tried to make a joke out of it. "Ah, saving yourself for marriage?"

He threw his head back and laughed that dorky laugh of his. I couldn't stop myself from smiling. When he calmed down he looked over at me, the distance between us mere inches. Our hands almost brushed on the edge of the bench.

"Is your dad going to kill you for this?" I asked, trying to keep my voice casual to cover up the guilt that had been creeping in ever since the coast guard arrived.

He shrugged. "Maybe. I couldn't care less."

Luckily the awkward moment was interrupted by a strong wind that kicked up noisily around us and I rubbed my arms for warmth.

"Are you cold or something?" he asked. I realized I was basically clutching myself under the thin blanket. Too bad Luca didn't have a suit jacket he could drape over me while complaining about what a dimwit I was for not being properly dressed for the cold evening. Perfect K drama moment wasted.

"A little bit, yeah. I'm wearing a short lace dress by the ocean. At night. Like a genius."

Luca smiled and his eyes swept over me, very quickly, a blink-and-you'll-miss-it moment. "You look good."

I had no sass at the ready for this genuine compliment. Just a meek, "Um, thanks." Luca was doing too good a job of the K drama hot-dude mixed signals. I looked anxiously toward the marina, wondering if my friends were there yet. I had texted them once the coast guard arrived.

I needed to dissect the hell out of this night with Fiona and Wes.

Suddenly, I felt Luca shoving something onto my head. "What are you doing?" I felt around my head and realized it was his beanie.

"To keep you warm," he said casually, hands already tucked back under his blanket.

I adjusted it so that it wasn't shoved into my eyes, its wool still warm from Luca's own head. "Thank you?"

He shook his head with a tsk. "Aren't you a science nerd? Everyone knows if you keep your head warm, you'll warm up the rest of your body."

I scoffed. "Okay, that's, like, if I'm *also* wearing a sweater. Heat doesn't transfer that quickly from your head to your body if the temperature difference is that drastic."

He shook his head. "Seriously, what is it like on your home planet of Vulcan? Just wear the beanie. Jesus!"

Hmph. I kept my mouth shut and let the beanie work its magic. And I couldn't be sure if it was the beanie or the *idea* of wearing Luca's beanie that kept me warm the entire ride back.

When we reached the pier, I looked for Wes, hoping that he hadn't ditched me and left with some other girl, which wouldn't be beyond the scope of normal Wes behavior.

"Desi!" Fiona was walking toward me with Leslie at her heels.

"What *happened*? Wes is freaking out—" She stopped short when she noticed Luca.

"Oh, hey Wo—uh, Luca, right?" she asked. Smooth.

That face-punch smile slowly spread across his face. "Yeah, and you're . . . ?"

I stepped between them. "That's Fiona and her *girlfriend*, Leslie." Just call me Smooth Jr.

I spotted Wes then, carrying my jacket. "Wes!" I waved him over. His expression switched from worry to annoyance, but when he noticed Luca next to me, he smiled smugly. I could almost hear his self-satisfied voice saying *Nice*.

"You must have been *so* worried," I said, throwing my arms around Wes's neck. I whispered, "Play along or die."

He wrapped his arms around me, too, almost crushing me. "*So* worried, babe." A little bit of barf rose in my throat.

When we pulled apart, Luca was openly staring at us. Before I could plan my next move, some people from the coast guard approached Luca. "We've got a few questions for you, son. Your father will be arriving soon."

"Whatever," he muttered. He looked so dejected that I quickly moved away from Wes and walked toward him.

"Hey, do you want me to stay?"

"*Des!* Your dad said midnight, yo!" Wes yelled. Argh.

Luca looked over at Wes and his mouth formed a straight, unamused line. "Nah, it's cool." He forced a smile. "Thanks, though. And hey, see you after break."

Oh *no*. I had completely forgotten that we had the next two weeks off for the holidays. That meant no Luca, no K drama steps time!

I tried to keep my face from looking crestfallen. "Oh yeah. Um, you, too. Bye," I said lamely, feeling myself deflate at the anticlimactic ending to the night. I held up my hand for a wave, but Luca grabbed it midair.

He stepped in closer. My breath caught in my throat. He slowly lowered our hands, then dropped mine. "Sorry, just wanted to say something," he said quietly.

"Hm? Do you want your beanie back?" I managed to squeak, reaching for it.

He shook his head and furrowed his brow again, eyebrows and lashes almost touching. "I just—be careful. That guy Wes seems sleazy as hell, dude."

Hot *and* perceptive. Won Bin was proving to be worthy of his code name.

STEP 10:
Find Out the Guy's Big Secret, Preferably through Excruciatingly Repetitive Flashbacks

Despite hating every day that passed without seeing Luca (and worrying about whether his dad really did kill him for the boat incident) and putting my K drama steps on hold, the holiday break passed by quickly in a blur of finishing up my college applications, a couple of snowboarding trips with Fiona and Wes, and K dramas with my dad.

The night before school started up again, I was watching another drama with my dad in the living room. A law-themed one that was basically a Dramaland version of *Legally Blonde* called *Prosecutor Princess*.

"Did Mom also like dramas?"

My dad dropped down from the pull-up bar in the dining room doorway. His Anaheim Ducks sweatshirt was soaking wet and his hair was pulled away from his face by a sweatband that was probably older than I was.

"Your mom?"

I nodded from my bundled-up position on the sofa, the drama paused on the TV. "Yeah, did she like them as much as you do?"

My dad stood with his hands on his hips. "No-o-o, ha-ha. Your mom, she was . . . snob." He said *snob* slowly, as if testing it in his mouth. "Yeah, snob. Snobby about telebee. She only watched news or animal channel. Always make fun of Appa for Korean telebee." Good ol' telebee. "Just like you. But now you *love* them like Appa."

I scoffed but couldn't help but smile. It was true, I was a certified K drama–obsessed fanatic. I mean, my dad's Christmas gifts to me this year were imported box sets of drama DVDs and sound tracks.

But something my dad had just said made me ask, "I'm a lot like Mom, right?"

My dad jumped back up and grabbed the pull-up bar. He lifted himself to the bar with a grunt. On his way down, he exhaled and said, "Yes, in all ways. Study hard, like Mom." He lifted himself back up, and while his chin was hovering above the bar, he said, "Always have to be best, like Mom." Another pull-up, then, "Impatient, like Mom." He dropped down again, bending over to catch his breath. "Not romantic, like Mom."

"What! What do you mean?"

He took a swig of water and sat down on the carpet by my feet. I pushed my foot into his back so that his festering sweatshirt didn't touch the sofa. He heaved all his weight against my big toe and I finally gave in and let him collapse onto the sofa.

"What I mean is, you don't like boys because too busy studying. Good. But, no good for Appa when he went to school with Mom." My parents had been high school sweethearts in Korea— my mom the top of her class, my dad the tough punk with a heart of gold. He had followed her to the U.S. when she got into Stanford med school. They got married soon after and moved to Orange County when my mom started her residency in Irvine.

It was a real once-in-a-lifetime romance. Good girl falls for bad boy. They stayed together against all odds. It was only as I grew older and listened to my dad talk about her that I realized they had the real thing, what K dramas are constantly dreaming up. And that sort of thing doesn't just disappear because one of you dies.

"Appa, it's not that I'm not romantic. I'm just . . . focused on other things," I lied through my teeth.

He hit my foot. "*Ya*, Miss Focus, what are you doing watching this? You have school tomorrow. Go to bed."

"Fine, but don't watch any more *Prosecutor Princess* without me!" I reluctantly went into my room and looked around. My bed was immaculately made—soft gray linen duvet cover accented by lavender pillows. A fluffy cream quilt folded neatly at the foot of the bed. Floor-to-ceiling shelves built by my dad were filled with books, trophies, photos, and awards. Everything arranged by color, size, and subject. My white lacquer desk sat under a window, completely cleared off except for a cup filled with mechanical pencils, highlighters, and red pens.

Everything just right. Yet. I pulled the list out from my wallet and looked at step 10: *Find Out the Guy's Big Secret, Preferably through Excruciatingly Repetitive Flashbacks.* I knew he was an artist and he'd told me about his arrest. What I still couldn't understand was why he didn't want to date anyone. I plopped down on my bed and carefully wrote these notes down in the notebook.

Then I opened my laptop to do some good old-fashioned stalking. Even though I had already done it several times during break, I typed *Luca Drakos girlfriend.* But still, nothing. I just knew there had to be more to his story.

I went to his Facebook page. A page I had been to a billion times before. But this time I scrolled through all the photos he was tagged in, to find any signs of a girlfriend. I clicked through so many photos. So many. To the point where I felt a little sick at the amount of time I was spending, not to mention my horror at the idea of him somehow *knowing* that I was doing this, that the little spy that lived in my computer was reporting all of this to Luca at this very moment.

And then. There it was. Some two-year-old photo hidden deep in the far recesses of his photo album. It was him and a girl tangled up in each other's laps, sitting on a blanket in a park or somewhere else with lots of grass. Luca's face was absolutely *glowing*, and he wasn't wearing a beanie.

And the girl . . . well, the girl looked like someone who should be Luca's girlfriend. Someone who was every guy's dream girlfriend. Effortlessly gorgeous—glowing light brown skin, Naomi Campbell bone structure, a wide, laughing mouth, and arched eyebrows paired with huge green eyes. Wearing cutoffs that showed enough lean muscle to make my legs feel like elephant trunks. A loose-fitting white tank with thin straps showing zero tan lines on sculpted yet delicate shoulders. An obscene amount of thick, wavy bleached-blond hair parted deeply to the side, pushed there so casually, so cool. She looked like California: a sunny mix of so many different beautiful things.

My stomach clenched. These were the girls who had boyfriends. Not girls with keratosis on their upper arms, or morning breath, or who spent an inordinate number of evenings watching K dramas with their dads, or . . . girls who at the age of seventeen still hadn't had boyfriends.

I clicked on the name tagged in the photo: *Emily Scout Fairchild*. That name, unreal. It brought me to her profile—a veritable treasure trove of stalkery laid at my fingertips. But before I could click through her photos, I noticed her latest post.

Last breath of Ojai air before heading down south to tie up some loose ends . . . peace & love.

Down south?! Like, Orange County south? Also, didn't she have school tomorrow? Did Ojai schools have a longer holiday break than us?? I scrolled down her profile page to see the occasional drawing posted—a lot of abstract stuff with shapes and

124

colors and inspirational or cryptic sayings scribbled on top of them. Another artist, it appeared. I snorted. "Goody for you, Picasso." She also seemed to post a lot of song lyrics or quotes from books by Old or Dead White Men. I'm *so sure* you love Bukowski and Leonard Cohen. I'm sure they, like, *totally* speak to you.

I flew through her profile. Not many photos of herself, just a few with friends. None of Luca except that one. Then my alarm popped up on-screen: **Stanford application due in one hour!!!** I had already submitted my application online days ago, but the official deadline reminder meant that it was already eleven and I had soccer conditioning in the morning. I flicked the photo of Luca and Emily with my finger before shutting my laptop.

Okay, stalking to reconvene tomorrow. I opened up the notebook and wrote down the plan for step 10, which began with calling Wes before I went to bed.

My phone was buzzing all morning. I had turned on notifications for all my social media updates so that I would catch Emily's. Because I was now following her under rando anonymous accounts.

Yes, I know. In my defense . . .

I needed to follow through on step 10.

While shoveling my sugar-coated cereal into my mouth that morning, I saw that she had Instagrammed a photo of her date-smoothie breakfast. (Gee, could you be any *more* from Ojai?) During second period, an uninspired shot of the ocean as she drove through Santa Barbara. Then a photo of the traffic in LA with a thumbs-down emoji.

And now, while I was sitting in French, the phone buzzed with another update.

Facebook this time: **Yum so glad to get my meatless In-N-Out fix in the OC.** A photo of her about to bite into a burger accompanied it. What kind of monster gets a meatless burger from In-N-Out?

Also: The OC. She was *here*. I knew it! I knew that's what her cryptic Facebook post from last night was about. Her end goal had to be Luca. If she saw Luca before I did . . . I didn't know. It worried me. Would they get back together? Had they already gotten back together over the holiday break or something?

And I had no idea if I would see Luca today. It was already three periods into the first day back from break and I was beyond impatient to see him. It had been two weeks! That was *years* in Desi Lee time.

So when the bell rang, signaling the end of French and the beginning of lunch period, I bolted out of there and ran into the middle of the courtyard, hoping to find Luca. If I saw him first, then maybe I could remind him of the sparks we had on the boat. That is, if I hadn't imagined them.

Suddenly there was another buzz on my phone. A selfie of Emily pretending to lick a Viking statue. I wrinkled my nose until I realized it was *Monte Vista High School's* Viking statue. She was here. OMFG. I scanned the entire campus with a speed that almost made my neck snap. Where was Luca? He usually sat with the art kids during lunch, but he wasn't at their usual spot.

Wait a second. Maybe he was in the art studio. I knew that a lot of the Art Club kids were spending lunch working on their pieces for the show. I texted Fiona: Skipping lunch today, have some Won Bin business.

An immediate response: Don't make too many babies.

I tried to look casual walking toward the art studio. People waved and I waved back cheerfully. *Nothing to see here, just some casual stalkery, folks!*

And then I stopped—because I spotted her. With Luca. My heart lurched at seeing them together, even if they were walking pretty far apart from each other.

Do the right thing and leave them alone or . . . be sneaky and nosy? My head spun with visions of all the various sassy K drama heroines until it stilled on Bong-Sun from *Oh My Ghostess* spying on the hot chef as he talked to a drunk college friend. *Always be sneaky.*

But how? I couldn't hear them from this distance. I darted behind a row of (lovely) floss-silk trees in bloom, getting a teeny bit closer, and strained to hear them. Still nothing. Then I saw that they were heading to the art studio.

I dashed toward the classroom ahead of them, ran inside the

supply closet practically holding my breath, and bumped into someone. My heart leaped into my throat.

"*Excuse* me." The world's most obnoxious voice.

And there was Violet, brushing up alongside me, reaching for a jar of paintbrushes high above my head, as if rubbing in her height. Ugh! Why was she in here? Of all the freaking people . . .

I moved aside to avoid her bumping into me. "*Shh,*" I hissed.

I could tell she was about to spill some serious bile over that, but she was interrupted by the sound of footsteps heading to the closet.

We both peered around one of the shelves and found ourselves looking directly at Luca and Emily. We immediately ducked back so we were hidden from view.

Emily. She of the doll-like features, killer hair, and wedgie-inducing cutoffs.

And she was standing awfully close to Luca. "Why'd you drag me into this dark little corner?" she teased, her voice low and a bit husky, like a young Lauren Bacall.

Luca closed the curtain behind them. "In case someone comes into the studio. I don't want to air our dirty laundry out there," he whispered. "So why are you here after months of silence and acting like—"

"Like what?" she said with a little head tilt.

He made a disgusted noise. "Like you didn't completely screw me over! Letting *me* get arrested for *your* tags."

Holy crap!

Emily wrapped her arms around him, and he let her. Gah! She rubbed her cheek on his shoulder and said, ever so quietly, "I had to. I'm eighteen. If I got arrested it would be on my permanent record. You're still a minor; it's not that big of a deal!"

Luca pulled back so abruptly that she almost stumbled. *"Not that big of a deal?!"* he shouted. "Do you have any clue what I went through? What I'm *still* going through? My mom had to grovel to my dad to get him to pay for a lawyer. And because of that, I had to move here to be with him. He's been watching my every move since I've been here, by the way. I got in huge trouble recently for this boat thing . . . Never mind. Anyway, because of the arrest, I'm on probation for the next *three years."*

Her shoulders dropped a little. "I know, Lu. And I'm sorry. I never fully got to tell you *how* sorry I am, and how much I appreciated you taking the blame. You know my parents made me break up with you because of your arrest. They threatened to take away my car. They even switched my phone and monitored my e-mails and social media!"

Luca kept his arms folded in front of him, protective. "Is that why you wouldn't talk to me, even at *school*?"

"I had to make it realistic to get them off my back." She took a little step toward him.

"I don't believe you."

"C'mon, I drove all the way from Ojai and ditched school

today to make things right. I still feel the same about you." Her eyes never left his. "Besides, with the RISD early acceptance letters out, you can relax now."

I raised my eyebrows at Violet. She nodded in confirmation. I looked back at Luca, who seemed caught off guard. "How did you know that I got in?"

She rolled her eyes. "Of course you got in. What art school in their right mind would reject *you*?"

He scoffed. "I don't know, Em, I had to be honest and put the arrest on the application. There was a good chance I could have gotten rejected because of what I did! For *you*."

Emily started pulling her curls into a bun, the hem of her lacy white shirt lifting to reveal the tightest set of abs I'd ever seen. "Please. You got arrested for *graffiti* and you were applying to an *art school*. They love that stuff."

Some tension seemed to ease from Luca's face. "Actually, I did manage to spin it as a political statement in my essay."

Emily laughed and threw her arms around him. "I'm so happy for you, Lu! I knew you could do it."

He didn't pull away. Instead he smiled a little and his eyes softened as they looked at her. "Thanks. When do you hear back from SVA? That's still your first choice, right?"

She nodded. "I'm not finding out until *April*."

And then. Oh, Lord. She tilted her head at him in that way again, and I swear her face turned into a fuzzy, Vaseline-lens version of itself, just imploring to be kissed. And he did. He kissed her.

Oh God. I suddenly realized how wrong it was for us to be witnessing this. And by Violet's expression, she did, too. But we were stuck now. We could only stare at each other with wide eyes.

They broke apart and she grinned. "We make sense together, Lu. You in Orange freaking County? Does *not* make sense."

He laughed really quickly, honk and all. My heart lurched. "I know, right? This place."

She dug into her pocket then and pulled out her phone. "Let's take a selfie to commemorate us getting back together!"

Luca made a face. "What, really? No, c'mon."

Seriously, what a weird thing to do right when you get together with your ex-boyfriend?

"We have to!" She was already getting into the pose, pulling his arm around her shoulders.

He sighed. "Okay, but just don't post it everywhere. It's weird."

Tilting her head *just so*, she smiled and spoke through clenched teeth. "I'm just posting it to Instagram; I have a new account my parents don't know about. Everyone *else* has to know we're back together!"

He looked at her. "Why?"

She was already editing the photo, swiping as if on autopilot. Her eyes didn't move from her screen. "Because we're the hottest couple."

Violet's hands flew to her mouth to stifle a laugh and I bit back the urge to do the same.

"Can't we just enjoy this for, like, a *second* before sharing with everyone?" he asked, peering down at her.

"Hm?" Emily's fingers were tapping furiously. "I knew it. I already have seven likes."

Luca stood very still for a minute before sighing heavily. "What about commemorating alone? Since this is about us?"

"Alone?" She finally looked up from her social media blitz.

The silence crackled and I held my breath.

"You know what? Never mind." Luca stepped away from her.

Emily's smile faltered. "What do you mean?"

"You just reminded me how it's never been about me, or how you feel about me. How it's about manipulating your image, what it looks like to everyone else. How I can never tell what's *real*." *Manipulating*. I felt a little ill.

The smile completely wiped off her face, Emily narrowed her eyes and lowered her phone. "*What*? Don't act all holier than thou. It's always been about image with you, too. Don't tell me you didn't like dating the hottest girl in school."

OMG.

Luca laughed again, but not his honky genuine laugh. A harsh, bitter one. "Wow, do you *hear* yourself? I regret nothing. I'm glad I got arrested. Not only did it reveal *your* true colors, but it's probably going to help me get my scholarship."

"What are you talking about?" Her bitchiness was thinly

veiled at this point. "Why the hell would *you* need a scholarship? Your dad could *buy* RISD."

Luca shook his head, as if she was an idiot. "Did you *ever* listen to anything I said about him? My dad will only pay for college if I study anything *but* art. And you know my mom can't afford it."

Violet and I looked at each other again, totally feeling guilty and terrible about this entire ordeal.

Luca, on the other hand, was getting more relaxed by the second, his hands stuck into his puffy-vest pockets. "Anyway, the financial aid I got with my acceptance wasn't enough. So I applied for the biggest art scholarship in the country with a project that's going to win it. And your little Banksy phase inspired it. So thanks."

The graffiti.

Emily cracked her neck, suddenly all gangsta. "Well, I thought I'd give this a try—but I don't need this shit. What a waste of ditching school." I truly hated her. She gave Luca a condescending pat on the arm before walking by him with a passing, "Good luck with that scholarship, Lu."

She swept through the curtains with finality. Luca stood there for a second, hands on his hips. Then he knocked over a stack of canvases, the sound of them clattering onto the floor reverberating through the room.

I held my breath, trying not to make a peep. Clearly, his cool demeanor with Emily had been just an act.

He stared down at the mess he had made, breathing heavily. Then, after a few seconds, he knelt down to pick it all up, resigned and slow in his movements. It took every bit of my willpower not to run over and help him.

When he finally left the room, you could hear a pin drop. I felt light-headed with the deluge of knowledge that had just flooded me in the past five minutes.

"Oh. My. *God.*"

I startled, having forgotten that Violet was standing there next to me. She was shaking her head. "What the *hell* was that? I felt like we were in a damn soap opera!"

Without thinking, I responded, "I know, right? What a *bitch.*"

Violet held her hands up with an aghast expression. "She needs to *jugeo.*" I giggled at her use of the Korean word for *die.*

She continued. "I guess that explains the whole not-wanting-to-date thing? She let him get *arrested* for *her* shit? And then she *broke up with him*!"

It was true. That was it. That was why Luca was so elusive. His big no-dating secret. I'm sure jaded didn't even begin to describe Luca's take on relationships.

"Damn her," I muttered under my breath.

Violet looked at me then and her expression cooled, as if she suddenly realized that we weren't friends. "Well, I guess the coast is clear, huh? Now you can prove yourself to be the *good* girl." The bitterness was palpable.

"Um, I don't . . ." I trailed off.

She sighed. "It's obvious that for some reason he has a thing for you."

Really?!

"Trust me, I'm just as confused as you are. But actually, after seeing that drama train wreck, I can see why he'd want someone a little . . . tidier." She looked me up and down with an air of disapproval.

I scowled. "Am I supposed to thank you or something? You've been such a—"

"Bitch? So what? We like the same guy, and you annoy the crap out of me. Deal." She started walking away.

This wasn't right. "Hey! Violet!"

She stopped and turned, blowing her hair out of her face with irritation. *"What?"*

I took a deep breath. "I don't know what I ever did to make you so annoyed by me. It really . . . I don't know, *sucks* to have that directed at you for no reason, you know?"

"Wow, you are so full of yourself. You have no idea why I'd be annoyed by you?"

"No."

"Okay, first of all, we've known each other since we were little."

My mouth dropped open. "What?"

She shifted so that she was standing directly in front of me, arms crossed. "We used to be friends in Korean school. But back then we called each other by our Korean names; mine was

Min-Jee." Korean school? I hadn't gone to Korean school since I was seven; I barely remembered all those Saturday afternoons spent at a church learning the Korean alphabet and such.

Wait. Oh, God. *Min-Jee.* I suddenly remembered her. She had been chubby and shy. And liked to draw. A lot. She always drew Disney princesses and Sanrio characters for me at my beck and call.

She must have seen the recognition cross my face. "Yeah, right? Well, you were my only friend at that place back then, and you just bailed. Without a trace. And so imagine my surprise when I saw you for the first time, here, freshman year. Like, yay! It's freaking Hye-Jin. But you didn't remember me, and you were so involved in all this popular school shit, you would never talk to the art freaks who smoked pot. I actually tried being your friend, do you remember?"

I bit my lip, trying really hard to place this version of Violet but I couldn't. "I don't know. I really don't remember . . ."

Violet glared at me. "Do you realize how much *worse* that is? That you were so wrapped up in your own crap you don't even remember someone trying to be your friend? So *rude.* But now, oh suddenly, you're into art because of a *dude*? It's *lame.*"

That stung. Because it was true. "Sorry, Violet. I didn't mean to be a jerk or a snob, I just . . ." So many things were running through my mind. But something she had said earlier stuck. And my sheepishness gave way to anger. I crossed my arms, too, trying to keep cool. "By the way, I *bailed* on Korean

school because my mom died and we couldn't afford it anymore."

Violet blinked a few times, and I saw the swagger leave her,
and her arms dropped to her sides. She bit her lip. "Oh. I
didn't . . . God, I'm sorry." It was the moment I called the
"M-Bomb"—whenever I told anyone about my mom's death
for the first time.

I sighed. "It's fine, it was a long time ago. But yeah, maybe
that explains things. And maybe you could get over it now." I
brushed by her, leaving the classroom and stepping outside.

The sunshine blinded me and I took a moment to regain my
composure, dazed by the weirdness of the past few minutes. And
when I looked up, I saw Luca. And our eyes met.

STEP 11:
Prove That You Are Different from All Other Women— IN THE ENTIRE WORLD

Okay. Either he knows or he doesn't know. Astoundingly astute hypothesis, Des. Just pure science in that impressive brain.

I glanced away, my heart thumping. And then I heard the studio door behind me swing open and saw Violet duck out. She glanced at me briefly before noticing Luca. He gaped at the both of us, his expression growing incredulous. Uh-oh. I needed to explain myself, *stat*. I had started walking toward him when he turned around and bolted. *Ran away* from me.

Despair hung over me as I stood there staring after him. Now what? Had I messed it up for good this time?

But I already knew the answer. No amount of miscommunication ever actually ended a relationship in K dramas. In fact, it was like a chemical that made the relationship stronger in the end. Mutated and fortified it.

I dug my wallet out of my backpack and unfolded my worn-out list. Since I had messed up, I now had a perfect opportunity to make up for it by employing step 11: *Prove That You Are Different from All Other Women—IN THE ENTIRE WORLD.*

And I knew exactly how do it.

A few days later, Fiona and I were pulling up to a parking lot overgrown with weeds. She careened Penny into a spot. "You ready?"

I took a deep breath. "I guess. Somehow I've managed to not see Won Bin for four days. I think he's been avoiding me. He didn't show up to Art Club and I don't know if he'll come today so . . . as ready as I'll ever be?"

We were at a youth center in the next town over—basically "the other side of the tracks," where people weren't all racially and socioeconomically homogeneous. Fiona had been volunteering here since freshman year and I had suggested planning an Art Club workshop with her, complete with an art supply donation from a local store. In K dramas, it was always the pure goodness of the heroine that really pierced through the guy's Rochester-like cynicism about love. I was hoping that watching me interact lovingly with children would appeal to some biological straight-guy instinct. For him to come to the conclusion that I wasn't actually a nosy weirdo, but rather an angelic, maternal type whom children flocked to. Classic K drama heroine. And the complete opposite of Emily.

So it was time to be that girl.

After getting a very reluctant Fiona to help, I also managed

139

to convince Mr. Rosso to have our Art Club spend a Friday afternoon at the youth center and teach them some art.

Fiona and I walked into the big playroom in the rec center and started arranging tables and chairs into groups for the kids to work at together. We had arrived earlier than everyone else; the rest of the Art Club kids were taking a bus from school. By the time they showed up, the room was pretty much *Lord of the Flies*–level mayhem and Fiona and I were trying to get things under control. I saw Violet pop in, and she immediately beelined toward Cassidy after glancing at me quickly. Hm. I couldn't tell if her hate for me had cooled down a bit since the M-bomb had been dropped or if she was just still embarrassed by the entire sneaky art-closet ordeal.

And for the billionth time in my life, I was looking for Luca when Mr. Rosso walked up to me, panama hat perched jauntily on his head. "What did you sign us up for here, Desi?"

I shot a pleading look at Fiona. She said, "Don't worry, I got this."

Then she whistled so loudly that a few kids dropped to the floor on their knees and covered their ears. "*Sit down. NOW.*" Her growl literally rumbled through the room. The thirty or so kids all scrambled to find seats on the bright orange plastic chairs arranged around the tables.

And then there he was.

Flutter. Pitter-patter.

Hovering in the doorway, he was looking into the room coolly.

Trying not to be discouraged, I assigned the Art Club students to each group, two of us to a table. We were supposed to get the kids started on some sketches and then eventually have finished work by the end of the workshop. When it was my turn to pick Luca's group I tried to get his attention but he kept his eyes on his phone.

"And, um, Luca, you and I can work with this group." His head snapped up and we made brief eye contact before he strode over to the group and plopped himself into a chair. *All right. This is how you wanna play it? I got all day for this, buddy!*

Our group was made up of two boys, named Micah and Jessie, and two girls, named Christine and Reese. (Named after Reese Witherspoon, as she proudly announced promptly after settling in to our group.) They ranged in age from six to nine and were all *very excited.* Normally they just played outside or had to do homework, so this was a bit of a special day for them.

Luca leaned back, still staring at his phone. I frowned and clapped my hands. "Okay, guys, so today we're going to work on some fun art! Let's start with some sketches! Do you guys know what sketching is?"

The four kids stared at me. Micah burped.

"Hm, okay. Sketches are rough drawings that you do to warm up before you start the real finished piece you want to do."

Luca cleared his throat loudly. I glared at him. "Do you have something to say or are you just *killin'* it on Candy Crush right now?"

He didn't look up from his screen. "Sketches don't have to be unfinished, they can be their own finished pieces, too."

Jessie waved her hand in the air. "So sketches are art, too?"

Before I could reply, Luca answered, "Yeah, art is whatever you want it to be." He looked up at me. "Don't let narrow-minded people try to define it for you."

Laying it on thick, Luca. I smiled directly at him. "Thanks for that. Not surprised that someone whose first word was *Impressionism* would have such a thorough knowledge of art."

Luca tilted his head and looked at me with a smile. "Are you stalking my fan pages?"

Reese threw up her little arms. *"This is boring!"*

I focused back on the kids. "Okay, sorry. Everyone grab some paper."

I had envisioned a peaceful afternoon of me gently guiding the youth to see the beauty of the world through art. It started off okay: the kids sat quietly and drew for the most part. I walked around, trying to be helpful and suggest ideas. Luca even straightened up and started chatting with Jessie about his SpongeBob sketch.

But as soon as Micah discovered the markers and drew a tattoo on himself, it went downhill.

"Look, a tattoo!" Micah said, proudly holding up his arm, which now had a giant cat drawn on it.

"That's a stupid tattoo," Reese sniffed, but she immediately reached across the table and grabbed a fistful of markers from the Tupperware box of supplies. Jessie and Christine immediately followed, and they all started scribbling on themselves.

"You guys!" I cried. "Stop that! Right now! We're supposed to be working on our sketches!"

Markers were clearly a bad idea and I scrambled to try to get them back, but I ended up playing tug-of-war with Reese instead. "Reese, we're not using these anymore," I said sternly.

She yanked my hand. "It's not fair, I want to use them!" We were both standing now, each of us clutching the bundle of markers with both hands.

"Too *bad*," I said through gritted teeth while keeping my grip on the markers firm.

Her green eyes suddenly welled up with tears. Uh-oh.

A third pair of hands enclosed mine, warm and firm. "Okay, why don't we compromise?" I looked up at Luca standing over us, a literal halo of sunlight lighting him up from behind.

"Reese, if you promise to only use the markers on paper, I'll draw you Elsa from *Frozen*," he said with a little wink.

Her tears seemed to retreat into her eyeballs. She sniffled. "Okay."

He raised his eyebrows at me. I rolled my eyes and let go of the markers, reluctantly disentangling my hands from Luca's.

Luca turned to Reese and held his hand out for a high five. She shyly gave him one, then scurried back to the table giggling. No one was immune to Luca's charms.

"Same goes for the rest of you, okay? Draw on the paper or

you're dead meat!" Luca pointed at each of them to accentuate the point. They all giggled and immediately went back to work on the paper.

Well, Maria von Trapp I was not. I turned to Luca. "You're good with kids."

He shrugged. "I used to babysit a lot."

"You *did*?" The incredulity slipped out before I could help it.

"Yeah. Why, is that so hard to believe?"

"A little?" I smiled. "I imagine it was hard to squeeze in babysitting while being an art genius."

He pressed his lips together but a laugh escaped anyway. "Okay, so you've done a thorough Google search on me."

What was the point in pretending I hadn't? It was my turn to shrug. "Kind of."

Our eyes met and while it was a bit uncomfortable, I felt some of the weirdness between us thaw.

I gulped nervously. "Luca, I—"

"Teacher, teacher! I don't know how to draw a hairy jellyfish!" Micah shouted.

"That's my cue," Luca said, turning on his heel to sit down next to Micah. *Micah, you little—!*

The next couple of hours flew by, and I barely had time to talk to Luca while trying to help Christine paint a seven-horned unicorn, then embellishing Jessie's very detailed portrait of Steph Curry with glitter. But every once in a while I would sneak a peek at Luca with the other kids as he patiently showed them how to draw perspective or mix paint colors to create other colors. But it was his ease with them, his absolute faith in their creativity that made me want to scramble across the table and plant a kiss on that mouth of his. He was in his element, and the kids adored him.

And then it was suddenly five o'clock and parents started picking up their children. They took their artwork with them, proudly showing it off to their parents. It was very sweet and I was pretty touched by it all—even if the good deed *had* been inspired by the K drama list, it felt nice to have spent an afternoon making these kids happy. The Art Club members seemed to feel the same way, and everyone was grinning as they cleaned up and said bye to the kids.

When the last of them had left, I fell back into a small chair. "Man, they're high-energy," I said to Fiona.

She picked up some scraps of paper off the floor. "I know, right? It was nice to have other people help out today."

"Let me know when you need it again. I think everyone enjoyed it."

Fiona laughed. "And add another extracurricular to your life?"

Before I could answer, I saw Luca walking toward the door. And while things had thawed slightly between us today, I would hardly call my attempts to be a beatific maternal type a success. Not only did I want to apologize for the closet incident, but I also had no idea if any of this had worked.

"Luca!" I called after him. He turned around and I walked

over to him while Fiona oh-so-subtly shot across the room to clean up another table.

He looked at me expectantly. *Just do it, Des.* "Hey . . . so, um, I meant to say earlier that I'm really sorry about the other day." I was dying with every word. "I didn't realize I was going to overhear that conversation. And neither did Violet," I added, glancing over to the back of the room where Violet was gathering her things. "We just kinda got stuck there." This was true for Violet. Just a teeny white lie on my part.

Luca appeared mortified for a second, too, and we just stood there, two statues of awkward. He finally broke the silence. "Okay."

"Also, sorry if you got in trouble for the boat incident."

He shot me a questioning look. "Why? It wasn't your fault."

Guilt zap. "Oh, but still . . . didn't you get grounded again or something?"

"I was when I was with my dad over the holidays. And now I'm at his beck and call for chores."

I smiled. "Oh! That doesn't sound so bad!"

"Also, I have to walk my stepmom's dumb dogs every day." He pouted.

"That sounds *horrible*. Do you also have to give up your weekly *allowance*?" I asked with a straight face. He laughed, not the big honky one, but still a little laugh.

And then I suddenly remembered. "Hey! And congrats on your early acceptance to RISD! That's awesome."

He stared down at his shoes for a bit and my heart started sinking lower into my stomach. Did I just remind him of the closet incident again?! Then he looked up with a small smile. "Thanks, but I still can't go until I figure out the scholarship stuff."

I nodded. "Right. Well, hopefully—"

Mr. Rosso yelled out, "All right, everyone back on the bus! Thanks for planning this, Desi and Fiona. It was great, we'll have to do it again!"

Luca tugged at his beanie and walked away, saying, "See ya."

And that was that. My face flushed as I hastily helped Fiona finish cleaning up. I fought back tears so that Fiona couldn't see my disappointment.

And that's when I spotted a pile of drawings by Luca.

I stopped to flip through them. One was an excellently rendered SpongeBob. Another, a pair of shoes that I remembered Micah wearing. A robot cat. A ninja princess. I flipped through various hilarious sketches until I reached one that made me freeze.

It was a drawing of me, sitting at a table with my head slightly bent, resting on my hand. Who knows when he caught that moment. But it wasn't just the fact that he'd drawn me that made me pause. It was how he'd drawn me. The careful and sensitive lines, the quiet moment captured.

It was so intimate, so studied. So . . . knowing. A little smile grew into a huge grin.

I drew out the K drama list and stared down at it lovingly. Fiona walked up to me and looked over my shoulder at it. "Everything work out okay?"

I kissed the list with a smack. "Crisis averted. Saved by the list once again."

STEP 12:
Life-Threatening Event Makes Him/ You Realize How Real Your Love Is

"I can't even *believe* we're doing this right now."

It was maybe the first time in my life I had ever seen Fiona sweat. Physical exertion and she were not the best of friends. We were walking in the middle of Stony Point Drive with the sun beating down on us, a mile away from my house, while Wes was setting up cones and yellow tape at either end of the street.

It was the week after the Art Club visit to the youth center. After seeing that drawing Luca had done, knowing that he had feelings for me whether or not he wanted to admit it, I was impatient to get rolling. I wished I could just skip to our first kiss, but I knew I still had some work ahead of me. So all weekend I had brainstormed to figure out step 12: *Life-Threatening Event Makes Him/You Realize How Real Your Love Is.* I had watched a few dramas with my dad and had finally come up with a plan.

I scattered a handful of nails on the street while Fiona dropped one and darted her eyes. Not a soul to be seen on this quiet side street in one of the eerie empty neighborhoods of Monte Vista. For a city with near-perfect weather year-round, people hardly ever stepped out of their air-conditioned homes.

Pulling her hair into a high ponytail, Fiona stared intensely at me. "Des, how exactly are you going to pull this off again?"

I tried to remain patient while explaining the plan to her. "We'll get a flat tire, hit the curb, and I'll pretend to hit my head. Then I can go into this damsel-in-distress mode and Won Bin will be overcome with his concern for me. Thus realizing he loves me."

Those large amber eyes pierced through me. "Wow. That's some high hopes. Also, what if someone gets hurt? Out of all the steps, this one seems the most extreme."

There was that little tug of guilt that had been increasingly persistent lately.

"Yeah, I know, this one is over-the-top. But they're just teeny nails, the worst thing that can happen is we get a flat tire. Which is what I'm counting on. And man, I am *so close*. I can feel it. That drawing he did of me . . . I think this will be the clincher. Plus, don't you know that going through stress causes the body to emit certain endorphins that can create *intense* bonding with whoever else you go through it with?"

She walked up ahead, throwing a few nails carelessly into the wind. "Yes. I, too, watched *Speed*."

I looked at our handiwork, hands on my hips. "It's really nuts. I might actually graduate high school with a *boyfriend*."

Fiona turned around and shot me a level stare. "Desi. You are someone who is going to go to *Stanford* to become a *doctor*. Not having a boyfriend in high school is freaking small potatoes. Boyfriends are overrated." She paused. "So are girlfriends, for that matter."

"Easy for *you* to say," I said with laugh, glancing at my phone. "Okay, we're cool, let's head back."

Fiona threw one last fretful look behind us as she said, "Okaaay. So, you're really not worried someone else might drive over this?"

"Fi! I told you, people in Monte Vista *will* obey the cones."

I linked my arm through Fiona's, even though I knew this sort of girlie BFF behavior drove her nuts. "So what's new with you?"

She made a face. "Why?"

"What do you mean? I'm asking how you're doing!"

"Is this a ploy to get me to help you with more weird shit?" she asked, stopping abruptly to look at me.

My heart sank a little. Life had been K drama steps 24/7, and it hit me now that this was the first time in a few weeks that I was actually asking Fiona about what was going on with *her*. I squeezed her arm extra-tight. "No, it's not a ploy. And sorry that it's been all Won Bin all the time around these parts."

She shrugged. "I get it. First-boyfriend stuff. I forgive you." But she gave my arm a squeeze back, and I knew she appreciated it nonetheless.

"So how are things with Leslie?" I asked as we walked down the middle of the empty street toward Wes and her car.

Fiona made a very unladylike fart noise. "She's getting so clingy. *Over* it."

"Fi!" I admonished her. "You're every girl's worst nightmare, you know that?"

"I think you mean *dream*," she said in her sultry way, leaning her head in toward mine. I moved it away with a rough push on her temple.

"I'm being serious! My worst freaking nightmare is Luca thinking that way about me."

Fiona's eye lasers sliced through me. "There are worse things than having a relationship fail, you know. And speaking of . . . if there's one thing I've learned with all my girlfriends, it's that you eventually have to stop playing games. How much longer are you going to keep this up?"

Why was she being such a Negative Nancy about this? I unlinked my arm from hers. "When it's *done*."

I strode ahead of her, annoyed. Couldn't she see how close I was? There was no stopping now.

Wes stayed behind to guard the cones and Fiona drove me back to school where she spied on Luca while I helped the student government crew set up for a pep rally. At 5:02 she texted me from her hideout that Luca was leaving the art studio and heading toward the parking lot. I took a deep, shuddering breath. Like, my body shuddered inwardly into itself. *Here goes nothing.*

My clomping footsteps hid the apprehension that was bubbling up inside me as I walked rapidly across the parking lot in my sandals.

"Luca!"

He froze in the middle of a cool-guy stretch, his arms above his head so that his shirt rose up ever so slightly to reveal a peep of tan abdomen. "What?"

I was momentarily distracted by that one inch of skin. *Perv.* "Hm? Oh. By any chance, can you give me a ride? Fiona was supposed to take me home but she had to bail. Something about her cat." Fiona's family had a twenty-year-old cat named Chubbins who was basically always on the brink of death. So my lie wasn't *that* much of a stretch.

Luca looked like a cornered animal for a second. *Geez.* Getting him to warm up to me again would be no easy task.

He cleared his throat. "Uh, well, I don't know if we live close to each other."

"What! We both live in *Monte Vista*, how freaking far could I possibly be from your house?" My nonchalant act evaporated as I frowned at him.

You'd think I'd asked him to make a colonoscopy appointment, the way he dragged his feet. "Fine. Whatever. My ride's over there."

We walked over to a battered old blue Honda Civic. I ran my hand over the dented hood. "Sweet ride."

He shot me a haughty look. "You OC people and your devotion to the *new*."

Oh, Mr. Mister. He had no idea what he had just unleashed.

"*Actually*, I was being completely devoid of sarcasm. The Si is the crown jewel of Civics, at least here in the U.S. Five-speed trans, tight suspension with stiffer sway bars, and even a strut bar." I walked around it, surveying the little masterpiece. "Lower profile and wider wheel-and-tire setup make this a great-looking *and* -feeling daily driver, but also an awesome platform for a tuner," I said as I glanced at him.

I was in the zone and prattled on. "I mean, for a car to get around thirty miles per gallon with this kind of performance back in '99 was really impressive. I guess that's the beauty of VTEC, huh?"

That's when I noticed that Luca was staring at me. Oh crap. I had unleashed another layer of nerd on Luca. I flushed but then remembered Hae-Soo from *It's Okay That's Love*, and how she was always so badass whenever she shut people down with her doctor knowledge. For ultimate crush-baiting, be very, very, capable or informed about an unexpected thing to shock and awe those around you in a very cool manner.

I mustered a smile, as if I was super-proud of the car talk. Confidence, Des. Exude who you wanna be.

"*Why* do you know all this?" Luca yelped, yanking open the passenger-side door for me. That little gesture did not go unnoticed, and I mentally thanked his hippie mama for raising him right. He continued ranting. "Do you also read the Kelley Blue Book in your spare time when you're not building robots in your creepy basement?!" The incredulity made his voice a little honky, like his laugh.

I slid into the seat and waited until he got into the car before answering. "My dad's a mechanic. Duh." Although there *was* that one summer in middle school when I studied the Kelley Blue Book out of curiosity.

Luca did that car-backing-up thing where you twist your entire body to the right and drape your arm across the back of the passenger seat. Where I was sitting. His hand brushed lightly against my hair and I got a whiff of boy sweat and breath mints. Somehow an intoxicating yet gross cocktail.

"A mechanic. That's kinda cool."

"I think so."

"Not a job that a lot of the parents of people at this school have."

I shrugged. "No, but it's not like anyone really cares. I think the most redeeming part of California is that there's a spirit of true meritocracy here that's absent in older parts of the country."

Luca laughed again, his hand deftly maneuvering the steering wheel and his eyes moving rapidly between mirrors and windshield. Huh, he was a very meticulous driver. Why I found that so hot, I don't know. Daughter-of-a-mechanic weirdness.

He glanced at me briefly. "You have this way of talking . . ."

"Yeah, yeah, like a Vulcan."

He laughed. "Exactly."

"Make a left," I said with a smile. I was suddenly aware that we were both in a small car together. Alone. And it felt really, really intimate. Like, could he smell my breath? I breathed into my palm subtly.

A couple of turns later and we were almost to the street where Fiona and I had dropped the nails. Oh, man, it was about to happen.

"Gotta tell my dad to pick up some milk," I lilted as I pulled out my phone and began furiously texting Wes, who was waiting to hear from me. **Just turned on Linda Vista. Be there in less than 1 min.** That was his signal to move the traffic tape and cones. I got an immediate text back: **Done.**

And then I directed Luca to turn left onto Stony Point Drive. I fiddled with my phone nervously. We were right about to drive over the nails . . .

Smooth sailing.

What the heck? I craned my neck to look out the window at the road. The nails were there, they were even visible as we drove right over them, glinting in the fading sunlight. I glanced at Luca, but he didn't seem to notice anything.

Well. Okay, let's just do this again. "Oh crap! I just realized

I left something at school." *Lightning-quick thinking, Des.* "My calculus book, which I need to do my homework tonight. Can we pretty please go back to school? Sorry."

Luca seemed unfazed. "Oh, okay, sure." As I hoped, he quickly pulled a U-turn and when we had driven back far enough, I smacked my forehead with my palm. "Oh, I'm such an idiot! I actually forgot I left it at home, so we're good."

"Are you sure?" Luca glanced over at me, and I could almost feel his faith in me leaking out of him.

"Yup, I'm sure! Sorry."

So we U-turned again.

I held my breath. We'd be coming up on those nails right about—

And then I heard an explosive pop—the unmistakable sound of a tire blowing out. Holy crap, that was way more intense than I thought it was going to be! But before I could even really register *that*, the car immediately skidded to the right, and Luca clutched the wheel with an "Oh, shit!" But he couldn't control the car fast enough and we bumped violently up onto the curb, a loud *crunch* piercing the air as something beneath the car scraped against the curb.

"Watch out!" I yelped, instinctively covering my eyes with my hands. Then I felt something heavy smash into my torso—something heavy but gentle. I opened my eyes to see Luca's right arm stretched across me. Doing the Mom-arm seat belt. Before I could register how adorable that was, I actually found myself being thrown back into my seat by the Mom-arm seat belt. And then a giant *boom* as the air bags went off in the blink of an eye, smashing me in the forehead.

There were a few seconds of silence as the air bags immediately started to deflate. Then I felt Luca's arm move, on my lap where it had landed. He felt around, his hand grasping my thigh before stopping abruptly. "Are you okay?" I heard his muffled voice. I was still looking straight ahead, trying to register what had happened.

I nodded, stunned but feeling okay.

"Desi?" I heard slight panic in his voice and turned to look at him, his head also back against his seat, but turned toward mine. Dark eyes worried, beanie askew.

I blinked a few times, seeing actual stars. "Yeah, I'm fine. Are you okay?" I asked.

He also nodded, looking as stunned as me. "Yeah, but I think . . ." He felt under his left eye where a giant welt was forming. I winced for him, feeling very terrible for causing it. For some reason, in all my machinations, *minor car accident* never actually involved real injuries.

He fumbled with the visor, popping it down and looking in the mirror. "Am I going to get a black eye?!" he screeched as he started to inspect his face. He let out a whimper when he touched the spot where it was tender. I was about to tease him except that this injury actually *did* look painful.

We got out of the car and circled it. Other than the popped

tire, it looked like his transmission had been dislodged after the car jumped the curb. Crap, way more damage than I had anticipated.

I felt really shitty.

"Are you sure you're okay? Should we go to the hospital?" I fretted while looking at Luca's eye again.

"I think it's fine . . . I'm going to call a tow, though. I don't think we can drive this thing. Can you go talk to those people who are coming out of their houses and tell them we're okay?" he asked, already on his phone. I looked around and saw a few people coming over to see what was going on. Ugh.

After I had reassured everyone that we were fine and had called for help, I suddenly heard a very familiar honk. Two short staccatos followed by one long blare.

I turned around slowly to see my dad in his garage's tow truck—Towjam, as it was endearingly dubbed. *Noooo!*

"Uh, who did you call for a tow?" I asked, my voice high-pitched.

"Papa's Auto Shop, why?"

Lord. I closed my eyes. How in God's name did he pick my dad's auto shop of all the auto shops in Monte Vista, in all the world. "Um, it's just that—"

"Desi?!" my dad shouted out the window. Oh *no.* I felt light-headed as I watched him park the truck wildly. *Shit, shit, shit.* I waved and smiled, so he would immediately know I was fine. "Hi!" I hollered. Luca looked at me and then at my dad.

My heart was beating like crazy and I was breaking into a sweat.

"Are you okay?" Luca asked, that little furrow showing up between his eyes.

I shook my head. "No, that's my dad. And he's probably freaking out!"

He looked confused. "But it was just a little accident?"

"Yeah, and my mom *just* died from a pulmonary embolism is all," I snapped.

His eyes grew wide but he looked confused. "What does that have to do with—"

Before I could say anything else, my dad was already hopping out of the truck and rushing up to me. His face was white with fear. "Desi! Did you get into an accident? Are you okay? What happened?" His frenzied line of questioning made my heart lurch and I kept my smile pasted on my face.

"I'm fine, Appa. Just a small fender bender. Everyone's okay."

The worry eased from his forehead, and I felt myself relax slightly as well. He started inspecting my head, not noticing Luca yet.

"Um, Appa, this is my friend Luca."

My dad shot me the briefest of looks before turning to greet Luca. "Hi, Desi's friend. I'm her dad."

Luca held his hand out. "Nice to meet you." Then he quickly added, "I'm really sorry about the accident."

My dad took Luca's hand. "No need for sorry, accidents are

called accidents because they're not on purpose, right?" Then he suddenly yanked Luca in close. "What happened to your eye? You hurt?"

Luca touched his eye, and I knew that he wanted to wince but he kept his expression cool. "Oh no, just a little bruise."

My dad squinted for a second, then patted Luca's arm heartily. "Okay, you tough boy!" Then he walked over to the car. "Okeydokey, so, whatchu going on here?" He started doing the mechanic crouch, bending over and shuffling around the car, peering under it carefully. I noted that relief seemed to wash over Luca, and I was touched by his (unnecessary) guilty conscience.

"Looks like you ran over some nails in the road," my dad said, holding up a couple in his hand. Oh brother. "What the heck are they doing here? Like cartoon?" he said, looking up and grinning broadly at us. I laughed weakly.

Luca crouched down next to him to look at them. "Weird," he mumbled. Then he straightened up, suddenly remembering. "Oh, we might have snagged the muffler, too." So proud of himself. Alas.

"Transmission," I corrected. My dad looked at me approvingly.

While they inspected the car (Luca was doing it out of bro-politeness it seemed; machismo was a little diminished every time he touched his face tenderly, though), I spotted Penny sputtering to a stop at the end of the street, with both Fiona and Wes inside. They were far away, but I was able to see their confused expressions. Fiona stuck her head out the window with a questioning thumbs-up gesture. I shook my head and waved her off until they finally drove away. I'd have a lot of explaining to do later.

My dad whistled, a low two-note call that he had used to summon me my entire life. I walked over to him and he wiped his already greasy hands on a cloth he kept tucked into his front pants pocket. "Desi, I'm going to sweep up these nails, then tow the car and take Luca to his house. You can walk home, right?"

"Sure," I answered, my heart sinking into a tepid pool of water. Not only had I actually injured Luca like some relentless villain, but now the entire thing was a bust.

But wait, I couldn't give up. Damsel-in-distress move hadn't been initiated yet. I walked over to Luca, where my dad couldn't hear me. "Hey, I don't want to worry my dad, but my head is killing me and I feel light-headed. Would you mind walking me home? He can give you a ride when he comes back." I held my breath, willing him to take the bait.

He shoved his hands deep into his puffy vest pockets. "Yeah, sure. Sorry about all this." Guilt punch again. I waved my hand dismissively. "Don't worry, I think I just need to lie down."

I went over to my dad and gave him a hug. "Luca's going to walk me home. Can we just give him a ride later?" He squeezed me *very* tightly before letting me go. "Okay, go rest."

As we walked away from the accident, I was able to relax for the first time since my dad arrived on the scene. *Appa crisis averted and step 12 still in effect.*

We walked a block in silence. I saw Luca glance behind quickly, where my dad was already sweeping up the nails. I bit my lip, not liking leaving a mess for my dad to clean.

Luca cleared his throat. "So your mom died?"

"Um, yeah." I cursed myself for dropping the M-bomb back at the accident.

But. To be truly K drama, I needed to capitalize on the M-bomb. *This* was my tragedy, this was how Luca would see me differently—compassion for my hard knocks in life. To admire me for my bravery in the face of tragedy.

Yes, ladies and gentlemen: I had to exploit my mother's death to get a guy. I waited for lightning to strike my eyeballs, one bolt in each.

Mom, I have no idea if you would have been the type of mother to hit me upside the head for doing this, or someone who would have just been so disappointed that you'd cry alone in your room at the monster you'd raised. But I gotta do this. Sorry.

Luca was looking at me expectantly and as we walked under the breezy shade of fragrant eucalyptus trees, I chose my words carefully. "That's why we live here. She was a neurosurgeon at UC Irvine. She died when I was little. And because it was so sudden and unexpected, it makes my dad worry about me, maybe more than other parents. That something could happen to me, too."

He looked at me straight-on with a sad smile. "I'm sorry," he said simply. And the sweetness of it hit me like a ton of bricks.

"It's okay, no worries. I was only seven when it happened, so . . ." I trailed off, my familiar go-to phrase left hanging in the air.

He frowned. "Seven. That's not *that* young. It's still, I mean, not to make assumptions, but it's still old enough to be traumatized."

There was so much I could say to that. How everyone assumed you were this fragile, damaged person when you lost a parent. How that was never the case with me, how my dad was the best mom *and* dad I could have ever had.

We reached my street and I breathed a sigh of relief. Necessary tragedy or not, I needed to fast-forward the romance *stat*.

Luca cleared his throat. "So you're like a disaster magnet."

"How do you mean?" I tried to keep my voice cool as a cucumber. A lying cucumber.

"So far, in the few times we've hung out together, we've been lost at sea and then in a car accident. Adventure seems to follow you wherever you go."

I laughed nervously. "What can I say, I'm a regular Paul Bunyan."

"What?"

"You know, Paul Bunyan, the giant lumberjack from American folklore who had all sorts of adventures?"

"Yes, I know who Paul Bunyan is—aw, never mind," he said with a defeated little laugh. "Anyway, your dad's cool."

"Yeah, he's the best."

The strange expression on Luca's face made me defensive. "What?"

Another inscrutable smile. He replied, "Nothing. It's just . . . nice. That you're so nice about your dad. I have no idea what it feels like to like your own father." An uncomfortable silence settled over us. I wasn't sure how to respond and bit my tongue before I said something flailureish.

"Here's my house." I made an abrupt turn off the sidewalk to walk across my lawn.

My house was a two-story cream stucco like all the others, with light blue shutters, an attached garage, and a spacious driveway. But unlike the rest of the houses on our street, our front yard wasn't just lush and green (not that the entire state was in the middle of a drought or anything), it also contained several raised vegetable-garden beds. And a few random tires lying around. And a general feeling of *A man without a wife takes care of this house.*

Luca stood awkwardly on the sidewalk as I started to walk up the path to the front door. I turned around and looked at him questioningly.

Shoving his hands into his pockets, he said, "I can just call a cab to take me home."

No!

"Oh, really? Um, I don't know, I still feel kind of crappy. Would you . . . Would you want to come in for a bit?"

The question hung in the air between us like the most obvious seduction ploy ever. After a moment of soul-crushing silence, Luca took his hands out of his pockets and strode over to me.

"Sure."

I opened the door and held it as he brushed by me into the house.

Oh shit. *Luca's at my house.* Now let's make him realize he likes me.

STEP 13:
Reveal Your Vulnerabilities in a Heartbreaking Manner

I instantly noticed all the embarrassing things you notice about your own home when looking at it through the eyes of a first-time visitor.

The cool-at-the-time-but-now-outdated teal-painted living room walls. The ratty and obviously overused recliner. That one window that never got proper curtains so it had a bizarre paper screen propped over it—a screen with a popular Korean cartoon bear pattern.

Power through, Des. Power through.

"Shoes off, please," I ordered breezily as I dropped my back-pack onto the cold tile floors of the entryway and kicked off my sandals. But Luca had already started unlacing his black high-top Vans, bent over with one hand balancing himself against the wall. Hm, for some reason, his Asian house-training appealed to me.

"You can go sit in the living room." And then my voice faltered. "Huh . . . I feel . . . light-headed . . ." I stumbled over to the sofa, where I had already set out a pretty gray-and-white-striped throw and a nice fluffy pillow that morning. I resisted the urge to bring my palm up to my forehead. That would be taking the damsel-in-distress thing a bit too far. Maybe.

I peeked to see Luca walking toward me, but he was clearly distracted, picking up a copy of *Popular Science* on the way over. "Did you hit your head on something?" he asked as he absentmindedly flipped through the magazine. Annoyance shot through me—when he hurt *his own face* he sure was concerned!

"I don't know," I responded weakly. "Can you maybe grab me a cold washcloth?" I had conveniently set a fresh one on the kitchen sink next to a small pink plastic tub (a staple in every Korean household). "The kitchen's that way." I pointed.

"Sure." I heard him rummage around in there.

I readjusted myself on the sofa so that he could either sit next to me or kneel by me. I fixed the hem of my sweater so it covered all rolly bits of my belly, then moved my hair off my forehead so that Luca could place the washcloth there all gently and lovingly—

"Catch!"

I looked up to see a frozen pack of peas headed straight for my face. My hands went up to catch it instinctively.

"Those will be *way* more effective than a washcloth," he said with a smug *you're welcome* tone in his voice.

"Er . . . thanks." I placed it gingerly on my head. "Hm, so . . . Yeah, might need to take a little breather."

Luca was bounding away from me already. What the heck, where was this energy coming from? "So what's up there?" he asked at the foot of the stairs.

"Uh, just the bedrooms, you know? Like in a house," I replied, annoyed that he wasn't tending to me in my current state of distress.

"*Your* room?" He turned around with an eyebrow cocked.

"Yeah?"

He started up the stairs. "Cool, let's go see it."

I sat up straight and scrambled over to him. "Wait, what? No, don't go in there!" My room was *not* part of the plan. No way did I want him in there—he would see the full range of Overachieving Dork, especially when he saw . . .

When I walked in to my room he had already plopped down on my bed, checking out the wall of shelves to his left. "What *is* all that?"

I was momentarily distracted by Luca *sitting on my bed!!!* *SQUEAL.* I gathered my wits and replied, "Well, sir, these rectangular paper vessels are called *books.*" I swept my arm Vanna White–style across the shelving. "Anyway, let's—"

"I see the books—you know what I'm talking about. All *that.*" He lifted his chin toward the Shelf.

Ugh. Too late. It was filled with awards, certificates, old science fair inventions, sculptures I made for my dad as a kid—the living proof of my Type-A DNA. And usually I was proud of my Shelf o' Overachieving Dork. But in front of Luca, I was mortified. I doubted Emily had a Shelf o' Overachieving Dork. Unless it was a shelf filled with Beat poetry and bongs. And, like, lacy lingerie tossed carelessly over vintage books.

"It's stuff. Okay, now let's—" I was interrupted by the swift, almost dancerlike grace of Luca leaping up to take a closer look at the shelf. The most athletic thing he had ever done.

He whistled. "Perfect attendance *seven* times? Best handwriting, first place at the science fair, first place at the science fair, first place at the science fair, first place—yeah, yeah. Top Girl Scout Cookie Seller. Arbor Society Award for Most Trees Planted. Christ . . . Wait, what's this one?" He held up a golden Korean flag statue with Korean writing etched into the plaque below it.

I grabbed it from him and placed it back on the shelf. "It's . . . this thing." He waited patiently for me to go on. "Um, the local Korean American newspaper gives it to students who get perfect SAT scores," I rushed.

Luca nodded his head slowly. "Yup. Okay, this has been a very revealing five minutes." Exactly. Way too revealing. Yet, despite seeing my lunacy in the harsh light of day, Luca seemed to find it amusing, not repulsive. The grin never left his face as he picked up object after object. I watched him while marveling at how I managed to be living the list without even trying. This potentially embarrassing moment was totally step 13, *Reveal Your Vulnerabilities in a Heartbreaking Manner.* If my freakish accomplishments could be considered vulnerabilities, that is.

"Hm," I heard him mutter as he peered at a framed photo. It

was one of me, Fiona, and Wes dressed up for Halloween last year. (Rock, Paper, Scissors. We were super-proud of this idea.) Luca jabbed his finger at Wes, who was Scissors. "Seems like you guys have history."

Every part of me wanted to yell, *I would never in a million years*. But I kept my mouth shut. No harm in dragging out the love triangle. Instead I grabbed Luca's arm to move him along, keeping my other hand clutched around the stupid pack of peas on my head.

"Wait, what's this?"

I wanted to cry. Damn curious weirdo! He was bent over my desk, looking at another framed photo.

"This photo is . . . awesome," he said, bent over and pointing. The Family Portrait. I had a vague memory of when the photo was taken—on the car ride to the studio, my dad had been insistent on wearing a newsboy cap and my mom was threatening him with divorce because of it. As with all their fights, it had ended with laughter and someone caving. My mom, in this instance.

In the portrait, we were posed in classic triangle family-photo pose. My dad standing behind my mother, who was seated, holding me in her lap. My dad was wearing a deep burgundy sweater and that gray newsboy cap, a thick lock of hair showing dashingly through. His hands were resting awkwardly on my mom's shoulder and his smile was one of pain more than joy, a toothy grimace. I was four and wearing a cat-print dress with my hair curled and tied back with bright yellow ribbons, eyes shut tight and mouth open in the middle of some silent-horror-movie scream.

A true parade of pain until you panned over to my mother. In the midst of all the awkward and bad, the chaos stopped and froze around her delicate frame. Her long, soft hair framed a face with sparkling, amused eyes and a wide grin showed off a set of teeth that never had to see braces. Intelligence and good humor radiated from her.

"I see you get your charms from your father," Luca said drily. I hit him. He stood back and looked at the photo a while longer. He glanced at me and smiled shyly, the first shy-anything I'd ever seen on him. "She was really pretty."

She was pretty. I felt a constriction in my chest and a familiar gnawing. Not necessarily because I missed my mom—I did, but just a bit. My memories really *were* hazy. Rather, it was something I felt for my dad, for the loss that our little family suffered so long ago.

"Yeah, she was," I said matter-of-factly.

Luca grinned. "How did your dad end up snagging her?"

I elbowed him and straightened up, moving away from my desk. "What do you mean! My dad's a total catch."

"Don't get me wrong, your dad's cool. But your mom was a total fox. Dr. Fox." He waggled his eyebrows.

I sat on the edge of my bed. "Yeah, well, my dad was a fox, too, back in the day. Their love story is ridiculous."

He sat down next to me. "Oh, yeah? Tell me."

We were sitting close and I felt every hair on my body stand on end. My right hand was numb from holding the peas to my head. "Well, they met in high school and she was the most popular, smartest girl in class. And my dad was a total punk."

"Wow, high school sweethearts?"

"Yep. They fell in love, and of course my mom's snobby, fancy parents didn't approve, so it was this whole star-crossed-lovers thing throughout high school and even when she was in college. They shipped her off to the U.S. for med school, hoping that would end things."

Luca was rapt. "Wow, that's extreme."

"Total dramatic-parents-type behavior. But it didn't work because my dad just saved up money working and followed her. Here, to California. When her parents found out they were living together, they disowned her and my dad worked as a mechanic to pay for her tuition. And when they got married, my grandparents *finally* caved and took her back." I always held those disowned years over my grandparents. I had met them a couple of times but I got the distinct feeling that I only reminded them of painful memories. They sent me fancy Korean beauty products every birthday and a check, and that was pretty much my only interaction with them.

"Your parents' story is right out of a movie," Luca said. "I think my parents met on a blind date."

I finally dropped the peas from my head; my arm was getting

tired. "Yeah. My dad's never even considered dating since she died."

"Really? Wow, it must have been total heartbreak," Luca said with a little smile.

I flinched. "He doesn't need to date anyone, though. He has me!" I laughed.

Luca gave me serious side-eye.

And then I felt the ol' flailure specter hanging over me. "We're like two peas in a pod. Happy as clams." *Please, more food analogies, Des.* "We don't need anyone else." Those words landed in the room with a thud. What's hotter than hearing a girl talk about how all she needs is her father and *no one else*?

When I finally gathered the nerve to look up at Luca, his strange expression said it all. And then the late-afternoon sunlight created a Michael Bay–esque lens flare and I could practically hear our Korean love ballad blast in jarringly in the background. "You okay?" he asked suddenly, dark eyes concerned, mouth set into a frown.

Oops, I guess I had just been staring at him. I nodded. "Yep, just fine and dandy." *Ugh, why.*

He laughed his honky little laugh, and his face cracked into a wide smile. "Okeydokey then!" Pretty good impression of my dad. Then his eyes dimmed. "Sorry, I should have been driving more carefully."

My heart melted into a pool of guilt. "You couldn't have seen those nails. Don't be sorry," I said in a low voice. Was that sexy? Too sexy? Ah! How did people do this?!

His eyes met mine and suddenly . . . suddenly it felt real. I wasn't faking this, this intensity I was feeling. And damned if he wasn't shooting intensity right back at me. The wounded-damsel act—holy effective romance enhancer. *This was it. Kiss time. Holy crap.*

A wave of heat passed between us—the vibration of our bodies' atoms and molecules transferring heat. *Yep, just like conduction heat transfer, Desi. Very romantic.*

And then he blinked. And the moment passed as quickly as it had come. He straightened up and took off his beanie, running his hands through his hair. A gesture I now recognized as a nervous habit. Then a door slammed downstairs and my dad's voice echoed through the house. "Desi! I am back!" I scrambled off the bed.

"Appa's home!" I chirped, pushing Luca out of my bedroom. "Do you want to stay for dinner?"

He hesitated just long enough for me to feel embarrassed. Was that too bold? Too lame to ask him to have dinner with my dad and me? But before I could backpedal, he nodded. "Sure!" I bit back a smile as we headed downstairs.

STEP 14:
Lock That Baby In with a Kiss!
~~Finally.~~ Maybe.

When we got to the kitchen my dad was washing his hands in the sink. "Okay, Luca, your car needs new transmission. But also, oh boy, lots of other problems, sorry to say. It got very damaged and it's already kind of old thing, right?"

Luca nodded. "It was my mom's car before I started driving it. And I'm one hundred percent sure she didn't really take care of it." He looked at us quickly, self-conscious for some reason. "I mean, she's not irresponsible or anything—she just wasn't ever interested in things like taking care of the car."

"Sounds kinda different from your dad," I said, pulling out scallions, thinly sliced brisket, tofu, and eggs from the refrigerator.

He leaned back on the counter and nodded. "Yeah, they couldn't be more different."

I opened the pantry to grab three packs of ramen.

"Ramen?" Luca asked, voice laced with doubt.

"Yup, food of the gods." I handed my dad a pot, which he

immediately filled with water. Once it was filled, we swapped—I placed the pot on the gas stove and he took the tofu and scallions from me. A cutting board was already set on the counter ready for him, swiftly placed there by me while he had been filling the pot. He started chopping while I cracked the eggs open over a metal mixing bowl.

"You guys are like a well-oiled machine," Luca said with admiration. He straightened up and stood in the center of the kitchen, looking uncertain and shy. "Can I help?"

Helpful, obedient Luca was a whole other world of charm. Whipping the eggs, I looked around. "Hm, I think we have it covered." Then I remembered something. I took a hard-boiled egg from a Tupperware container of them we kept in the fridge, still nice and cold, and handed it to him. "For your future black eye," I said with a smile.

His hand reached for the welt on his face instinctively and my dad walked over to Luca and peered at his face. Then he laughed, really loud. "That's just baby black eye! You'll be okay, tough boy."

Luca managed to look embarrassed about his wimpiness for a second before staring at the egg curiously. "What do I do with this?"

My dad took it and placed it under Luca's eye, then repositioned his hand so that his palm was open and holding the egg in place. Then he rolled it slowly on the area where he was hurt. Luca was very still and, I guessed by his strained facial expression, just a teeny bit weirded out. "Asian-style remedy to help with black eye," my dad said sagely.

I bit my lip to keep from laughing. My dad was totally milking this ancient oriental act. "Okay, Appa, I think he gets the picture. He can probably take over now."

My dad shrugged and walked away, leaving Luca to stand there rolling the egg under his eye awkwardly.

"Since I'm clearly useless, can I learn how to make this masterpiece then?" he asked, stepping over next to me and subtly placing the egg on the counter. Luca's physical proximity always released something purely chemical in me, and I stepped back slightly so that I wouldn't turn into a malfunctioning giggly twit in my dad's presence. I'm sure he didn't find this unusual at all—*a random hot guy hanging out at our house.*

"Why are you making scrambled eggs?" he asked.

Cutie dum-dum. "Not scrambled. These are going to go in the broth near the very end. They'll cook and make the soup all nice and thick."

"I like lot of eggs but Desi she gets stomach problems if too many," my dad said helpfully, tossing the sliced scallions and tofu into the boiling water. I dropped in the thin slices of brisket right after. Really, Appa? Let's talk about my bowel movements some more. I gave him a furtive *look* and he shrugged innocently.

Luca smiled. "Learned the hard way?"

My dad guffawed and nodded his head vigorously. "Exactly right!"

They both laughed and I continued to beat my eggs into a frenzy. "Ha-ha," I said. "Hey Luca, can you open the ramen packages, then hand me the noodles?"

Luca tore open the packages and handed me the rectangles of dehydrated noodles. "I used to eat these 'raw' as an after-school snack," I said proudly.

I felt a knuckle grind the back of my head. My dad gave me a *look*, too. "Don't remind me." I laughed, then focused back on the ramen. "So watch carefully, Caucasian lad, this is how you make our superspecial ramen." I dropped the noodles into the water and then started breaking them apart gently with chopsticks. In the meantime my dad was grabbing a jar of kimchi from the refrigerator.

Luca was watching us intently, like he was actually fascinated by this entire procedure.

"We only use a little of these powdery seasoning packets," I said, shaking one and then ripping it open and pouring its contents into the pot. "We'll save the other ones for later," I said while sweeping them aside. "The real goodness comes from here." My dad tipped the kimchi jar ever so slightly over the pot so that a bit of the juice dribbled into the soup. Everything boiled deliciously.

"Want to do the honor of pouring the eggs in?" I asked Luca.

He nodded and grabbed the metal bowl and was about to tip them in when he hesitated. "Wait, so like this?" It actually felt very nice to be showing Luca how to do something.

"Yes, the whole thing, dump it in." As soon as he did, I started mixing the eggs around with my chopsticks. "This is basically done; the eggs will continue to cook." My dad had already started setting silverware and bowls out onto our tiled kitchen counter where we ate most of our meals.

I turned off the stove and set the boiling pot onto a cat-shaped trivet. "Ta-da! This is how *fancy* Korean folk eat."

Luca clapped. "Epic. Really."

We made eye contact and I grinned. I couldn't help it. He grinned right back and for a second I forgot my dad was two inches away from me.

My dad settled on a stool at the edge of the counter and waved Luca over. "Sit down and eat before it gets cold!" I placed a small dish of kimchi on the counter as the final piece and we sat down.

"Cheers," Luca said, holding up his chopsticks. I clicked them with my own, my dad reaching over to join us.

"Thanks for dinner, Mr. Lee," Luca said as he stood up from lacing his shoes. He held out his hand.

My dad looked amused as he took it. "No problem. You're good at doing dishes, so you can come over every day!" He laughed and I joined in nervously. Ha-ha, Appa. Ha-ha.

"Drive safe," my dad said sternly as we stepped out.

I patted his arm. "I will."

He stood in the doorway watching us as we got into the Buick.

As I backed out of the driveway he waved at us, a dark and sturdy silhouette against the warm foyer lights.

Luca waved back and I gave a little honk. It was silent for a while as we drove down the dark streets, lit in neat intervals by faux gas lamps.

"So where do you live?" I asked.

"On Marisol—it's a little north of the cove," he said, sticking his arm out the window, letting his fingers drift idly along the waves of the breeze. "You and your dad . . . It's killer to witness."

The radio played quietly in the background, something kinda Johnny Cash. "What do you mean?" I asked. My eyes stayed on the wide, pristine road.

"That kind of relationship. The way you guys are. I've never seen anyone like that with their parents." He was complimentary but there was something sad hanging on the edges of his words, as if this nice thing highlighted the crappy thing in his own life.

"Do you get to see your mom often?" I ventured gingerly. The music switched to something distinctly Elton John.

The breeze whipped through the car, lifting our hair, our voices. He nodded his head. "Yeah, she kind of freaks out if she doesn't see me at least a couple of times a month. I spent a few days over holiday break with her." His voice was wistful rather than annoyed like most teenage boys' would be talking about their mothers. He glanced at me. "I bet you find that weird."

I shrugged. "I get it. I'm an only child, too, remember? We're not weird."

He pressed his index fingers into a little steeple between his nose and mouth. When he spoke, his voice came out muffled. "You *are* weird. I know you think you're normal—but you're weird."

I fiddled with the radio. "Hm."

"Everyone's weird, though. If you're not even a little weird, you are *truly* weird. In that bad way. Not in the good way."

"Uh, did we suddenly get high without me knowing?"

"I'm serious!" Luca's voice took on a jovial tone. His guard down, just completely earnest. It reminded me of when he'd talked about his art project. The only time Luca seemed to wake up from his lazy-cool-guy slumber. "You know what I mean. People who have absolutely no weird in them, they're so boring it's creepier than anything a weirdo can do. Like, actually, when I first met you, I thought maybe you were of that variety."

We stopped at a red light and I braked sharply. "Gee, thanks."

"I said *when I first met you.*"

I looked over at him. "Ha! And now? After seeing me in my natural environment you realize that I am a special, special snow-flake?"

He practically cackled with glee. "More like—I realize you're human. With a lot of hilarious trophies."

I'm sure he meant *despite* my trophies. But when I glanced over at him he smiled. "It just adds to the appeal."

My pulse quickened. "Oh, yeah?"

"Yeah."

"It's nice to know you're a little odd. Otherwise you're so . . ."

I tensed up—I knew what he was going to say. "Let me guess . . . controlling? Uptight? Crazy?"

He smiled at me in that bratty way only he could get away with. "Well, as long as you're aware—"

"Listen. Do you know what being in control does? It gets stuff done. Do you think I was good at soccer when I started? No, I sucked. I tripped over the ball the whole first season. But I forced myself to practice—morning fitness runs, days hitting the ball against my fence, nights studying YouTube clips. Until one day, I was good. Really good."

He held up his hands in defense. "I believe you, Des. You win at soccer! It's just, I mean, you know you can't control everything?"

I gripped my steering wheel. "Why does *everyone* say that? You *can*."

"No, you *can't*. You of all people should know that."

The car lurched forward as I accelerated when the light turned green. "What does that mean?" I asked calmly, knowing exactly what he meant—my mom.

I felt his discomfort from my side of the car. He shifted uneasily and cleared his throat. "I just mean, look, shit happens in life. You'll only drive yourself crazy trying to control *everything*. That energy could be expended on other things . . ."

The breeze coming in through the open windows cooled me off somewhat. "Like what? Living life to the fullest?" I scoffed.

"Something like that . . ." His voice trailed off in a strange way. A few seconds later, he pointed out the window. "Hey, you can pull over here."

The beach parking lot we pulled into was empty. "Do you live near here?" I looked around at the large homes lining the street across from the beach.

"Yeah."

I put the car in park and looked at him, but his head was turned away, gazing out the window. And then, before I could blink, in one purposeful swift motion—he took off his seat belt, reached over the space between us, and pulled my head toward his.

Lips met mine, soft, a little chapped, and warm. My eyes were open in true K drama heroine fashion. *What in the world?* My mind was registering what was going on, but my heart was going berserk, running in circles. FIRST KISS, an alarm was blaring. MOTHER OF DRAGONS, THIS IS MY FIRST REAL KISS. Was I doing it right? Oh my God, was I supposed to open my mouth now? Wait, close your eyes first, you freaking creep. Okay, eyes closed. Now wait, do I breathe? *Aaaaaah.*

But then everything stopped and the world was muffled—the waves were silenced and the car around us disappeared. My chaotic inner world just froze. And Luca and I were alone, suspended in space. My lips parted and his fingers brushed the back of my neck. All that existed was that hand and the mixing of our breaths.

For the life of me, I couldn't tell you how long the kiss was, but then it was over as abruptly as it had started. The hand left my neck, leaving it cold. I touched my fingers to my lips and looked up. Our dazed eyes locked. Luca looked perplexed for a second, brow furrowed, eyes narrowed.

Then he leaned back into the seat with a smile, head still turned to me. "Sometimes it's nice to be surprised, yeah?"

I struggled to find words to match the buzz and hum of my body—everything simultaneously frantic and languorous. Before I could actually think of a response, he drew my hand onto his knee and pulled out a pen from his pocket. Sticking the cap into his mouth, he scrawled something on the soft skin on the inside of my wrist. His phone number.

I was mute the entire time and didn't actually have a chance to speak because what he did next gave me zero time to think: he slipped out of the car, bent over to pop his head back in, and said, "Thanks for dinner."

And then he was gone, strolling across the street.

It had happened. Luca and I had kissed.

And then I started laughing and couldn't stop, covering my mouth with my hands. Because guess what, Luca? Surprise or not, this *was* all going according to plan.

STEP 15:
Fall Deeply into Cringe-Inducing Mushy Love

The next day I sat on my front step and stared at my phone.
I typed in one word: Hi.

Somehow that didn't look cool and effortless. No, that was the text equivalent of just staring at someone. I deleted it.

Can I see you?

Good God, way too serious.

Want to go graffiti together today?

Ha-ha.

So about that art project . . .

Oh, shut up.

Do you like me?

Why don't I just throw myself down a well to die a slow, painful death.

I like you.

Thrown into a well to die a slow death with two broken legs.

After a startling first kiss, what would a K drama heroine do?

I wanted to relax and feel like I'd accomplished something, but I remembered Song-Yi from *My Love from Another Star*, and how after her first kiss with the alien love interest, he avoided her like the plague. (Well, granted, he could die from the physical contact. But still.)

It was a Saturday, so I had no reason to bump into Luca. And I wasn't sure if I could survive the weekend without knowing what the heck he was thinking. Did he like me? Did he feel sorry for me? Was it just *lust*? I flushed thinking about it.

I started to text Wes and Fiona to get their sage, masterly make-out advice, but realized that the conversation would just turn into a crapfest of jokes and opinions. I told my best friends everything, but the kiss with Luca was a little too fresh and special to share with them.

I glanced at my K drama steps list, which was next to me on the front step. Oh, wonderful, wonderful K drama steps. You who have brought me my first kiss. Hm, the next few steps were post-kiss, all the blissful mushy stuff to follow.

So I needed to make sure the mushy happened. Just do it, Des. I straightened my spine and texted Luca: Hey, what are you doing right now?

I hit Send. Then shoved the list in my shorts pocket and got up to dribble a soccer ball in my backyard. Hell if I was going to sit around waiting for a text from a guy.

I was balancing the ball on my knee when I felt a vibration in my pocket.

The ball dropped onto the grass. It was a text from Luca.

Working on my art project. Wanna join me?

Heart catapulted off my ribs and into my throat. Should I wait a little—

Sure—what are you defacing today? ☺

I think it's totally cool if your dad drops you off on a date. When you're seventeen.

"Bye!" I slammed the door and waved goodbye with a big toothy smile so that he would just zoom off. Instead, the car patiently idled as he watched me.

I looked around but couldn't see Luca—just a bunch of tourists. "Okay, Luca's meeting me inside the mission!" I said to my dad brightly, not wanting him to witness whatever awkward greeting Luca and I would have post-kiss.

"Okay, have fun. Pick you up at six!" With that he was off, waving to me out the window. I squinted after the Buick, wondering if his chillness was just an act and he was secretly freaking out about his precious daughter going out with a boy. Or maybe my general lack of boyfriends made my dad trust me to an embarrassing degree.

I walked up to the Mission San Juan Capistrano—a beautifully maintained Spanish-style compound built in the 1700s, complete with ruins of a chapel and a plaza of lush gardens. Once I reached the pool filled with lilies, I pulled out my phone to text Luca.

"Hey."

I looked up, already smiling at the sound of that voice. "Hey."

When standing so close to him, I could smell his deodorant—which I was oddly flattered by. No puffy vest for this unusually warm January day, just a short-sleeved white T-shirt and jeans. Black high-top Vans and beanie still part of the uniform though. (And a backpack full of spray paint, of course.) Also, up close, I noticed a zit or two on the jawline of his otherwise flawless face. And weirdly enough, those two zits relaxed me. Like they were saying, "Hey, we're not perfect either." I also noticed, with relief, that his black eye from yesterday had almost all but faded already.

I thought there would be an awkward shy moment, or maybe he would act like nothing had happened and we would be back to being friends, but those fears were instantly dashed when he grabbed my hand. "Ready?" he asked.

Ah!

Here's the thing. A kiss is the *ultimate*, I get it. In K dramas they take a billion episodes to get to it, and it's replayed over and over again from fifty different angles. And the kiss is so chaste and close-mouthed that it's almost comical to your typical Western audience used to open-mouthed kissing followed by panting and groping. (But K dramas understand the importance of the *sweetness* of the moment, too. And all the anticipation, woo boy. All those episodes building an agonizing tension so taut that when their lips *do* meet, you are *dying.* Anyway.)

And last night's kiss felt like that, for sure. But it was so sudden, because despite all my planning, I hadn't anticipated it coming at that moment. So after a night of agonizing over what that kiss meant—whether Luca liked me or if he was just caught up in some moment—holding hands with him right now created the same heart-thumping adrenaline rush. Holding hands was also something you didn't do in the heat of the moment, it was something you did while *thinking*, purposely. To make a public statement about your relationship to each other.

We started to weave through the crowd and I said, "So, uh, I'm guessing we're not tagging on the actual mission?"

His silence made me freeze midstep. "Luca?!" I yelped.

He squeezed my hand. "You're way too easy sometimes. What kind of monster do you think I am?"

"Well, you *do* deface public property."

"So a mild one?"

"Yeah, mild monster." My grin almost cracked my face open. He led me farther away from the mission and toward the quaint San Juan Capistrano train station until we reached a gate covered in bright fuchsia bougainvillea. Suddenly I felt a little nervous. "Luca, what if we get caught? Aren't you on probation?"

"Don't worry, this place is totally hidden." As if on cue, he flipped a flimsy latch and slipped through the gate, taking me with him.

I felt and heard a deep rumble from somewhere not that far away, and I clutched Luca's hand. Or I should say, attempted to. Our hands were pretty sweaty at this point, to be honest. "I hear a train!"

Luca cocked his head. "You're right. Let's go over here," he said while pulling me toward the tracks.

I yanked his hand back and stood perfectly still. *"Luca!"*

He glanced back at me, genuinely surprised. "What?"

"You can't . . . You can't just cross the tracks!"

"Why not?"

There was a list of reasons. Before I could answer, Luca let go of my hand and hopped over the tracks in two seconds. The rumbling grew louder as he stood on the other side motioning for me to cross over.

Screw it.

I sprinted and nimbly hopped over the tracks, landing on the other side, right into Luca's outstretched arms. He wrapped them around me tighter and I fit against his chest like it was the most natural thing in the world.

"Hi." His voice was quiet but I could feel the smile before seeing it.

I looked up. "Hi. For a wimp you sure don't mind putting yourself in danger."

The train whizzed past, my long braid coming undone in wisps that whipped across both our faces. The earth vibrated beneath our feet, and this time I stood up on my tippy-toes and brushed my lips against his. Soft and a bit hesitant. And he kissed me back just as softly, with a little pressure at the very end.

And when the train finally passed us, we were left with a whole lot of silence.

He leaned his forehead against mine and I swore I couldn't feel my feet. Did I have feet?!

"Yeeeah. I like you," he breathed.

I heard the words but couldn't register them.

"Hm?" My voice was abnormally loud.

"Desi. You cute nerd. I like you."

I pushed him away, laughing. "So romantic." But I couldn't stop smiling and my hand covered my mouth to hide it.

He tugged on his backpack straps impatiently. "Is that it?"

"Is what it?"

He stared at me.

Oh.

"Anyway, so where's this graffiti we're graffitiing over?" More silence as I walked ahead of him, pretending to be absorbed in finding the tagging spot. "Is it, like, on a wall or maybe some old railroad equipment . . . ?" I let my voice trail off. I was going to milk this for all it was worth.

Then I felt something hit my back. Something blunt but still a little heavy. I whipped around to see Luca standing in the same spot, wielding a rotting avocado. His feet were surrounded by them—all mushy and gross after days in the sun.

My mouth opened to speak, but I shut it quickly. Let him

suffer. I turned around, and instantly felt another thud, on my butt this time. I yelped, "Gross! It's going to stain my clothes!"

He grabbed another one off the ground and drew his arm back as if to toss it. I screeched and ran out of the way. He started chasing after me, the occasional avocado pelting me on the arm or back. I ran into a thicket of overgrown morning glory vines and live oak trees, safely away from the train tracks.

I was hiding in there, holding my breath, my eyes trying to adjust to the dark when I felt hands grab me from behind.

"I said I liked you." His voice was muffled, his lips on my hair.

I shook my head, feeling the top of it rub against his face. "I like you, too."

And that was that. Those simple words ended a very complicated few weeks. The K drama steps *worked*. Nervous relief unburdened the pressure of all this scheming.

Luca's voice broke through my thoughts. "I really resisted this, you know. When I had to move here, all I wanted to do was get the next few months over with and have zero connections to anyone here. Especially a girlfriend," he said, and I felt his smile against my hair.

I turned around and looked at the shadowy outlines of his face. "Girlfriend?"

And although it was dark, I could see his happy expression falter for a second. "Oh, do you—can you not date? Or . . ."

I mentally squealed into a megaphone so big that the sound

reverberated into space, reaching Pluto, then bouncing back. I responded with an articulate, "I—no—I mean—"

How to reveal to this hot guy that I had never had a boyfriend? He probably started dating when he was three years old. The Mr. Darcy of Montessori School.

And then I thought of how endearing it was when K drama heroines were inexperienced in love, like Hang-Ah from *The King 2 Hearts*. How it drove the prince crazy to find out that this strong and hot soldier lady was so innocent.

I swallowed. "To be honest, I've never dated anyone before."

And there it was. The truth in all its humiliating starkness. I waited for some jaw dropping, some disbelief, or perhaps a snort of derision. But he just bit his bottom lip and looked at me in that inscrutable way of his.

"I'm your first boyfriend?" he asked.

I couldn't even—boyfriend? *Unreal!* "Yes," I replied simply.

"What about Wes?"

Ohmygod. I kept a straight face. "Nah, that was nothing important."

He paused. "So . . . I'm your first boyfriend?'

"Yes."

He kissed my forehead. "Nerd."

STEP 16:
Pick Your Very Own Love Ballad to Blast Jarringly Over and Over Again!

That night, Luca and I didn't sleep.

Because we were *talking*. On the phone.

I glanced at the clock. It was 4:34 a.m. My comforter twisted around my legs as I burrowed deeper into my bed. I positioned my head so that my phone didn't dig into my cheek as much.

"So now what are you doing?"

I giggled. "Um, pretty much the same thing I was doing the last time you asked."

His voice was scratchy on the other end of the line. "I don't know, you could have started a plan for a citywide tree planting in those fifteen minutes."

"True. What are *you* doing?"

I heard a muffled sound on the other end. "I'm . . . I just moved onto the floor."

"Why?"

"My bed got too hot."

Visions of an overheated Luca in bed was enough to make me kick off my blankets entirely. "My dad likes to sleep on the floor sometimes," I said.

"For some reason that doesn't surprise me."

I smiled. "It's not because of eccentricity. He grew up sleeping on the floor. A lot of Koreans still do it, not because they can't afford beds or anything, but because they find it more comfortable."

"I bet my mom would dig that. She does this thing called grounding. Have you heard of it?"

I shifted to my back. "Um, I know what it means in physics, but I doubt it's what your mom does."

"What's it mean in physics?"

"Well, it's this way of removing excess charge on an object by transferring electrons between it and another object of a pretty big size . . ." I could hear him snoring, or pretending to. "Hey! Look alive, buddy."

He made a fake startled noise, like he was being jolted awake. "Oh, uh, what were you saying?"

"*Anyway.* What's it mean according to your mother?"

More shuffling noises on his end. "It's kind of *amazing*. In a way that you will, of course, mock. It's this idea that you should walk barefoot outside a few times a day, to literally touch the earth. People believe there are benefits to this."

"Oh please, tell me those benefits."

He let out a honk of laughter. "I can practically feel your *glee* over the phone. Anyway, the main benefit is that a plant's electric energy goes into the ground and then directly into your body." He paused. "Got that? So all these medical benefits come from having the earth's good, natural energy enter your body."

I tried to keep my voice composed. "'Kay, like what?"

"Improving blood flow for one. And helping with fatigue, poor sleep, inflammation. And, um, it may eliminate diabetes."

My entire body started shaking with laughter as I kept my hand clasped over my mouth. He could sense it. "Are you still there? Or are you writing to all the major medical journals about it?"

"I'm here. Wow. Grounding. You learn something new every day."

"I'm sure you think my mom's a total nut."

I shrugged even though he couldn't see me. "I don't know. She sounds interesting."

A noise that sounded suspiciously like a yawn carried over. "Mm, she is. We've been through a lot together. Compared to other moms, I'm sure she can seem kind of flaky. But it's always been us against the world." He paused for a second and I listened to his breathing. "Although sometimes I feel like we're equal parental units to each other. Like I take care of her as much as she does me. Does that make her sound bad?"

I lowered my voice, even though there was no way in hell my dad was still awake. "No, I get you. I mean, obviously my dad is in charge and has done everything for me. But I like to think that I've also taken care of him over the years."

"You do. I mean, almost everything you do is about your dad." He definitely yawned this time.

I yawned, too. My eyes fluttered closed. "Whaddya mean?"

"What I just said. You're like a little helicopter watching over him. Are there such things as helicopter daughters?"

I barely registered what he had said and murmured, "What are you talking about, you weirdo? I think we're getting . . . delirious."

"You are but not me. I'm as awake as"—a huge yawn—"as coffee."

"Awake as coffee?"

"Yeah, you heard me."

I started cracking up when I heard a door open in the hall. I froze. "Uh-oh, my dad's awake. I think I have to go for real."

"Nooo . . . pretend to sleep."

My dad's heavy footsteps padded by my door, then stopped. I shoved my phone under my pillow in one swift movement. The door opened just as I shut my eyes. The bright light in the hallway sent diffused halos through my eyelids and I didn't move a muscle until I heard the door shut again. When I was sure my dad was back in his room, I pulled out my phone. "Luca?" I whispered.

No answer.

"Luca?"

A few seconds of silence passed and then I heard it. Soft breathing. Rhythmic. I smiled and whispered, "Sweet dreams," before falling asleep to Luca's breathing.

I stood back and admired Luca's handiwork.

It was late afternoon the next day and we were back at the train tracks by the mission—somehow still standing after just a couple of hours of sleep. Luca hadn't been able to finish before my dad came to pick me up yesterday so I agreed to join him again today. His "canvas" was a wall on a dilapidated little shack that he had somehow found in one of his searches for good graffiti. It was hidden from the passing trains by a thicket of oaks and eucalyptus. The other side of the shack faced a large open field, part of a nature preserve. The late-day sun transformed the tips of the grass into gold, the temperature dipped suddenly, and the air took on a slightly metallic scent.

When we had first arrived at the wall yesterday, it was a masterpiece of ancient graffiti. It was like every tagger in Orange County had at one point visited this shack. Layers and layers of color: words, tiny animals, symbols. All jumbled and packed in this small space.

So when Luca splashed the wall with paint thinner, I almost had a heart attack. But I kept my mouth shut, sitting back and watching him go about his business. The graffiti had started to smudge and drip, creating a mass of swirled colors.

Then he had grabbed black spray paint and started covering the wall in great big swaths of black—leaving the middle visible in a soft circular shape. He left bits and pieces around the circle visible as well, so that color peeped in as blurry-edged shapes. Eventually he took out some gold and silver paints and dotted the black with little splashes and pinpoints.

And when it was all over, I was staring at the universe.

When I said as much, he corrected me: "Nebula."

I raised an eyebrow. "Pretty specific there, art boy."

"There's something you can't outnerd me in, nerd."

"What?"

"Space."

"Like, all of space?"

"Yeah, like everything outside of this tiny, insignificant planet. All of that," he said, pointing up at the sky. With eyes turned upward, Luca's face took on a faraway look that I recognized from my dad's face when he was talking about his latest favorite K drama. "Space is . . ."

"The final frontier?"

He looked at me with a huge grin. "Yes. Live long and prosper."

"Did you ever want to be an astronaut when you were younger?"

The swiftest of replies: "Yes."

I imagined a little Luca staring out into space and I almost died from the preciousness overload. "Why did you give up on that?"

A slight hesitation, then he pulled me into another big hug. "I found out I had to be good at math." Mm, math. Arms. Luca's soap.

I looked up at him. "So, wait—when's the application due for your scholarship? I'm guessing this graffiti stuff is going in?"

Luca nodded, keeping his arms linked behind my back. "Well, the deadline for the scholarship was actually in November, but I managed to include the graffiti. After Emily and I broke up I got *a lot* of tags done. So those older ones made it just in time for the application."

"What's the scholarship? It seems like a lot is riding on this."

Letting go of me, Luca stepped back and looked hard at the nebula wall. "There *is* a lot riding on it. It's a pretty big one— the largest fine art scholarship in the country, in fact. It'll pay for half my tuition basically—for the rest I can take out loans."

My jaw dropped. "Wait, what! *Half* your tuition?"

"Yeah, if I keep up my grades every year. Some superrich anonymous donor is doing it."

"That's so much!" I sputtered. "There are some big ones for the sciences, for sure, but they're backed by huge pharmaceutical companies and, like, weapons manufacturers!"

Luca laughed. "Well, there's money in art, too, you know," he said.

"Geez, I guess!" I was still doing the math, knowing how much private art schools cost, while Luca snapped a photo of the wall.

"What's crazy is that the announcement's going to be made the day of the gallery show. Cosmic timing, right?" he asked, putting his phone away.

I helped pack up the supplies. "Whoa, totally. Are you nervous?"

He hoisted his backpack back on with a grin. "What do you think?"

Flutter. "You'll get it," I said firmly. "Believe me."

He reached for my hand. "Thanks, ye of too-much faith. Now let's take a train ride."

We hopped on the next train to San Diego, a few stops south, where we would catch a concert. The train lurched forward and I had to grab on to Luca's sleeve to catch myself from falling.

He looked down at me. "You okay?"

The boyfriendly concern made me blush, and I held his hand as we walked through the train to find seats.

When we did, a comfortable silence settled between us.

I stared out the window, watching the ocean and tall grasses zoom by us. Suddenly I realized what we would pass. I elbowed Luca. "Hey, Graffiti Gary, look out the window."

"Graffiti Gary," he muttered under his breath, but he craned his neck over to my side to peer out anyway. We were passing a long cinder-block wall, but after a few seconds I jabbed my finger on the window and grinned. "Look, the three buds!"

Painted on a row of storm-drain covers were three colorful

and slightly grotesque cat faces, each with a toothy grin—one was sporting sunglasses, one had a giant mole, the other had its eyes closed blissfully. I sighed happily and looked at them until they were receding shapes in the distance.

When I finally turned around to see Luca's reaction, I found him with his elbows on his knees, staring at me with mock wonder. My smile slid off my face. "What?" I asked.

"I think *I* should be the one asking questions. What the heck were you excited about? Those cats?"

"Yeah! They change every once in a while but have been there forever. Aren't they awesome?"

He tried to bite back his pitying smile. "Yeah . . . So edgy and neat!"

I reclined in my seat and snootily avoided his gaze. "Whatever, they're an institution. When I was little, I always looked forward to spotting them when we drove down to San Diego on the 5." I nodded my head toward the window at the traffic-jammed freeway running on the other side of the tracks.

Luca was still smiling at me. "That's sweet." And then I abruptly changed the subject, because I didn't know how else to bring it up.

"So what's the deal with Emily?"

He winced and I bit my lip, regretting how rudely that had come out.

He tapped his thumb into my palm before launching in.

"I was . . . really smitten. She was my first real girlfriend and we made a good team in a lot of ways. We bonded over our messed-up families. It was kind of obvious that art was our cathartic release from our mediocre family lives," he said drily.

Smitten. First girlfriend. Hmph. A unexpected surge of jealousy coursed through me but I squeezed his hand to encourage him to keep talking.

"But she was also . . . full of shit. In the beginning, I was so into her that I didn't really notice, you know? But I caught little glimpses here and there. She was really good at manipulating people, at getting her way by pulling the damaged-rich-girl act, or just by batting her eyelashes."

Manipulating. Like following a bunch of steps to get a guy to like you? My breath caught for a second, and an iciness trickled down from my scalp to my toes. But *no*. Emily was different . . . She hurt Luca. My K drama stuff was just to get me on level footing. So that Luca and I even had a chance. And it had worked. I brushed the dread aside and continued listening to Luca.

"And in the end, I was just one of the many suckers who fell for her act. She was just using me—she knew I would take the fall for her if she ever got caught tagging. And not to mention, I got her a ton of attention online, too."

I kicked his foot playfully. "According to Wes, you're Tumblr famous."

He didn't even look embarrassed. "Yeah. I don't know how

that happened. Anyway, once I got arrested, I figured it all out. The blinders I'd been wearing fell off. She was just this lying little opportunist. And so, yeah, I haven't had a high opinion of girlfriends since then."

Again, I shoved that shadowy sense of guilt off to the side. "That's pretty harsh, to take all girls to task for one jerk's duplicity."

He leaned in to me, mouth inches away from mine. "Not *all* girls, I guess."

"Good," I whispered, then fell back in my seat.

I gazed out the window—tall grasses flying by, a strip of everpresent blue sea alongside it. I realized it was the perfect moment for the ol' classic K drama move of falling asleep on your love interest's shoulder. I channeled a K drama hero this time, Jin-Gu from *Plus Nine Boys*, when he takes the bus home with his crush and purposely moves her head onto his shoulder when she falls sleep. A few minutes passed and then I took a shallow breath and willed myself to drop my head onto Luca's shoulder.

At one point, I shifted slightly in my seat and rubbed my cheek onto his shoulder, making my hair slip across my face and onto his arm. But then my hair was tickling my nose something fierce.

Okay, just move your hand up to your face, as if drunkenly passed out and not realizing what your body is doing, then casually move that stupid piece of hair off your nose . . . and as my hand inched across my lap on the long trek to my nose, someone else's hand touched my face.

It grazed the lock of hair fanned across my eyes and the bridge of my nose, then gathered the hair together and gently pushed it to the side of my face—short fingernails brushing across my cheek.

Change the train—from the Surfliner to an underground subway in Seoul. And as the train zips through one of the stations in the heart of the city, the camera catches two figures in one of the windows. A girl fast asleep on a boy's shoulder. He's staring at her with conflicting emotions flitting across his face: tenderness, irritation, compassion, and finally submission.

I made a mumbled sleepy noise, moved in closer, and tucked my right leg up to my torso so that my entire body was now curled into his side. And I felt Luca's breathing match my own as we zipped along the coast.

STEP 17:
Worlds Have to Collide for Some Comic Relief

The next week passed in a haze. The only thing completely in focus was my time with Luca. Luca this and Luca that. I was in full-on, Bella Swan, obsessed-with-my-guy mode.

And you know what? It was a *pleasant* place to be. Do I think one's life should revolve around a boy? No. BUT. And here's a huge BUT: when you had spent almost eighteen years on this planet wondering who that first boyfriend was going to be, and then holy cannoli there he was, it was pretty freaking amazing.

Some amazing things:

- There is a person who thinks my color-coded charts for watering every plant in my yard are fascinating. And that person isn't my dad.
- Despite seeing my pores up close and personal, Luca still stares at me and says with wonder, *So pretty.*

- Having someone help you carry heavy things even if technically he is not as strong as you.
- Listening to music and suddenly understanding the significance of *all feelings* in *all songs*.
- Sharing your favorite everything with someone new—and everything you've loved forever taking on a fresh and exciting new light.
- Everything reminding me of him: ramen, pencils, T-shirts, ice, my house, the Buick, my bed, trains, morning glories, the ocean, breathing.
- Finding yourself fitting into the negative space of someone else's body perfectly.
- Feeling like the center of someone's life—that someone is waiting for you to wake up so they can text you *good morning* and send you a funny cat gif.

And that is just the tip of the iceberg, I'm sure.

On Saturday night, I nervously texted him: **Have you left yet?**

Within seconds: **Leaving now. Keep your pants on. Or not.**

I giggled. There was a whoooole lotta giggling going on lately, let me say. I was nervous because we were headed to a bonfire with my friends. And despite being together for a week, this was our big "public appearance" together as a couple. We'd been seen holding hands together and kinda canoodling at school but in a weird way I felt like we were "coming out" at this event. It would be the first time he hung out with my friends. Everyone had been busy and I had basically slipped away with Luca at lunch, alone, at every opportunity.

To be honest, I was nervous about the Big Meeting. My best friends . . . God love them, but they could be an obnoxious, critical duo. Wes called Luca Brooding Artist Boy and teased me endlessly about him. Fiona—well, she just hated everyone until she didn't. They were both excited for me when they found out about the kiss and subsequent mushy moments, but a little cautious, too—as if they couldn't quite believe I had actually done it. I couldn't blame them. Also, I had to remind them one billion times not to accidentally call him Won Bin.

I skipped over to the kitchen, where my dad was cleaning out the refrigerator. His head and upper body were barely visible as he grumbled while moving things around wearing a pair of pink rubber gloves. "How many leftovers you going to bring home and never eat?!" he demanded as he tossed a box filled with moldy fries at me.

Catching it deftly, I threw it into the trash bag that my dad had set up at his feet. "If we had a dog, we could give it to her."

"No dog!"

I sighed and went into the pantry to dust off the picnic basket we kept in there. After three of my gerbils died consecutively, we'd had a strict no-pets policy at our house. But the past few months I had been pestering my dad to get us a dog, which he found really confusing, I'm sure. But I hated knowing that after I left for college, my dad would be alone. "A dog would be so good at chasing away Señor," I cajoled.

Señor was the neighbor's cat and my dad's nemesis. He was constantly shitting in the vegetable beds and leaving dead mice on our doorstep. My dad's facial expression indicated that he was definitely weighing that pro for a moment.

He straightened up and pushed a lock of hair out of his eyes with his forearm. "Where you going again?"

I started filling the basket with various bonfire foods—hot dogs, marshmallows, graham crackers, chocolate, and some pickles for good measure. "The beach, for a bonfire."

"Which beach?"

"Vista Dunes," I answered dutifully. "We'll be there with Fiona and Wes and lots of other kids from school. Call the police if I'm not home by midnight."

"That *late*?" he yelped comically while emptying curdled milk into the sink.

"Yup," I chirped, adding some napkins to the basket.

He pulled open the produce drawers in the fridge and inspected the contents tentatively. "Okay," he responded amiably. "Luca's driving his dad's car?"

Luca's car was still being worked on by my dad. Apparently, there was *a lot* wrong with it and I had my suspicions that my dad was prolonging the fixes as a bit of a pet project. He loved Honda Civics from that era.

"Yup." My phone buzzed just then. "It's him, gotta run, Appa." I ran over and smacked his butt with my basket. "Don't go too crazy partying with all the kitchen appliances tonight!"

He mumbled something about me being a brat and continued tossing rotten produce into the trash bag.

I ran outside to see a zippy little BMW idling in my driveway. The driver's-side window rolled down and Luca stuck his head out to yell, "What up, babe, like my riiiiiide?"

"You're disturbingly good at that." I crawled into the tiny passenger seat, shoving the basket between my feet.

He immediately leaned over and kissed me. My skin buzzed, every part of me alert and alive.

"Hi," I said, unable to keep the smile off my face.

He smiled back. "Hi."

I mean.

We drove with the Beach Boys blasting and didn't feel the need to talk. But constantly hold hands? Yes.

We pulled into the beach parking lot, which was brightly lit and full of cars. The pitch-black shoreline was dotted with glowing bonfires. It seemed like all of Monte Vista High was jam-packed onto the beach.

"Ready to be officially initiated into Monte Vista High School debauchery?" I punctuated the question with a weird dance involving puppetlike bent elbows.

He held up his hands and wiggled his fingers. "Can't wait, nerd."

Fiona and Wes were standing under a parking lot light waiting for us, arms full of grocery bags, wood, and blankets. No sign of Leslie since, true to her word, Fiona had broken up with her. Wes made a porno-ish *bow chicka bow bow* sound as we approached. I rolled my eyes. "Just so you know, Wes is the worst."

"Is that why you spent seven minutes in heaven with him?" Luca asked in a low, teasing voice.

I bit my lip to choke back a laugh. My instinct was to reassure him and shake my head and say, *Gross!* but being completely honest with him would make that entire night suspicious. Instead, I shrugged. "We're over that weird blip in our relationship. You're my one and only."

His lips twitched. "Are you being sarcastic?"

I hugged his arm. "Yes and no."

And then there we were, me and Luca facing Fiona and Wes. I cleared my throat. "Hey guys. Um, this is Luca. I mean, you guys have already met but I mean . . ." I just stopped talking and shrugged.

Luca held a hand up. "Hey."

Wes lifted his chin in response. "What up, man. So you and Desi, huh?" I saw Luca's eyes get all squinty again.

Fiona elbowed Wes. "Don't be lame." Then she smiled this scary smile at Luca. "So what are your intentions with our darling Desi?"

I started choking on nothing and Luca took my hand, very casually, very coolly, and said, "Being forever life partners."

Wes looked horrified but Fiona burst out laughing. "Okay, cool. Ready to hang out by a giant fire?"

We all walked toward the beach and found a fire pit, which we filled with wood, then lit. I had started unpacking my picnic basket when I noticed Violet and Cassidy. "What the heck, look who's here!" I whispered to Luca. He looked over and waved at them. "I invited them. Is that okay?"

What! "Sure . . . I mean, you can do what you want. But why didn't you tell me?"

He looked at me with a sheepish smile. "To be honest, I didn't want to be outnumbered by your friends. Fiona scares me." I was going to argue but then saw Fiona viciously taking Wes to task for not skewering his hot dog correctly, and realized he had a point.

Violet and Cassidy walked over and for a moment we were all standing there staring at anything but one another. "Hey guys," I finally said with a wave.

Cassidy said hi enthusiastically, but Violet hung back a little bit. We hadn't really talked since the crazy supply-closet sneakiness incident. I announced I was going to make some s'mores. Fiona had taken the supplies I had brought and started walking toward the designated s'mores bonfire pit a little farther away, so I jogged to catch up with her, skewer in hand.

We set up our marshmallows and held the skewers over the

fire. Fiona nudged me, dripping some melty marshmallow into the embers. "Hey, so you did it."

"Hm?" I kept a close eye on my marshmallow so that it didn't catch fire like Fiona's always did.

"I mean, I can tell what you and Luca have is real. You got your boyfriend."

I couldn't stop myself from smiling like an idiot. "I did."

"So now you're on your own, right?"

"What do you mean?"

"What I mean is, you don't need the K drama steps anymore, right? It's done!" I could sense relief in her hushed tones.

Damn. My marshmallow caught fire and I blew it out quickly. "I don't know. I mean, yes, I got the guy. But barely. We've just started dating! And I don't know. Knowing I have those steps ready for me, whenever, kind of keeps me feeling confident."

"But what possible new steps do you need to take now? Haven't you basically reached your happy ending?"

Handing Fiona my skewer, I furtively pulled my wallet out of my back pocket and unfolded the list. "I guess you're right. But I can't abandon it yet." The idea of leaving the K drama steps completely unnerved me, and I felt like I was suddenly plummeting from the sky without anything to hold me up.

Fiona grabbed the list and quickly skimmed it. "Des, the rest of the stuff is, like, terrible. Misunderstandings and betrayal city. You're not going to plan *things going wrong*, too, right?"

Although we were far from Luca and everyone else, I kept my voice low. "No, of course not! Those other steps were just part of the formula found in dramas that I wanted to document. But I don't know . . ."

Suddenly Fiona was holding the list over the bonfire. "Let's just get rid of it, once and for all."

My heart leaped out of my chest and into my throat. I muffled a scream. "Fiona! No!"

The list fluttered above the flames and Fiona looked at me steadily. "Why? You're done. Why do you need it?"

Before I could answer, my body went into motion. I shoved Fiona away from the fire and grabbed the list out of her hand. Relief flooded me as I held it to my chest. Then I put the list back in my wallet and glared at Fiona. "What the heck, Fi! This is my list, *I* decide when to toss it."

She shook her head and held her hands up in surrender. "All right, all right. Clearly you're freaking attached to that thing. But don't say I didn't warn you."

We finished making our s'mores in silence and then walked back to our group. I handed Luca his s'more and he accepted it with reverence. Fiona sat down next to Wes, who was wolfing down a hot dog. With the list back safely in my wallet, my heart rate returned to normal.

Wes smacked his lips, wiping a bit of mustard off the corner of his mouth. "So Luca, can you eat fine roasted meats on the beach where you're from?" Violet giggled, which made my eyebrows shoot up into my hairline. I glanced at Cassidy, who was looking at Wes with *Sailor Moon*–heart eyeballs. Oh, Lord.

Noticing that it took me 0.5 seconds to scarf down my s'more, Luca carefully broke his in half and handed a piece to me. "No. Sadly, we eat our vegan meats in holistic yurts."

Everyone cracked up and I could feel Luca relax next to me. He looked around at everyone. "How long have you guys known Desi?"

"For, like, *ever*," Fiona drawled.

"Really, though?" Luca asked patiently.

"For real. We've known each other since second grade."

Wes chimed in. "And I've known her since sixth grade. Back in the day when she insisted on wearing jorts."

"Ha! I have you all beat! I've known her since preschool."

Everyone's head swiveled toward Violet.

"Really?" Wes asked, looking at her curiously.

She shot him a sly, sidelong glance. "Hasn't Desi mentioned Korean school?"

"What is that, a school to learn how to make kimchi?" Wes cracked himself up.

I kicked sand at Wes. "Yes. Kimchi. We made vats of it. As preschoolers."

Violet shrugged, unperturbed. She looked at Wes. "We had to learn how to read, write, and properly speak Korean. On *Saturdays.* Anyway, um, we recently realized we knew each other from those days." She took a swig of beer and I telepathically sent her a *thank-you* for not going into the more dramatic elements of that story.

Luca opened my Squirt for me. Totally not necessary, but it was one of those small boyfriend gestures that I loved reveling in. At school he insisted on carrying my books, too, although I could tell he kind of regretted it whenever my giant physics textbook was involved.

Fiona tossed a dirty napkin into the fire. "Desi and I met in, like, a terrible way."

I groaned. "Ugh, *Fi*, doooon't!"

Luca looked between us. "What? Tell me!"

I buried my face in Luca's puffy vest–clad shoulder. "Noooo."

Wes chuckled. "I'll tell him, then."

Fiona cleared her throat. "No, *I* will tell the story since I was the one who saved the day." She settled into a comfortable position, reclining like an Egyptian queen surrounded by her male slaves. "Well, one day in second grade, Desi's dad packed her a juice box. And she drank that entire box right at the end of lunch, in five seconds, just, like, huddled in a corner sipping at that little straw all greedily. Like some troll."

I burst out laughing. "Shut up, Fi!"

"No, for real, it was, like, disturbing how much you needed that juice. Anyway, a couple hours later we were in class, school was about to get out, and she kept squirming next to me. And just so you know, we were *not* friends yet. I was hanging out with the cool outdoor-playground kids and Desi liked to boss every-one around in the mini-kitchen."

I wrinkled my nose. "Everyone was always so *messy* in there and putting stuff away in the wrong places."

Fiona rolled her eyes. "I rest my case. Anyway, so she's sitting there, getting all antsy. And I notice this antsiness because she's usually so obedient and perfect. And that's when I notice her get completely still. And her eyes get huge. And then . . . I spy dripping."

Luca groaned. "Oh, *no*."

"Yup. She was peeing her pants."

Violet, Cassidy, and Wes burst out laughing. I huffed. "It's not that funny, you guys!"

Violet almost choked. "Yes, it *is*."

Cassidy wiped a tear off her cheek. "Sorry, Desi—but—"

"Dude, you peed your pants!" Wes yelped. "We're *allowed* to laugh."

Fiona shushed everyone. "Yeah, she peed—an entire puddle at the bottom of her chair. And she didn't utter a word. I was so grossed out and about to raise my hand to tell on her"—Fiona's huge smile faltered a little as she looked at me—"when I saw one giant tear drip down her face. It hit me then that it wasn't some-thing she wanted the teacher to know. But how could you cover *that* up?"

I interrupted her then. "So Fiona did something as a

seven-year-old that defines the Fiona we know and love today. While the teacher was busy in the supply closet, she pulled me out of my seat, mopped up my pee with her Anaheim Ducks sweatshirt, then gave me her pants to swap out for my wet ones— wearing just her underwear and getting in big trouble." Everyone started laughing. I grinned. "She just created a bigger distraction that stole my pants-peeing thunder."

Violet slow-clapped. "Whoa, that's true friendship right there."

Fiona shrugged. "Well, let's be real, walking around in my undies was no big sacrifice."

I shook my head. "Yes it was, don't try to be all humbly bumbly right now," I said. "It was the beginning of a beautiful, dysfunctional friendship." I smiled and looked at Luca then, expecting him to have loved this story, but he had this strange expression on his face.

"Hey, I'm gonna dip my feet in the ocean," he said, standing up and brushing sand off his jeans.

"Right *now*?" I asked, startled by this sudden change in mood.

"Yep, be right back." And he jogged off before any of us could join him.

"Um, I'll be back, too," I said.

When I reached him at the shore, he was just standing there, a dark figure on a dark beach. The churning waves lapped at his feet, which were still in his shoes.

"What's wrong?" I asked, feeling my heart lurch nervously. Had I said or done something? I had been too confident, I knew it . . . I had let my guard down.

When he didn't answer right away, I nervously tucked my hands into my sweatshirt pocket. "Are you okay?"

His back still to me, he dropped his head and kicked at the sand. "I'm fine. Sorry, I just . . ." He trailed off, going silent.

I touched his shoulder lightly. He reached up and held my hand, turning around at the same time. He looked at me straight in the eyes and said, simply, "That story was sad."

My brow furrowed and I smiled a little. "The peeing one? What do you mean? It's embarrassing, sure, but also hilarious!"

He shook his head. "No. That happened in second grade, right? Was it after your mom died?"

I was still confused. "Mm, yeah, I think it was. Why? What's wrong?"

He hesitated before he spoke. "I'm sorry, I don't mean to make this into a big deal. I know how you feel about talking about it. It's just . . . It's *sad* because your mom had died." He let go of my hand and turned his head, digging the heels of his palms into his eyes. "I feel sorry for that little kid. I don't think it's funny that she peed her pants. I think it's *sad*."

I was stunned.

Because I was finally seeing Luca for who he really was. In all my crushing, in my obsessing, in all my scheming . . . I hadn't known *this* person had existed in front of me all along. Not just cool artist-rebel Luca. But kind, deeply empathetic Luca. The Luca who viewed a story about a little girl peeing her pants in second grade as tragedy rather than comedy.

And it was at that moment that I knew, for sure, that this person was who I wanted to be a *girlfriend* to. And I finally understood what that word meant. It was something beyond giddy hand-holding and stealing kisses. It was sharing yourself with someone who deserved it. The weight of it almost took my breath away.

I instantly thought of one of my favorite K drama scenes: In *Healer*, Young-Shin discovers the mysterious Healer's secret lair, and finds him sick and emotionally distressed. When he pushes her away, *she* grabs *his* arm and hugs him, and he falls apart.

So I wrapped my arms around him and rested my cheek on his chest. We stood there for a long time, our breathing and thoughts entwined. "You're right. It was sad," I said into his shirt.

"You're allowed to admit that your mom's death is sad, you know?"

Those simple words, that little bit of permission, unlocked something in me, because it was the first time anyone had ever said it. I couldn't respond because my throat closed up. So instead I hugged him harder, arms wrapped tight to keep this person close to me.

"Okay," I said in a small voice.

"You can still appreciate your dad and be sad about your mom."

My vision blurred as I nodded.

When I got home that night, I peeked into my dad's bedroom, casting a small ray of light from the hallway onto his bed. I just stood there for a bit, watching him sleep—shoved all the way onto one side of the bed even after ten years of sleeping alone. Suddenly one of his eyes opened. "Huh? Desi, is that you?"

"Yeah, sorry to wake you up," I whispered. "Go back to sleep!"

"Everything okay?"

"Yeah. Everything's okay." I shut his door with a gentle click. "Like it's always been."

When I was in my room, I picked up the K drama notebook off my nightstand. At this point, it was filled with my notes from everything that had happened. All my plans and their results, faithfully documented. I took the folded list out of my wallet and flattened all the creases out.

"Well, list, you've been good to me. I'll never forget you, but it's time to go into retirement." While I couldn't destroy it, it was time to let it go. I placed the pages back into the notebook, closed it resolutely, and set it on my nightstand.

A scribbly cartoon heart squeezed itself out of the pages and floated into the air, its drawn wings flapping, and I felt my own chest grow lighter as I slipped into sleep.

~~STEP 18:~~

~~Meet His Family and Win Them Over~~ CHAPTER 18

I watched Bob Ross videos until my eyes bled, but I still couldn't paint a sycamore tree that didn't look like a piece of broccoli.

It was hours before the California State Parks fund charity show, where all the Art Club kids and I would finally show our work. And in very un-Desi fashion, I was finishing up my painting at the very last minute. I added a final blob of purple paint to one of the branches. When I had shown it to Luca a few days ago, he had explained to me, with the utmost patience, that you could see unexpected colors in everything if you only switched off your literal perceptions of the world around you. Unfortunately, I was very used to seeing things in literal terms. In physics, the law of gravity didn't shift based on the time of day like the colors of a leaf did.

When my phone alarm went off, **Art show!** flashed on the screen. I pointed a fan at the painting to help speed up the drying process, then ran upstairs and nervously viewed my outfit choices. Not only was it the art show tonight, but I was about to meet Luca's dad and stepmom. After dating for a few weeks, I had insisted on meeting them—not only because it was the proper thing to do, but because I *wanted* to meet them. I was so curious about this mysterious jerk dad whom Luca hated.

My dad was working until the show, so I had the house to myself before Luca picked me up. I blasted Beyoncé, and thirty minutes of hair-curling and leg-shaving later, I was standing outside waiting for him. The Dad BMW pulled into view and I waved, smoothing down the black floral-patterned dress I was wearing (with red Keds so as to avoid being *too* stuffy) while holding my painting in the other hand.

"Pretty," Luca said once I got my painting safely situated in the backseat, leaning over to kiss me and brush aside a strand of curled hair.

Still not used to boyfriend lavishness, I blushed. "Thanks. Wasn't sure what to wear."

Luca gestured at himself—wearing a blue flannel and black jeans. "Dress code is *fancy*."

"Clearly," I said, laughing and pulling on his beanie. He reached over for my hand, then held it as we drove. We dropped the painting off at the gallery with Mr. Rosso, then headed to Luca's dad's.

At one point, we passed the beach parking lot where we'd had our first kiss (the sight of which made my fingers and toes tingle);

then we drove up a sandy road on a hill until we entered a private driveway.

"Whooaaa," I breathed as the house came into view.

It was ridiculous, but beautiful. The architecture was both Spanish and ranch style. Huge windows, some with intricate stained glass, dark wood trim, and a riot of hot-pink bougainvillea crawling over the walls and onto the many balconies. Ancient oaks and young olive trees surrounded the estate and various succulents and desert plants dotted the landscape, creating a truly old-California feel. I was reminded of the house that the dad owned in the original *Parent Trap* movie. I had dreamed of living in a rambling ranch-style mansion ever since I'd seen it. You know, that old dream.

"Home sweet home," Luca muttered, parking the car haphazardly near one of the oaks.

I squeezed his hand. "It's really beautiful," I said almost apologetically.

He shrugged. "I have nothing against the house. It's who owns it."

We walked up to the door and I braced myself to meet the larger-than-life douchebag, Daddy Drakos. Then the tall wooden double doors flew open.

"Desi! So glad to finally meet you, darlin'!"

The man who greeted me was *not* who I was expecting. Rather than the pink-polo-shirt-wearing slimeball I had envisioned, I was greeted by . . . well, kind of a hot geek.

225

Tall, taller than Luca even, he had short, thick brown hair, messy and disheveled in a boyish way like his son's. He wore black-framed glasses on a face featuring some fantastic bone structure—straight nose, strong jaw, pronounced cheekbones. With a wiry build, like a long-distance runner, and exuding a real kinetic energy, his dad enveloped me in a warm hug and I caught a whiff of sandalwood on the crisp white shirt he was wearing with jeans.

Before I could recover, a tiny woman clutching two barking chocolate Labs shouted, "Hi Desi!" Even while holding those two happy beasts at bay, she was stylish with her straight blond bob, slim black pants, and gray silk camisole.

Once the dogs calmed down she came up to the door. "Don't embarrass Luca, already," she said to Daddy Drakos with an exaggerated eye roll. The tiny woman beamed a huge smile at me and held out a perfectly manicured hand, making her chunky bangles clink together. "I'm Lillian. It's so nice to finally meet you! These two monsters here are Hansel and Gretel." Lillian of www.dailylillian.com—I recognized her immediately from her fashion blog that Luca had showed to me to make fun of her.

"Come on in! We'll have a little chitchat and drinks here and then we can drive over to the show together," Daddy Drakos said. "And by the way, please feel free to call me Ned."

I had just been nodding my head mutely during this entire scene and finally snapped out of it. "Nice to meet you, too! Thank you for having me over." I held out a small potted succulent I had clipped from my backyard that day.

They both smiled warmly at me in response, and Ned took the plant. "Thanks, Desi! What a great addition to our little desert garden! Let's hope we keep this guy alive." Impeccable politeness? Check.

We walked into the house, Luca still holding my hand, and his grip got almost imperceptibly tighter. I couldn't imagine why—his dad was pleasant as hell so far. We went past the giant tiled foyer, complete with a rustic antler chandelier that was bigger than my bedroom, and my jaw dropped when we fully entered the house.

It was both rustic and palatial—huge windows and French doors overlooking the ocean and the setting sun. Candles were lit everywhere, and colorful tapestries and soft animal-skin rugs accented brown leather furniture. It was luxurious *and* cozy and I wanted to live there forever.

"Wow, what an awesome house!" I exclaimed.

"Thank you!" Lillian exclaimed just as enthusiastically. "You should have seen the place before we got married—a real bachelor pad."

Really? I mean how bachelor pad–ish could this beautiful house have been?

"You mean before you moved in," Luca said drily "You got married like two years after already movin' on in." I threw him a sharp glance but Lillian didn't bat an eye, and Ned shot him a warning look while pouring us some drinks from the bar off the living room.

"Yeah, that's what I meant," she countered easily.

I squeezed Luca's hand gently, trying to communicate to him without words: *Chill out*. He seemed to relax slightly, but I couldn't tell from his stony expression.

Ned handed me an ice-cold glass filled with a bright red beverage. "Just a Shirley Temple, don't worry." He tossed Luca a can of root beer. "Your favorite, right?" Even I knew that Luca didn't like root beer and I'd been his girlfriend for a mere month. I willed him not to say anything mean. Instead he kept a blank expression and placed the can on a side table.

"I had to Google you because Luca was keeping you so mysterious," Lillian said, curling up on the sofa with a glass of white wine. "Pretty impressive—your parents must be so proud of you."

Hm, *parents*. Looks like Luca *really* didn't talk to these guys that much. I took a sip of my Shirley Temple. "Thanks, but it's just my dad and me. My mother passed away."

Lillian and Ned looked stricken. Ned's mouth opened and closed before he said, "I'm so sorry to hear that, Desi. We didn't know . . ." He trailed off, giving Luca a look that was equal parts baffled and disappointed. I, however, wasn't surprised that Luca had never mentioned this to them. I was surprised they even knew I existed.

"Thank you, but it's okay, she passed away when I was little.

I'm very close to my dad, he played the dual parenting role pretty well," I said. Since Lillian and Ned had been so open and welcoming to me so far, I felt like I should reciprocate.

"Must be one great dad," Lillian said with a warm smile.

"He is," Luca said. "He's fixing my car, you know. He's a mechanic."

"Oh, really? Where's his shop?" Ned asked.

"Off Baker Road, near our school," I said. And we continued to talk easily about my dad, school, and a hundred other topics over our drinks. Lillian and Ned were curious about everything— the sports I played, what I wanted to study at Stanford, what part of Korea my parents were from.

"So Desi, what made you want to be a doctor?" Ned asked as he replenished my Shirley Temple.

"Thank you," I said, taking the drink. "I've always wanted to be a doctor because my mom was one. A neurosurgeon."

"Wow! Impressive lady," Ned said, taking a sip of his own cocktail.

"Yeah, definitely," I said with a laugh.

"But Desi loves all the gross biology behind being a doctor, too. Right, Des?" Luca asked with a nudge.

I stirred the ice in my drink with my straw. "You know it."

"*Beyond* science dork," Luca said with a proud smile.

"I guess I also like the idea of, I don't know, *literally* saving lives," I said. "I know that sounds so simple, and I don't know, scripted. But I'm an impatient person, you know? I like to see *direct* results from things I do—and while I admire the unsung heroes, I could never be content with the, uh, *long* game, you know? I'm not sure if I'm making any sense . . ."

Ned had been nodding his head from the second I started speaking. "Desi, you're making *complete* sense. It's what drove me to engineering and then specifically to medical equipment. A youthful impatience to enact change."

"Exactly! Luca told me that you patented the . . . well, he couldn't quite remember the name, but is it the CPR machine?"

"Ah, nope—the external auto-resuscitator."

I snapped my fingers. "I knew it! I guessed that first! Right, Luca?"

Luca was trying *very* hard to look like this entire conversation wasn't happening. But it was, and I wanted his dad to know that he had spoken to me about him. "Anyway, yeah, Luca told me about that and I was super-excited."

Ned beamed and Luca squirmed. I cleared my throat. "Can I get a house tour?"

I nursed the dregs of my Shirley Temple while getting the tour from Ned and Lillian. We left for the show shortly after, taking one car together. The show was being held at some fancy art gallery downtown. We were a little early but eventually people started trickling in, including Fiona and Wes. I introduced everyone and it was comfortable and easy and kind of lovely.

At a certain point, Luca pulled me aside while everyone was

chitchatting. "Do you remember that the scholarship recipient is going to be notified tonight? By e-mail."

I gasped. "Oh my God, how did I forget?"

He waggled his eyebrows. "I've been distracting you."

I laughed. "You have. Okay, well, do you know what time?"

"Midnight."

"Geez, dramatic much?" I said with an eye roll. That reminded me. "Hey, is your mom going to be able to make it to the show tonight?" I asked, trying to keep it light but feeling apprehensive. The idea of her showing up with Ned and Lillian around made me nervous.

Luca shook his head. "No, she's traveling for work."

"Oh, too bad. Would have been great to meet her," I said with a too-bright smile.

Just then I overheard Wes's voice loudly asking, "How does one become a fashion blogger?"

I groaned. "Let's go rescue them."

Before we could, though, Violet walked in with two people I assumed were her parents. While I wasn't sure if we were exactly friends, Violet and I definitely had reduced the hostility between us. I knew she hung out with Luca sometimes and just tried not to let it bother me. As long as she didn't flirt with him, that is.

Unexpectedly, Violet's parents made a beeline for me, filling me with dread. Oh God, Korean parents. I would have to be all Korean-y.

"Desi! Oh my gosh, look at you! You're so big now!" Violet's mother cried while pulling her beautiful cashmere shawl over her shoulders.

I did my awkward Korean bow and greeting to them— bending slightly at the waist and saying, *"Annyeonghaseyo,"* in a rushed, mumbling fashion.

Violet's dad gave me an awkward Korean-dad pat on the arm. "Wow, nice and tall!"

I laughed nervously. "Not as tall as Violet though!"

They both threw their heads back and laughed like I had told the world's funniest joke. *Ever.*

"She's too tall," her mother said with a cluck and a disapproving glance at Violet, who was slouching and practically hiding in her hair. Ah, the sly Korean deflection of complimenting their own children by warping it into a criticism instead.

"Violet says you're going to Stanford to become a doctor!" her dad bellowed.

I hid my embarrassment with a nervous laugh. "Well, not yet, ha-ha. I mean, I have to get accepted first."

Her mom waved her hand. "Oh, you will. Violet's always bragging about how smart you are."

Violet almost melted into a pile of hair and leather. "Eomma. *No*, I do *not.*" She glared at me. "Don't even think for an instant that my senile parents are telling the truth."

Her mom dug a knuckle into Violet's arm and tsked.

While I *thoroughly* enjoyed watching Violet get schooled by her mom, I noticed my dad just then. Walking into the gallery wearing a dark green sweater hastily pulled over his greasy T-shirt and khakis. Only the best for his daughter!

I quickly excused myself and ran over to him. "Hi Appa!"

He grinned and immediately scanned the gallery. "Hi, Desi. Where is yours?"

"Hidden in a dark corner somewhere." I pointed to the end of the gallery, my painting the last one before the hallway to the restrooms. Fitting.

"Let's go look together," he said, pulling me toward it.

"Okay, but first do you want to meet Luca's dad and step-mom?" I asked with some trepidation. While I knew they would all probably get along, I didn't want anything awkward to happen. I couldn't shake the nagging feeling that all of this could unravel at the slightest tug, the smallest mismaneuver.

"They're here?" he asked, looking around. Then he spotted Luca and waved his arm in the air—very high, and with a very expansive wave movement.

We walked over to them and I noticed that Wes and Fiona had scattered already. I smiled at everyone. "Ned, Lillian, this is my dad."

"Hi, Dad! Does Dad have a name?" Ned asked with a hearty grin as he reached over to shake my dad's hand.

My dad laughed. "No, to Desi my name is just Food Machine."

All the adults burst out into boisterous laughter. Where was this weird TV-dad humor coming from? I pushed my dad lightly. "Ha. Ha."

"My name's Jae-Won, but you can just call me Jae!" he said in the cheerful voice he used when he met the White People who couldn't pronounce his name.

"Nice to meet you, Jae! We love your kid, here. Desi's just the best," Ned said with a wink in my direction. "Luca's lucky she even bothers!"

So many dad jokes. I made a face at Luca and he crossed his eyes back at me.

We all walked around the gallery to check out the artwork. Some were good, like Violet's. Hers was this dark (surprise, surprise) abstract painting full of paint drips and shadowy shapes. Yeah, I could imagine it in some rich person's living room.

And then there was my painting.

"Ta-da!" I cried. "Behold, the mastery of rudimentary painting skills!"

Luca sighed. "Here we go again with the self-deprecating act." He looked around at our parents. "She's good! She just needs more practice."

I nodded. "Yes, definitely can't wait to get more practice. But I had a lot of help from Luca, thank God. Or you'd be looking at a very bright green blob on a brown stick."

My dad peered closely at it. "Yeah, it's pretty good, Desi! I've never seen you paint before, so good job!"

And then we moved on to Luca's piece, which had its own little room in the gallery. The Beach Boys were blasting in the dark, all four walls lit up by projected images. Images of the graffiti that Luca had painted over—but projected in a way so that the walls actually looked painted on. With the dreamy music floating in the background, the pictures would change every few seconds to match certain beats. There was a little placard by the entryway to explain the concept of his project.

"Wow." Lillian marveled while spinning around slowly. "This is *awesome.*"

Ned was silent, taking it all in. And then he looked at Luca. "Were you *tagging?*"

Ah, shit.

Luca shrugged. "Kinda. All of this stuff already existed, I just added to it."

Ned's jaw clenched. "First your arrest. Then the incident at the zoo, which could have been an arrest if the security guard had been a policeman. Have you learned *nothing?* You're on probation, how could you be so careless?"

Something switched off in Luca's face, turning it into an impassive mask that I hadn't seen since the early Luca days. A mask of boredom, of self-preservation.

I jumped in. "Um, Ned, it's not really tagging though. Like he said, the graffiti was already there, the whole idea is that he turned vandalism into *art.*"

My dad shot me a sharp look, signaling *Don't get involved.*

Ned was quiet for a second before his face relaxed. "Yeah, I guess I get the concept." And I could see in his controlled

235

expression that he was trying really hard not to get mad. "I don't have to like *how* you got there . . ."

"You don't get to have an opinion!" Luca exploded. Ned turned red and I saw Lillian freeze up. And I got it—the dynamic of Luca's home life. Tiptoeing around Mr. Grumples Teenager until one of them blew up. Even if things had gotten better between them, their history was always bubbling right under the surface, just looking for reasons to explode.

"*Luca,*" Ned whispered fiercely. "This isn't the time."

"There is no *time*, Dad! When do you want to talk? At home? We don't freaking *talk*."

Lillian's face blanched as she glanced over at me and I threw her a helpless look in return.

"Is it always *my* fault? When will *I* stop having to paying for this divorce? I've been trying for five years, Luca!" Ned's voice reverberated off the walls, mixing with Brian Wilson singing "Don't Worry Baby," and the entire scene was just surreal.

"That's the problem, you think you can just fix everything with money! Tossing alimony at us, thinking, *Well, that's that*," Luca said, using a low and douchey voice for effect.

Ned threw his arms up in the air. "Are you *kidding* me? Is having you move in just tossing money at you? It was your mom who kept you away this entire time!"

Uh-oh. Luca ran his fingers through his hair and laughed harshly. "Just stop. There's no way you can convince me that this is all Mom's fault, that *you* didn't cheat on her."

Oh *shit*. Even in the dark, I could see Lillian's face get red. My dad slowly made his way over to me. "Maybe we should go outside," he said in a low voice. But I couldn't leave now.

Ned was silent and Luca kept going. "And you only had me move in with you because you wanted to control me."

"No, no, that's where you're wrong." Ned's voice went back to a normal volume. "Yes, when you got arrested, I wondered if you needed more supervision. But it was . . . just an excuse. I had been looking for an opportunity to convince your mother to let you live with me, and the arrest was the one that finally did it."

Luca made a rude noise—something between a snort and laugh.

Ned ignored him and continued. "Do I think you need more discipline? Yes. Is it too late? Maybe. But I still wanted to *try* and get to know you before you left for college. I knew I'd never have a chance of seeing you in any real way after that." Ned's voice cracked. "I didn't want to miss out on *all* the big things."

Everyone was silent and my dad cleared his throat. I elbowed him.

Luca was still looking down at the floor, hands shoved into his pockets, and while my heart went out to him, I resisted the instinct to go and be with him.

"Luca, I just want to say . . . you're right." Ned waved an arm at the walls surrounding him. "I should care about this because *you* care about it. And it's *great*, I'm so impressed. And I'm so glad that I had the opportunity to share this moment. This is why I wanted you to move here. So I could get to know you better. And all this? Makes me understand you a little more. And I'm proud."

I held my breath. Luca continued to stare at the floor.

"Even if you did, maybe, break the law." The playful tone in Ned's voice seemed to knock something down, then, and Luca finally looked up. He didn't smile exactly, but he didn't look angry anymore.

"Thanks."

And right on cue "Good Vibrations" came over the speakers and a group of people came in and started chattering loudly with oohs and ahhs. My dad walked over to Ned and Lillian, and Luca headed toward me.

I bumped him with my shoulder. He looked over at me sheepishly and bumped my shoulder back.

"Hey."

He smiled, a little ray of sunshine breaking through clouds. "Hey. Sorry about that."

After darting my eyes around to make sure my dad wasn't watching, I pecked him on the cheek. "Don't be sorry. I'm sorry *we* were all standing here being awkward as hell."

He laughed and tugged a strand of my hair. "So? What do *you* think of the piece?"

I looked around with a blasé expression. "It's okay, I guess."

"Oh yeah?"

"Yeah. Could use a little more . . . I dunno, *purple*."

"Definitely."

"Yeah, it's no sycamore tree."

He kissed my ear. "No, it is most definitely not a tree."

I watched the clock.

Des, do not project your anxiety onto Luca's future.

Tick-tock. I willed my eyeballs to move from the clock to the tattered copy of *Beowulf* that I was trying to read. I settled back deeper into my pillows and dug my toes into my bedspread. *Chill. Just read. Luca will text you as soon as he hears.*

11:42.

11:43.

11:45.

My phone buzzed. I didn't even need to grab it since it was already propped on top of my knees, behind my book. I threw the book onto the bed and read Luca's message: I'm outside.

I scrambled over to my window and pushed the curtain aside to see Luca in the driveway, sitting on top of the BMW's hood.

My dad was already asleep, so I tiptoed past his door, then ran down the stairs, grabbing a blanket off the sofa to throw across my shoulders. I gently shut the front door behind me and walked out barefoot in my pajamas.

I went through my K drama cute-heroine checklist: *Hair in bun: okay but not ideal. Makeup scrubbed off but no acne medication dotting face: check. Teeth freshly brushed, so fresh breath all in order.* I wished I had a giant pair of glasses to finish the look.

Luca was staring at his phone when I approached him. "What are you doing here?" I whispered.

"I wanted to be with you when I found out," he whispered back. "Wait, why are we whispering?"

I hopped onto the hood next to him and he scooted over to make room. "I dunno. I feel like these neighbors see and hear *everything*. These houses, they have *eyes*." I looked around at all the houses with their lights off, the street eerily empty, silent, and blanketed by a foggy marine layer off the ocean lit up by the occasional street lamp.

He tugged on the corner of my blanket and pulled one end over his shoulders, drawing me closer to him. "Well, the neighbors will really have something to talk about when I don't get the scholarship and light myself on fire in the middle of this cul-de-sac."

"Ha-ha. Don't even joke about that. You're going to jinx it."

"You and your superstitions!"

I looked around me. "And there's no wood to knock on!" I reached under myself and pinched my butt. I caught Luca's expression. "What? You're supposed to pinch your butt when there's no wood around."

"Did some pervy guy teach you that?" he asked with a huge

grin, his eyes crinkling in that way they did whenever he was tickled by some new, bizarre facet of my character.

I sniffed. "No, it was my friend Amy Monroe in sixth grade, thank you very much."

"I think Amy Monroe was messing with you."

"Well, I have yet to have disasters happen after I pinch my butt, so . . ."

"Must work. *Science*." He shook his head sagely. I laughed and nudged his knee with my own.

Then we were both silent for a while, just letting our breath come out in puffs into the chilled night air. Both of us fully aware of the minutes passing by.

And then. A tiny chime on his phone, and then on mine. He looked over at me. I shrugged. "I set an alarm, too."

He smiled for a second, then looked nervously down at his phone. "Hm."

I also looked down at his phone, then up at him. "Well? Luca! Check your e-mail!"

He blinked, hand still, cradling his phone. "Wow, so. It all hinges. On this. Like, this upcoming moment will determine the next four years of my life. Isn't that just insane if you think about it?"

What was *insane* was that he wasn't checking his freaking e-mail at *this very second*. I willed myself to be patient. "Yeah, but, I mean, that's what all of us are waiting for! That envelope, that acceptance. Every high school kid goes through this, Luca. It'll be okay whatever the outcome."

Luca nodded. "Yeah. Yeah, right. I mean, obviously I knew it would all boil down to this. But now that I'm actually faced with *the moment*, it feels really strange. Surreal."

I resisted snatching the phone out of his hands. "Okay, worst-case scenario: You don't get the scholarship. You can still apply for some other scholarships at the eleventh hour *or* you can try talking to your dad about it?"

"Ugh." He made a face. "You know what, though. After the show tonight, I think he might have changed his mind about art school."

"Whoa, really?"

He shrugged. "Yeah, but I still want this scholarship. To prove it to myself. It'll mean so much."

I nodded. "I get it, dude." Then I stared at his phone. "Okay, please check your e-mail before I pee my pants."

He scooted away from me and I swatted his arm. He took a deep breath and looked at me, all big eyes and uncertainty. I squeezed his arm and smiled, trying to exude confidence. And reaching into the depths of my brain, I tried to will the result I wanted. *Concentrate on what I want.*

With a quick swipe his phone unlocked, and I watched as he tapped the in-box icon at the bottom of the screen. It popped up and there at the very top was an e-mail from the California Fine

Art Scholarship Committee. He glanced up at me and we held our gaze for a second before he tapped it.

At the very last second, I averted my eyes. Despite me being here, this was a private moment for Luca. And also, I really did think I was going to pee my pants. I stared out into my street, spotting a peach-and-white cat darting between some bushes. That was Señor, always prowling at night and getting into scrapes with the raccoons in the neighborhood. And let me tell you, raccoons here are vicious. Señor must be like a ninja cat to—

"Des."

My cat-based reverie dissipated into vapor above my head. "Yeah?"

His head was bent down and I couldn't see his face, just the top of that gray beanie.

"I got it."

"Wait. What?" I couldn't register without seeing his expression.

He looked over at me with a huge smile, the biggest smile I had ever seen on that perfect face of his. "I got it."

I covered my mouth with my hands and scream-squealed into them, kicking my legs up into the air. He started laughing and I threw my arms around him, the blanket falling off our shoulders onto the hood of the car.

"Ahhh!" I jumped off the car and started bouncing up and down. "I knew it, I knew it!"

He was still laughing when I grabbed his hands and pulled

him off the car to join me in my bounce celebrations. And he did—both of us clutching each other's hands, jumping up and down in the middle of my driveway at midnight.

Then suddenly we weren't jumping anymore—just a whole lot of kissing. He lifted me onto the hood of the car and had his hands in my hair while I wrapped my legs around his waist. When I thought we were seriously going to light the BMW on fire, he pulled away and rested his forehead on mine.

"Whoa," he breathed.

"Mm-hm," I said while blinking, eyes adjusting to the street lamp behind Luca's head. I took deep breaths. "So . . . RISD. Rhode Island. East Coast."

He nodded. "Y-e-e-a-h. Stanford. West Coast."

"We could be, like, rival rappers."

"Yeah, berets against beakers," he replied with a honky laugh at his own joke.

We were silent for a second, giving our heartbeats time to return to their normally scheduled programs. And then he pulled me toward him again and leaned his forehead against mine. "Good thing we always have naked FaceTime."

"Ha-ha, in your dreams," I said, bumping his forehead lightly. "Well, we can just plan on visiting each other every other month or so? I mean, it'll be expensive, but I plan on working and maybe your dad will fly you out here. And also we can make sure to check in every night, but we should make it clear that we're not *obligated*—"

Luca's hand clamped over my mouth. "Desi. Let's not think about this yet."

I pushed his hand off. "Yet?! It's not *that* early, it's almost the end of the school year!"

"Des, it's still February; we have *months* to think about it."

There was so much I wanted to say, to plan. But this was a happy moment for Luca, and I didn't want to ruin it. So I tugged on his beanie instead. "Are you finally ready to wear this beanie out of necessity? It's gonna get cold over there." My fingers brushed over his thick hair, marveling at the weird sense of possessiveness I had over this head of hair. Like, world, that hair was *mine*.

He shrugged. "You know, for all my intensity about getting this scholarship, I haven't really had time to think about what it all means. As in, moving across the country to where there's . . . snow and stuff."

"Sounds like everything you've been waiting for, right?" I asked, my voice more optimistic and perky than I actually felt.

He picked up the blanket and placed it over our shoulders again. "Yeah. I mean, yes. But now . . ." His gaze shifted from the street over to me, a small smile hovering over his lips.

My smile was sad, brimming with so many uncertainties—something I wasn't used to. "I know what you mean."

We sat there for a long time, our butts growing cold on the hood of the car, watching the fog lift slowly from the street. And inevitably into the sky.

~~STEP 19:~~
~~You Must Make the Ultimate Sacrifice to Prove Your Love~~ CHAPTER 19

Still feeling the high of Luca's scholarship a week later, I approached my Stanford interview with Full Intensity Desi Lee. This meant that in the days leading up to the interview on Saturday I:

- Cut my hair.
- Memorized the "Common Interview Questions" listed on www.ivyleagueorbust.com (even though Stanford isn't *technically* Ivy League).
- Practiced the pronunciation of all Stanford-related proper nouns.
- Whitened my teeth.
- Amped up my workout so that I was doing planks every night. A sound body is a sound mind, I always say (okay, not really, but it fit the occasion).

- Reread every single word in the Stanford brochures and on the website.
- Used Korean sheet masks on my face every night while watching dramas with my dad, which always freaked him out.
- Had every dress I owned dry-cleaned.
- Downloaded meditation tracks on my phone because I hear you're supposed to relax for this sorta thing. Hadn't listened yet, though.

So when it was the big day, Fiona and Wes came over to view my outfit choices and to offer last-minute support. My dad was at work but would come home early to drop me off at the interview.

I pulled out three different outfits in their own garment bags. Unzipping them, I said, "Okay so I am thinking three different looks. One is a no-nonsense pantsuit-type thing." Fiona made a gagging noise at the dark trousers and blazer. I tossed them on the bed.

"*Okay.* Second is a demure, girlie look." I held up the Peter Pan–collar shirt and cardigan with skirt. Fiona made an X with her arms while Wes nodded his head and gave me a thumbs-up sign. I hung it up as an option, then held up the last outfit. "Third is breezy and cool, like, I am being respectful but am not bending over backward to impress you," I said while holding up a slouchy black sweater and cropped houndstooth-patterned skinny trousers.

Fiona whistled. "That's the one, Desi."

Wes shook his head. "No, that one's too . . . flippant. She's going to be a *doctor*."

"What, and doctors dress like 1950s kindergarten teachers?" Fiona scoffed.

"Just because you dress like an extra from *Mad Max* doesn't mean that every woman wants to," Wes said, looking pointedly at Fiona's holey white tee and distressed army pants full of neon patches. "Also, Des, remind me again why you aren't telling Luca about your interview?"

I riffled through some socks in my dresser. "I told you—I don't want to steal his scholarship thunder."

I held up a pair of mint-green socks and Fiona shook her head. "No to the socks. And no to stealing your man's thunder. Luca's cool, he won't feel that way. Just tell him; it's weird that you're being secretive about it."

"I'm not being secretive! I'm just super-nervous and I'd rather get the interview over with and tell him *after*, when I'm not such a stress case anymore." The interview was nearby at an alum's house at five p.m. and I was supposed to meet the woman's family and have dinner with them. When she had suggested it, I high-fived myself because I knew that I *killed* at dinners.

Wes and Fiona were still looking dubious, so I changed the

subject. "So Fi, are you nervous about hearing back from Berkeley?" I asked as I finally decided on the black-sweater outfit. I made Wes turn around and started changing into it. UC acceptances were going to be mailed out at the beginning of March, and Fiona's first choice was Berkeley—as an undeclared major, of course. I had no doubt she would get in.

Fiona shrugged. "I'm not nervous really, although I'm banking on the scholarship. I hope my essay cinches it."

I winked. "Gotta play up your coming-out story for all it's worth." Fiona's essay was based on when she had come out to her family two years ago. Her grandmother had fainted and when her dad rushed over to grab her, he fell over a chair and broke his leg. I happened to be there for moral support but ended up having to take care of the injured parties while we waited for an ambulance. Luckily, everyone was fine, relatively. Her family eventually recovered, although they still weren't thrilled with her active love life. I'm pretty sure that would have applied to boyfriends, too, however.

"What are you guys gonna do without me?" Wes asked the wall since he was still turned around. His first choice was Princeton—he had also applied as "undeclared" since he wasn't sure if he wanted to be the next Mark Zuckerberg or the next Stephen Hawking. Typical Wes. Fiona tackled him into a hug and Wes protested as she pushed him onto the bed and mussed his hair.

"We'll make you visit Nor Cal as much as possible," I said,

already a little sad at the prospect. "I can't believe we're going to be *Nor Cal* people, ew."

"Yeah you better not start saying *hella* or I'm gonna have to *hella* kick your asses," Wes said, still lying on the bed but with his head hanging off the edge, near my nightstand. He craned his neck to look at something buried under some books. "Girl, is that the K drama notebook?" He rolled over and pulled it out.

I glanced at it. "Oh, yeah—been meaning to toss it, but I'm kind of attached to it. It's also fun to reread, like some anthropological study."

Wes flipped through it. "You put some serious detail into the notes section." He flipped through it some more. "I would burn it," he said, looking up at me. Just then, his phone buzzed.

He looked down at it. "Crap, that's Violet—Fi, we're late."

"Where are you guys going?" I asked, putting the rejected outfits away in my closet.

"New Spider-Man movie," said Fiona. "I'm there to chaperone." She waggled her eyebrows.

It begins. Violet and Wes had been hanging out a lot since the bonfire and love was blossoming before our eyes. Or, at the very least, a lot of make-outs.

Wes drew me into a firm hug that almost suffocated me. "Good luck, Des. *Kill* it."

Fiona also came over for a hug and then pinched my cheeks when she pulled out of it. "You got this, Desi!"

I watched them drive off in Penny, who honked twice in farewell. My interview wasn't for another few hours so I flipped my laptop open and pulled up my text doc with all my prep questions.

My phone buzzed from its spot on my bed. I grabbed it to see a text from Luca: **Where are you??**

I texted back: **Home!**

He immediately called me and his voice was shaky when I answered. "Des, I'm freaking—my mom's in some hospital in LA. Can you come with me?"

My brow furrowed in confusion. "Oh no! Is she okay? What happened?"

"I'm not sure, all I know is that she was visiting LA with some friends before this happened. The person who called me from the hospital wouldn't tell me—just that it's an emergency and my mom told them to call me. I have to go and find out what happened. Can you please come with me?"

Oh, God. There was no way I could miss this interview.

"What about your dad?"

"He and Lillian are out somewhere. Besides, my mom wouldn't want to see him. Please, Des. I'm scared. I need you." His voice was tiny, almost a whisper.

I was barely thinking when I responded, "Of course, I'm ready whenever." He said he would pick me up right away.

I glanced at the time on my phone. Okay, I had two and a half hours. LA was a forty-five-minute drive away if you drove fast. I could pop in and make sure everything was okay before grabbing a cab back immediately after. I could do this. My hands shook as I shut my laptop. I glanced down at my interview outfit. Luckily, I wouldn't be dressy enough for Luca to find it odd.

When Luca pulled up, I slipped inside the car and he instantly drew me into a hug. I rubbed his back. "Are you okay?"

"No . . . I'm not. I wish I knew what was going on!" His voice was raw and his eyes red with worry.

"I'm sure she's fine," I said calmly, not knowing anything of the sort. "Do you want me to drive?" His hands were shaking more than mine. His dark eyes were almost black as they darted around the car, unable to focus.

He hesitated for about a second, then nodded imperceptibly. We swapped seats and Luca turned on his phone navigation as we headed for the freeway. Reaching over, he tucked a piece of flyaway hair behind my ear. "Thanks for coming, Des. I thought I was gonna lose it earlier . . ." There was a hint of shame in his voice.

I reached over for his hand, as he had done so many times to me while he was driving. "Of course."

And while I absorbed Luca's anxiety, I was also watching the minutes tick by on the dashboard clock. Okay, worst-case scenario, I was a little late. But I was sure they would understand if I had an emergency. And seeing Luca this upset was really unsettling.

We didn't say much during the ride. Luca stayed curled up near the window, staring out silently. Even music felt inappropriate, so I turned it off. About half an hour into the drive my phone buzzed in my jacket pocket. I had to ignore it while driving, but then it buzzed five more times.

Luca glanced over at me. "Is that your phone?"

"Um, yeah, but it's okay."

"Do you want me to check for you?" He was reaching over into my pocket.

"No! Totally fine, probably just Fiona talking about Spider-Man and how hot Mary Jane is."

That got a smile out of Luca. "Nice." I laughed and squeezed his hand a little harder than I'd planned. When he pulled it away with a wince, I took the opportunity to slip my phone out and glance down quickly while Luca continued to stare out the window.

My dad. Shit.

"I have to use the bathroom, can we pull off here?" I asked, already getting off the freeway onto an exit with a gas station.

"Yeah, sure."

I parked, then ran toward the restroom, calling, "Be right back!" When I got into the restroom, I pulled out my phone to see a bunch of texts from my dad asking where I was. I texted him back: Luca had an emergency. His mom's in the hospital, I have to take him. I'll be back in time, don't worry!

My dad immediately called me. Crap.

"Hi, Appa."

"Is Luca okay? What happened?"

"I don't know, this hospital in LA called him but they won't tell him what's wrong."

"LA? But—but couldn't he go by himself or with his dad? Why call you when you have the interview?" My dad was confused, not mad . . . yet.

I leaned my head back onto the tiled wall of the disgusting bathroom. "He didn't know the interview was today and I didn't want to tell him. He wanted *me* to go with him, not his dad. And he wasn't in a good state to drive. He needed *me*."

"Desi."

"I know, please don't be mad. Also, I think maybe I might be able to make it in time." It sounded feeble, even to me.

A sigh that I had never heard before came from the other side of the line. Disappointment sigh. "This is big mistake, Desi. If Luca knew, he would not want you to do this. What if you're late and this affects admission?"

My palms grew sweaty. He was right and I knew it. "Well, it's too late now, right? We're almost there and I have to be here for him now." My voice took on a hysterical edge.

He didn't budge from disappointment. "I'm really . . . This is a very, *very* stupid thing you did."

Tears pricked my eyes. Regret flooded me and settled into a rock in my chest, heavy and flinty. My dad's disappointment crushed me. Every day of my life I worked so hard so that I would never hear that in his voice. And my own self-loathing was also oppressive. What could I do, though? It was done, and Luca was out in the car, waiting for me and worried out of his mind about his mom.

My dad was quiet for a second; then his haggard voice came over the line. "You go help Luca. Don't worry about Stanford while you drive. But call me *as soon as you find out*. Okay?"

I nodded, tears still in danger of spilling over. "Thanks, Appa."

"I love you."

"I love you, too."

As soon as he hung up, I took a few deep breaths and walked over to the sink to splash my face with water. As I grabbed a paper towel to dry off, the reflection looking back at me was as skeptical-looking as I felt.

There was traffic. There was always traffic on the 5. What could I have been thinking.

If only we were *really* in a K drama, then I could drive wildly through rush hour, wheels squealing as I pulled insane moves, not giving a damn if I left a trail of car accidents behind me.

Unfortunately, this was one thing I couldn't do no matter how much K drama heroine sass I summoned. I wanted to scream.

When we finally got to the hospital, it was four-fifteen—giving me precisely forty-five minutes to get back to Monte Vista. Which I would never do—I had seen all the opposite-flowing traffic that would await me on the way back. And when Luca grabbed my hand as soon as I was out of the car, I knew it was too late. Stanford receded into the distance, stuck in that traffic behind me.

We ran down the hospital halls holding hands, and visions of K dramas entered my head—because there was no drama in the universe that didn't have at least one hospital scene in it. By the time we reached reception, we were out of breath.

"Hi, my mom is a patient here. Rebecca Jennings. Can you tell me what happened to her, please?" Luca asked the young nurse behind the desk.

The nurse's blue eyes were warm and he gave us a sympathetic smile. "I'm sorry, I'm not allowed to release that information without her permission."

"What! She *did* give permission," Luca snapped.

I could tell by his facial expression that he was about to get really mad at this nurse. I put my hand on his arm. Before speaking, I glanced at the nurse's name tag. "Hi, Benjamin. The thing is, he got a call from someone here, so clearly she must have given some sort of permission or how would they have known to call him?"

Benjamin appeared skeptical but then he looked something

up on the computer with a few keystrokes and said, "What's your name?"

"Luca Drakos."

"I'm sorry. She did list you as next of kin and gave permission for us to release information to you. I expected someone older." He read from the computer screen. "Anyway, she suffered a burst appendix but the doctors were able to perform surgery." Luca exhaled a sigh of relief. Benjamin continued. "Yup, she'll be fine, but you'll want to talk to the doctor. Let me page him. You can wait over there." He pointed to some dark green chairs in the waiting area.

It hit me then: a burst appendix. Oh my God, *that's* why I missed my interview? I tried not to pass out as we walked over to the waiting room.

Luca rubbed his face with his hand. "Burst appendix. That's not a huge deal, right?"

I nodded, unable to speak right away. After a few seconds, I cleared my throat. "Totally, a very common condition. They've probably done a billion of those surgeries here." Luca's relief was palpable and I envied him for it.

My phone buzzed again. Luca was lost in thought so I pulled it out.

Did you get to the hospital yet? My dad.

Yeah just got here. His mom had a burst appendix but will be ok. She's out of surgery already. We're waiting for the doctor.

There was a long moment of that ellipsis hanging out in the text bubble before my dad finally texted back: I'm glad she is ok. But I think you are going to miss interview. Even if you leave now.

I had to sit down to text him back; my legs were in danger of full-on collapse. I know. I'll call the interviewer and tell her I had an emergency.

My dad texted back: No, you are not in good condition. Stay with Luca. I'll call her and see if we can reschedule.

I sent him her contact info. Thanks, Appa. I'll call you when we're headed home.

Tell Luca I am thinking of him. Bye bye.

I clutched my phone and saw a black middle-aged doctor in scrubs approach us. Luca got out of his chair nervously and I also stood up, to hold his hand.

"Are you Ms. Jennings's son?" the doctor asked, looking at Luca. He nodded, and I could feel his heart racing in his palm.

He reached out to shake Luca's hand. "I'm Dr. Swift. Your mom's had surgery to remove the burst appendix and she's recovering very well at the moment. Okay?" He smiled kindly at Luca, who relaxed visibly. "But it did burst, which is always a bit serious. When that happens, it spills infectious materials into the abdominal cavity, so we had to put her on some heavy anti-biotics." I nodded, listening attentively. He continued. "She should be able to get up and move around in a day. Then she should be set to go home a few days after that."

Luca looked at me. "That's all good," I clarified.

Dr. Swift smiled at us both. "She's weak right now but conscious, so you can go in and see her. Room 1004. I'll be in to discuss more details later."

Luca nodded and replied, "Thanks so much, Dr. Swift."

He nodded in response and walked away. Luca and I looked at each other.

"Thanks, missy," he said with a smile.

I reached for his hand. "Of course. Hey, don't you think you should maybe call your dad and tell him what's happened?"

He frowned. "Why? We're here now."

"Well, she's your mom, they were married once. Wouldn't he want to know this happened?"

"I doubt he'd care."

I shook my head. "Luca . . . of course he will."

Luca was silent for a second. "Fine. But first let's go see my mom."

"Oh, both of us? I—I thought maybe I could just hang out, give you guys some privacy," I stammered. "I'll meet her another time when she's feeling better."

Pulling me into a tight hug, Luca spoke into my hair. "No privacy needed. I want her to meet you. You saved the day."

Oh, God. "Okay, then, um, why don't you go see her first, see if she's up for it. I'll call your dad for you while you do that. And if you want me to come in later, I'll come in."

He kissed my forehead. "Okay, you're right. Thank you."

"You're welcome," I said into his neck.

With that, I reached for his hand and squeezed it again. He smiled widely and walked away with a little skip in his step.

My hands started shaking as I called his dad.

STEP 20: ~~You Are Not Allowed to Be Happy Until the Very Last Possible Minute~~
CHAPTER 20

Luca's mom was the most high-maintenance appendectomy patient ever.

"Come over here, sweetie, so I can see the girl who stole Luca."

Er, didn't sound like she was joking. I walked over to the hospital bed, holding the hand lotion she had requested. I had driven to three pharmacies before finding it.

"I'm sorry we had to meet under these circumstances," I said with a smile. "How are you feeling?"

Her eyes glinted. "As good as I can, I suppose," she said with a weak laugh. I placed the all-natural paraben-free lotion on the table by her bed. Luca was sitting at the foot of the bed holding her hand.

Luca's mother was beautiful, no surprise there. Thick, dark hair flowing over her shoulders, piercing blue eyes, and a wide, Julia Roberts–esque mouth. Even after suffering an exploded organ she looked good.

She was also kind of annoying. Aside from the weird lotion request, she had asked Luca to get her room changed because she didn't like the feng shui of this one. And then complained about how *simply awful* the hospital sheets were. Probably full of *chemicals*. (More like low thread count.)

"So Luca has told me all about you, Desi. How could anyone be so perfect?"

Every word out of this woman's mouth was a backhanded compliment. I glanced at Luca but he was smiling and totally oblivious. Her tone was nice but her eyes were steely and appraising.

I didn't know how to respond. "Ah, well, I'm sure he was being overly flattering."

Luca rolled his eyes. "*Okay,* Des. Mom, Desi's going to be valedictorian and is going to Stanford." My heart constricted. "Who would have guessed I'd fall for such a nerd?"

His mother's eyes scrutinized me more carefully than ever. "What does your dad do again? Plumbing?" Although I wasn't following the steps anymore, I summoned strength from my mental K drama catalog. I thought of Ji-Eun from *Full House*, and how she adorably sang a song for Young-Jae's uptight family and managed to break the ice and endear herself. *Just suffer through, don't let her ruffle your feathers, Des.*

I smiled, sunny and perpetually pleasant. "Nope, he's a mechanic."

"How lovely." Rebecca's voice indicated anything but. She

started to fuss about her blankets again and Luca got up to adjust them. Angelic K drama heroine or no, I still wanted to punch her in the face.

A quiet knock interrupted my thoughts. It was Ned. I practically ran over to him in relief. I gave him a hug and whispered, "Thank God you're here."

Ned whispered back, "I hear ya, sister."

"Ned?" Rebecca's voice was sharp. "What the hell are you doing here?"

He walked over to her and placed a bouquet of hot-pink peonies on the nightstand. "Glad to see your spirit has yet to be trampled, Becca," he said drily.

She frowned and looked at Luca. "Did you call him?"

Luca looked at me nervously. "Yeah, Desi thought it would be a good idea to let him know what happened but I didn't know he was coming." He shot his dad a smile, a small one, but I caught it and so did Ned.

Rebecca started complaining and Ned took off his glasses and rubbed his eyes.

I cringed and made eye contact with Luca, who was hovering protectively over his mom. I tried to communicate telepathically: *let's get outta here.* He got the drift.

"We're gonna go get some food so you guys can commence with yelling or whatever," he said, walking over to the door with me.

I rushed out of there with Luca close on my heels. Once we

were well out of earshot, Luca let out a huge sigh, as if he had been holding his breath. "I know it's good to have Dad come, but . . . they're so annoying when they're together."

I couldn't imagine what it would be like to have two parents hate each other so blatantly. "I'm sorry, I didn't know he'd show up either—another stressful thing to add to the stress pile?"

He draped his arm across my shoulders. "No, I'm actually glad he came. And I'm glad you're here," he said. A few seconds passed before he added, "Hospitals are the worst."

"Let me guess, you think you're going to catch whatever everyone else has in here?" I teased. The more I got to know Luca, the more his subtle neuroses revealed themselves.

His nose wrinkled. "Well, yeah. In fact, does this look like a rash to you?" He pulled up his sleeve in earnest, showing me a patch of normal skin that had just recently been scratched.

I pushed his arm away. "Get out of here. You're, like, every doctor's worst nightmare."

"I suppose I'll have to get used to hospitals, since my girlfriend's going to be a doctor someday."

Normally I would have been thrilled to hear that—the planning ahead that the sentence implied. But instead I felt my throat close up. Stanford hovered over me and with every second that passed, the gravity of what I had done weighed more heavily on my shoulders. *I might not be able to have my Stanford interview.* Eighteen years of nonstop work. Not only me, but my dad, too.

My dad who brought me food at midnight when I was doing all-nighters, who took me to all my SAT classes, who mended my cleats when the toes blew out.

I needed to get my mind off Stanford, so I delved into trickier territory. "So . . . your mom . . ."

We reached the elevator and Luca glanced over at me, warily, pushing the Down button. "I know. She's annoying."

I almost tripped into the closed elevator doors. "What! But I mean, you're so close to her."

He shrugged. "I never said she was perfect. But she's my mom, and I'm loyal to her."

While I wanted to say a million things, like *She doesn't deserve your loyalty!* I kept my mouth shut, because everyone had their own private family dynamics. Who was I to judge?

When we got to the cafeteria my phone buzzed with a text from my dad: Got a hold of interviewer. She said to call Stanford Admission first thing Monday morning.

I woke up Monday morning screeching—with cold water dripping down my face.

"Good morning!"

"Appa!" I yelled, using my sheets to wipe the water off my face. My dad stood at the foot of my bed with a spray bottle he used to mist our houseplants.

"What? It's almost seven a.m.; you need to be prepared to call Stanford right when their office opens at eight-thirty."

"That's an hour and a half from now, Appa!"

"What, don't you like being prepared?"

Touché, Appa. He was right but I didn't appreciate the tone.

When my dad had called the interviewer on Saturday she had said that we had to check with Stanford to see if I could reschedule. Despite the dread that had been hovering over me since my dad told me that, I was optimistic this would all work out. I had spent the rest of the weekend cleaning the house inside out to distract myself. The gutters were officially ready for a torrential rain and my dad's tools were now organized by size, color, and application.

"Let me know how it goes," my dad said sternly. Well, as sternly as one could while wearing a Mickey Mouse T-shirt and basketball shorts. He left my room on that ominous note.

At eight-thirty I was in first period, calculus. When my phone buzzed with the alarm I had set, I raised my hand during Mr. Farhadi's lesson on derivatives. "May I use the restroom?"

He nodded and I grabbed my phone and rushed out of class with a quick glance at Fiona, who looked at me quizzically. Luca had driven me to school, so I hadn't told her about the interview yet.

I walked out to the courtyard, the day overcast and chilly. My phone was already set to the admissions number and I tapped it as I paced the gravel path between the purple and green grasses (fescues—native, drought-tolerant grasses I had convinced the school to plant when they re-landscaped last year).

The line rang and an operator answered. After a few transfers, I finally got the right person on the phone.

"Hi, Mr. Lipman. This is Desi Lee. I had an interview scheduled with Sandra Munoz Saturday but I had an urgent matter come up and need to reschedule. Ms. Munoz told me to contact you in order to do so?" I kept my voice upbeat as I tucked my phone against my shoulder and placed my hands on my hips, striking the pose that made me feel like Wonder Woman. I read once that it was *actually* called the Wonder Woman and made you appear confident even if you totally didn't feel that way.

"Ah yes, Miss Lee. Is everything okay? Ms. Munoz e-mailed us saying that you'd had an emergency."

"Yes, thank you. My boyfriend's mother had emergency surgery and I had to drive him up to LA." Crap, *boyfriend* slipped out before I could stop myself—coming from the mouth of a teenage girl, that word sounded so flimsy, so damning. There was a beat of silence and I rushed to fill it. "She's okay now, and I'm happy to reschedule the interview."

Again, a bit of silence.

"I'm sorry to say, Miss Lee, that we can't reschedule."

Heart stopped. Just. Stopped.

"As you know, we hold the interviews over the course of one month, and you got one of the last slots—in fact it was the very last day we held interviews everywhere. I'm sorry."

I shook my head, phone stuck to my ear. "But I can do it today! She lives fifteen minutes away, I'm sure I could just call her—"

"Miss Lee—the time has passed. Again, I apologize. But you know, the interviews aren't mandatory."

I could no longer understand the words coming from my phone. I melted out of the Wonder Woman pose and slid down onto the gravel.

"Miss Lee?"

I struggled to speak. "Um . . . but will this affect my application?"

Another beat of silence. "Well, it doesn't mean you're *disqualified* from consideration," Mr. Lipman offered optimistically.

I laughed, a harsh, scary noise. "Well, what a relief!" All politeness had left in the wake of knowing that I had probably just deducted points from my application to Stanford.

Mr. Lipman's voice changed in tone from fake sympathetic to curt. "I'm not sure what advice I can offer beyond this point."

"Can I please speak to your supervisor?" I willed myself to keep my voice calm.

"I don't think that would make any difference," he said, voice stiff.

"Please transfer me to your supervisor."

"Fine." And I heard a click as the call was transferred to another line, ringing. It stopped eventually and went to voice mail.

Damn. I left a clipped and urgent message and hung up the phone.

I was staring out into the grassy courtyard in silence when the clouds rumbled loudly. I looked up and a raindrop fell on my face. And the weight of the humidity and disappointment filled my lungs.

~~STEP 21:~~

~~Betrayal Time—One of You~~ ~~Kinda-Not-Really Betrays the~~ ~~Other~~ CHAPTER 21

It's a funny feeling when your entire future is erased within seconds. It's like space—a whole lot of nothingness. After the denial and the will to fight, there's . . . nothing. Because at the end of it all is a black hole where your future used to be.

"Don't you think you're overreacting?" Fiona asked a few days later as I brooded in her car as we headed to school.

I shot her a dirty look, almost as potent as one of Fiona's own. "Overreacting? If I don't get into Stanford, I am seriously, majorly screwed. And it's all my fault."

"That there, Desi Lee, is what I would call an overreaction. Why the hell would you be screwed? You'll get into all your safety schools and you'll be a doctor no matter what."

"Because it's always been Stanford, Fi!"

Fiona pulled the car over dramatically and we screeched to a stop as she put Penny into park. She turned toward me with a very un-Fiona-like serious expression.

"Desi. That's the thing. *Why* is it so important to you that you go to Stanford? I know your mom went there, but that's just not . . ." Fiona trailed off, uncertain how to say what she wanted to say.

"What? Not important?" I demanded. "Not a good enough reason?"

Fiona shrugged, her face turning red. "Yeah. I mean, not to be a total bitch about it, but is it going to bring your mom back if you go to Stanford?"

I flinched. Fiona was right. It wouldn't bring back my mom. I leaned into my seat and stared up at the ceiling. "No, it won't. But Fi, that's not the point. I want my dad to know that I can be the best, like my mom was. Stanford is . . ."

Fiona also leaned back in her seat. "Symbolic," she finished for me.

"Yeah. Symbolic."

"Of your dad's good job raising you."

I nodded.

"Desi, everyone knows that your dad did an awesome job raising you. *He* knows that." Her voice softened.

My best friend's sympathy broke something in me and I felt tears prick my eyes. "I just—I want him to always be proud. To never worry."

She laughed kindly. "Des, parents are going to worry no matter what. You can't always protect him, no matter how perfect you try to be."

I swiped at my tears. "I know that. But I'm always convinced I can do it."

"So what was his reaction? If I know Appa, he didn't ground you for disappointing him."

I managed to laugh. "No, of course not. He was definitely bummed at first but then instantly tried to cheer me up, saying it wasn't a big deal and that I still had a good chance. Then we binge-watched an entire drama series."

Fiona pulled the car back onto the road. "See! Don't even worry. Now, with Appa covered, when are you finally going to tell Luca about this whole thing?" she asked.

Luca. I had avoided him the past few days, using a bunch of student government things as an excuse. I didn't want him to see me so bummed and I wasn't ready to tell him about Stanford yet. I knew he would feel guilty and I just didn't want to bring another slew of emotions into my life. And I didn't want him to feel guilty about my own stupid decision.

"Not sure. Soon, though."

She threw me an unconvinced look as we pulled into the school parking lot. "Soon, for sure," she said firmly. When I got to my locker, there he was. Leaning against it like some hunky 1950s boyfriend.

"Hey, stranger," he said to me with a smile.

I gave him a hug before saying apologetically, "I know, it's just been kinda nuts lately. Sorry."

He stepped back as I opened my locker, and shrugged. "No worries. Can you hang out tonight?"

My instinct was to avoid it, but I knew Fiona was right. I had to tell him soon. "Sure!" I grabbed my books and shut the locker just as the bell rang. "I have a French Club meeting at lunch and soccer after school, so we'll figure it out tonight?"

He gave me a kiss on the forehead. "You got it, missy."

But when Luca texted me that evening, I was in slug mode. My dad was out at dinner with friends, so I was home alone, lying on the sofa watching *Kill Me, Heal Me,* and had lost all motivation to do anything.

His text said: **Meet me at Boba Palace?**

I was wearing leggings, my dad's old basketball-league jersey, and my hair was a frizzy pile. Public-ready I was not. And for the first time since we started dating, I just didn't feel like putting my best foot forward. Or grinning and bearing it. Or whatever platitude fit the bill. I just wanted to wallow.

So I texted back: **Sorry Luca—not sure if I'm feeling up for seeing half of Monte Vista population tonight** ☹

You ok?

Guilt ate away at me. But I honestly felt like, for the first time in a long time . . . just not doing anything. **I'm fine, sorry. Just** feeling kinda meh. And as soon as I sent that text, I regretted it. Crap. Who wanted to date a Debbie Downer?

He texted back: Sorry ☹ Need anything?

I wouldn't be able to hide my bummerness around him if he came by, so I texted something that I *knew* would keep him away: I'm already taking a ton of Pepto, I think I have the stomach flu, probably best if you don't come over 🤢

As anticipated, there was a long pause before Luca's response: Eek, ok, feel better D. Miss you xoxo.

I was relieved but also disappointed in myself. Alas. I just wasn't ready to tell him. My dad texted shortly after to say that he would be out a bit longer with his friends, so I had a whole night of pure wallowry ahead.

In my room, I stared mournfully at my Stanford sweatshirt and T-shirt, then tossed them into a trash bag to donate to Goodwill. All my Stanford brochures went into the recycling bin.

I ate an entire jar of pickles.

In the middle of the final episode of *Kill Me, Heal Me*, the doorbell rang. I started. Who the hell was *that*? I decided to ignore it, since I looked and felt like utter crap anyway.

But it rang again, and then came a tentative knock. Ugh.

I dragged myself off the sofa and peeked through the peephole. *Ah!*

It was Luca! *Nooo.*

Why was he here? I didn't have time to change my clothes

or fix my hair, my face . . . my everything. With a giant sigh, I opened the door.

Luca held up a bunch of bananas and a giant carton of yogurt. "Luca's stomach flu remedy to the rescue!"

Despite my annoyance, I couldn't help laughing. "Bananas and yogurt?"

He raised his eyebrows. "Bananas stop *you-know-what*. And according to a few disgusting Google searches, I found out yogurt helps repopulate gut bacteria."

Gut bacteria.

And just like that, it hit me: I could be myself with Luca.

Luca, who could sense I was feeling shitty and needed to be with someone. Luca, who came over when I was sick. Luca, who hated being around sick people. Luca, who cared about *me*.

Weeks and months of anxieties melted off, layer by layer.

He truly liked me. It *really* was done.

Carrying this revelation like a fluttering key in my chest, I practically floated on air as I followed him into the kitchen. I watched as he scooped out the yogurt into a bowl and cut the bananas into slices. He refused to let me help, making me sit on the counter instead. "Do you have any honey?" he asked while sliding the bananas into the bowl of yogurt.

I tried to appear normal and not like a person who had just had an emotional breakthrough of epic proportions. "Yup." I made a move to grab it from the cupboard, but Luca held up his hand. "Nuh-uh. The patient must rest. Just tell me."

Staying perfectly, comically still, I said through barely moving lips, "That upper cupboard to your right."

He grabbed the plastic honey-bear bottle and squeezed a healthy dollop into the bowl. I widened my eyes. "Whoa, mama, that's a lot of honey, Dr. Drakos."

"Sweets for my sweet," he said in a high-pitched trill. I laughed and took the bowl when he handed it to me with a flourish. He sat on the opposite counter. I lifted a spoonful of the yogurt up toward him. "Don't you want to sit next to me and share?" I teased.

He squirmed. "Um, I know you're my girlfriend but I don't know how romantic it'll be spending the night in the bathroom side by side."

I shook my head. "Who knew I would end up dating such a germophobe?" His response was to lean back, the picture of comfort, and grin his cocky little grin. As was always the case, I couldn't help but crack a grin, too—my body's response whenever he looked at me like that. After this snack, I would tell him about Stanford. Again, relief washed over me, and I felt lighter and lighter as every minute passed.

After finishing the yogurt (I held back from telling him that most yogurt didn't have enough units of bacteria to actually help repopulate microbes), I slid off the counter and started doing the dishes. Luca scrambled over and took the detachable

276

faucet from me. "No! I'm here to tend to your every need, missy."

This was getting ridiculous. I wasn't even sick! "Luca, let me do this, you've been very sweet and all, the *perfect* boyfriend, really."

He cracked up. "Ooh, perfect boyfriend."

I wrestled the faucet from him. "Yes, a prestigious title! Now let me just—" Suddenly, the faucet flipped over in my hands and sprayed water all over Luca. I dropped it and covered my mouth with my hands, stifling my squeal of laughter.

He looked up slowly, staring at me through dripping-wet locks of hair. "You're so dead." He grabbed the faucet, flipped the lever to full blast and sprayed me. I shrieked and bolted to the other side of the kitchen. "I'm *sick!*"

A moment of hesitation before a stream of water hit me in the butt.

"Oh my *God!*" I yelled before running toward him to exact revenge. He dropped the faucet in the sink and ran out of the kitchen, laughing his ass off.

"Even sick I'm faster than you!" I shouted, following him up the stairs.

He fled into my room and slammed the door shut. I jiggled the knob but he had locked me out. "Luca!"

He shouted at me from the other side of the door, "You're not allowed to come in here until you call truce!"

"*Truce*?! I sprayed you once by accident and you sprayed me, like, three times! If you played any sports you'd know how unsportsmanlike that is!"

Silence. I banged on the door. "What are you doing in there?"

I heard the distinct sound of a body plopping down onto my bed. "Just making myself comfy," he called out.

My bed was unmade and all my linens probably needed a good wash. *Lord.* "Luca! Come on, let me in."

"In due time, girlfriend," he said. Then I heard him walking around the room. "First, I'm going to look through your underwear. I've been curious ever since that first day you dropped your pants in front of me."

"What! That was an accident!"

"Suuure." I heard some shuffling noises—as if he was looking through papers or books. Eep, I hoped he hadn't discovered my tree scrapbook. I'd never hear the end of it.

"If you're looking through my tree scrapbook, I hope you're being careful not to let the pressed leaves fall out!" I waited for a smart-ass response, but heard nothing. "Luca?" Instead I heard more paper shuffling noises.

"What's a K drama?"

What? Then every part of my body froze over—every hair, every organ, every inch of skin. I jiggled the doorknob again. "Luca, let me in!"

"Wait, are they those Korean soap operas your dad watches all the time? You've been studying those, too? Des, your nerdiness knows no bounds."

No no NO. I kept jiggling the knob, as if I could actually get the door open. "I'm serious, Luca, please let me in. Stop reading that, it's private!"

He didn't respond. And with each passing second of silence, I felt myself dying. And then suddenly the door whooshed open, and I stumbled forward.

When I looked up, Luca was holding the K drama steps in his hands, staring at me with an expression that made my breath catch in my throat.

I reached for the notebook, but he swiftly moved it out of my reach—instead holding it up to his face to read out loud from it. "Take Wes to Gwen Parker's party and make Won Bin jealous . . ." He was reading my notes scribbled for step 8: *Be Caught in an Obviously Lopsided Love Triangle.* His voice shook as he continued reading. "Ask Won Bin to take me home, cause minor car accident."

"Luca . . ."

He stood there staring at the notes for what seemed like forever, in silence. "Let me guess, I'm Won Bin."

I gulped for air. "No! I mean, yes, but—"

He started to pace the room but continued to read, throwing tiny little daggers into my heart with every word. "Prove that you are different from all other women—in the entire world. Side note: You are the only person that can prove his jaded conceptions of relationships and love are all wrong—that you, of pure heart and soul, are the exception to the rule that all women are hateful, untrustworthy creatures." A derisive snort, then he kept pacing, reading and muttering. When he finished, he looked up at me again. "Who *are* you?"

"Luca, please stop reading that. It's stupid, it doesn't matter anymore . . ."

He stopped in his tracks and shook the notes violently. "Oh, no, it matters. It matters a lot. You planned all of this." His voice shook. His posture was slumped, all traces of his usual cockiness gone, and the sight of him so defeated, so undone, crippled me with guilt.

I shook my head. "No, wait. You don't understand. It was because I liked you . . ."

And then, everything changed. He went from pacing and agitated to completely still. "So you followed these steps to get a boyfriend? This is a real thing you did?"

I kept shaking my head, unable to do anything else with my body. "No, no. Not a boyfriend. *You.* Luca, it was for you."

The harsh, mocking sound he made was like a slap to my face. It wasn't his honky laugh, the one he did with his entire body, the one he did when I copyedited menus at the local sushi place or when I made him change parking spaces because we were one inch into the red curb. No, this was a different laugh.

"This was for me? Wow, this all sounds so fucking familiar."

Emily. Oh, God, he was comparing me to Emily. "No! No, Luca, please, listen to me. I know this seems crazy!"

Luca pointed at me. "*Seems* crazy? It *is* crazy, Desi. This is *beyond*. I knew you had it in you to go overboard, but I always thought it was harmless. Endearing, even. Not manipulative, like some scheming . . . like Emily." His eyes blazed, the recognition clicking.

"You're just like her."

My chest hurt, my face hurt. It all hurt.

He straightened, controlling himself with a tight precision that panicked me more than him yelling or screaming. And when he spoke, his voice was calm again, measured. "Except, actually, you aren't just like her, are you? You're worse." My eyes filled up with tears and I choked back a sob.

He watched me cry with that familiar impassive expression I'd seen on him when he spoke to his dad. Then he slowly turned to the shelf in my room. "You know why you're worse? Because with you, I was just another trophy on that shelf, another accomplishment to check off your list. *None* of this was real."

I tried to choke out words between sobs. "No, Luca. What I felt for you, what I still feel for you, is real. Please, believe me!"

"You're a liar. Everyone around me is a liar. My dad, the cheater. My ex-girlfriend, the manipulator. And you . . . you're the same." He dropped the notebook on the floor.

And that was my moment, the moment I needed to explain everything.

Except I couldn't. I was paralyzed in my own waking nightmare. Everything—Luca, Stanford—was vanishing before my very eyes.

I walked over to him and grasped his sleeve. "Luca, please—"

He shoved me away. *Shoved.* "No."

Then he walked out the door. Down the stairs. And out of my house.

And I just stood there. Heart broken in half, the pieces laid at my feet.

~~STEP 22:~~
~~At Your Lowest Point, Your Life Is~~
~~Only Made Up of Flashback Montages~~
~~of Good Times~~ CHAPTER 22

So I suppose the next month of my life was the blank pages of breakupdom in *The Desi Lee Story*. And unlike Bella Swan, I couldn't just sit in a chair for months and stare out my window, unfortunately. I still had to go to school, go through the motions. And while I wore a convincing Normal Desi mask for my dad, I immediately took it off when I got to school.

The last few days of February crawled by. Those days were spent alternately crying or being delusionally hopeful that Luca would forgive me. Then March inched its way toward April and I went from sad to angry. I hated everyone. I refused to watch K dramas and the excited end-of-school-year buzz just deflected off my dark-energy force field. A period where Wes referred to me as Des Vader. But then the anger eventually cooled to a numbness—giving me a nihilistic outlook that made me *real* fun to hang out with.

It was while in one of these delightful moods, in April, that I found myself walking out into the courtyard for lunch. The sun was too bright, the air too cold. I yanked my sunglasses on and threw my sweatshirt hood over my head.

I spotted Wes and Fiona at our usual table but veered away from them, heading for the pizza stand. They saw me, though, and their concerned faces made me want to scream. For the first couple of weeks, they had insisted that it would blow over, that Luca would forgive me. And if he didn't, Fiona said she would happily castrate him. But now even they could tell the breakup was a done deal.

It was shockingly easy to avoid Luca. We never saw each other. Once I dropped out of Art Club (the first time in my life I'd ever dropped out of *anything*), I never had any reasons to bump into him. As far as I knew, he had died. Just kidding. (But it felt that way.)

Three giant greasy slices of pizza teetered in a pile on my plate, which I topped off with some peanut-butter cookies. You know how some people lose their appetites when they go through a breakup? WELL, NOT I! I craved calories right now—the crappier the better. More grease and butter, please. And heaps of sugar to boot.

When I finally got to our lunch table, I noticed that Violet and Leslie were there, too. Wes and Violet had started dating officially, something I had managed to notice even while living in my own personal production of *Les Misérables*. And it was no surprise that Leslie and Fi had gotten back together as well. Happy couples all around. Yippee.

Everyone said hello but I could *feel* the concern vibes and I was so over it right now. I grunted my greeting and sat down with my heart-attack food.

Wes broke the awkward silence. "So should we end senior year in a blaze of glory and rent a Hummer limo for prom?"

"Are you serious?" Fiona asked with her lip curled. "I'd rather eat a dick."

Violet started choking on her food while laughing.

Prom. Ugh. In my misery I had totally forgotten about it. We had made plans a while back to go as a group—which included Luca, of course. The thought of going now made me feel sick.

"Um, yeah, count me out," I muttered as I bit into my pizza slice.

"Come on, Des, you have to go!" Wes whined as Violet took a surreptitious peek at my plate of food. It probably contained all the calories she usually ate in a month.

Fiona pulled a leg up to her chest and rested her chin on her knee. "Normally I'd be all for rebellious Desi, but it would be weird to not have you there, Des. You're the face of our senior class. It wouldn't be right."

I didn't answer, just kept my eyes on my food. Wes tossed a football up into the air, then caught it. And threw it up to catch it again. My eye twitched.

285

"No, you guys go and have fun," I said, trying to smile.

"It'll be your loss," Wes said, tossing the football again. But he fumbled catching it and it landed on my plate of food, knocking a few cookies off the table and a slice of pizza onto the grass. Everyone was instantly silent.

Wes scrambled to pick up my food. "Sorry, Des," he said quickly, awkwardly placing the grass-covered slice back onto my plate.

My instinct was to be nice, to not let my annoyance show, but I immediately thought of K drama heroines and how they only existed under a rainy cloud of misery when going through heartbreak. Specifically, any of the leads in the Four Seasons dramas when one of them was dying (they are all dying at some point).

So I just smiled blandly at Wes. "Whatever."

I felt everyone exchanging uneasy glances. I took off my sunglasses and looked around. "Okay, I love you guys but I can't handle the pity faces right now." I stood up, tossed my plate into the trash, and stalked away.

I heard Fiona cry out, "Des!" But I just kept walking.

When I got home that day, I headed straight for my room. I threw my backpack onto the floor and flopped into bed. The force of that made something clatter on my desk and I looked up to see my family photo lying facedown on my desk. How appropriate. The photo had landed right on top of the draft of my valedictorian speech. It had been sitting there gathering dust since the Luca/Stanford implosion.

Stanford. I would be hearing from them in a couple of weeks. I was nervous, yes, but something interesting had happened in the past month: I cared, but just not that much. I'm sure some of it was owed to my current numb state—but it also felt like *one* piece of my life. Part of a bigger picture. And I had gotten into Boston University and Cornell already, both of which had higher ranked premed programs than Stanford, might I add. It felt scary and unfamiliar, this not caring. But in a way it was also liberating.

I looked over at the draft of my speech and felt guilty for about 0.5 seconds before closing my eyes for a nap.

Before I could settle into the covers, my door flew open and my dad stomped in.

"Appa!" I snapped. "What the heck, don't you knock anymore?"

"Appa never knocked!" True.

He came over and took me by the arm, dragging me out of bed. I struggled and swatted at him. "What are you doing?" I yelped.

"Appa sick and tired of you *doing* nothing. Get up and help me outside."

I groaned. "I don't *want* to."

He stopped and stared at me. "You what?"

My body straightened immediately. I knew I could only push my dad so far. "Never mind," I muttered, following him outside. The garage door was open and there was a car sitting in it, lifted on some jacks. And not just some car, Luca's car. What the hell. I glared at my dad. He shrugged. "I have to fix it still and thought I would do it at home."

He got onto the creeper, the flat rolly thing that goes under cars, and wheeled himself beneath the Civic. "Okay, you get on the other one, put on headlamp, and keep the tool kit near you." I sighed heavily and dragged the giant tool kit over to the car and then lay down on the other creeper, pushing my bare feet against the garage floor to get under the car.

I turned my headlamp on to look at the underbelly of the Honda. My dad pointed and explained the situation. "The oil and fuel filters and spark plugs are old and are totally no good. They need to be replaced or it will never pass smog test. You're going to help me swap out the filters, okay?"

I knew what that entailed and started to disassemble the heat shield with a socket wrench. While I did that, my dad watched with an eagle eye. After a few seconds he asked, "So, Appa always curious, how do spark plugs actually work? They're just made of metals!"

I worked at the filter, squinting to make sure I wasn't going to make anything explode somehow. "Well, I think because there's electricity that makes a spark at the tip of the plug, which ignites the gasoline, causing combustion."

My dad made a thoughtful noise. "Ohhh, okay. That makes sense." That was his polite response whenever he didn't really know what the eff I was going on about. "Hand me the bigger socket wrench now." I rolled out from under the car and dug around the tool kit until I found it. I handed it to him, sitting up and letting my dad take over.

"So what are you going to do about Luca?"

I started. "What do you mean? We broke up." While I had tried to keep my sadness to a minimum around my dad, I had told him about our breakup because there would be no other explanation as to why Luca was never around anymore.

My dad grunted. "When did you become quitter?"

"Sometimes you just have to accept the shit that life hands you," I said. The self-pitying words were out of my mouth before I realized whom I was speaking to.

"Yes, I know. I know very well, okay?" He rolled out from under the car, wiping his hands on a cloth he kept on his creeper.

"I know you know," I said in a small voice.

My dad sat up and took a swig from his water bottle, then looked at me. "Will you finally tell me what happened?"

I had avoided going into it with my dad. I was so embarrassed by the entire ordeal. But I was ready now. And I told him everything.

Afterward he was quiet for a second. "So . . . that is why you watch dramas so much lately."

I managed to laugh, the first time in weeks. "Yeah, but also I like them now."

"You know, Luca must think you're very crazy."

"Yes, I know."

"Because this is very crazy thing, kind of."

Kind of very crazy. Summed up perfectly by my dad, as per usual. "Yep."

"Why did you do this, then? Why couldn't you just get him to like you normal way?"

We sat side by side on our creepers in silence for a minute, my dad ever so patient as I tried to piece together what to tell him—the patchwork of flailures and insecurities brought on by not feeling control over this one thing in my life.

But despite everything, even after a lifetime of trusting my dad with all the minutiae of my life, I couldn't tell him. I couldn't tell him that despite all his hard work and love and care, I was terribly insecure about this.

"You know me, have to follow the steps to feel comfortable, Appa."

"Ha, just like your mom."

Yeah. Uh-huh. I'm sure my mom never needed a list.

My dad cleared his throat. "You know what? If not for Appa, you would not be born."

I cringed. Shades of our sex talk from years ago . . .

"Because your mom, she was *worst* at quitting on us. I had to fight many times to keep her from throwing in the blanket."

"Throwing in the towel."

"Yeah, what I said. Anyway, she so many times almost gave up. In high school, when her parents hated me, she said we had to stop loving each other." I smiled at my dad's choice of words. "When she knew she had to move here, she was ready to say bye-bye. I had to prove it would work, I moved here and I knew *no* English and we were very poor. So many times your mom cry and say this was bad idea. But I never give up."

He scooted over to me and put his hands on either side of my face, gently. "You cannot control who you love, Desi, but you can always control how hard you fight, okay?" His eyes crinkled with his grin. "Yes, you did a bad thing, but not *so* bad that you cannot explain it and have him forgive you."

I rubbed my eyes with my sweatshirt sleeves. "Appa, trust me. I have some pride, you know? He won't even answer my texts— there's no *way* to even explain it!"

"Then you need to find a way to be heard."

Those words reverberated in my brain hours later as I lay sprawled on my bed, trying to slog through *A Man for All Seasons*.

How could I make myself heard?

I was tossing the book aside on a pile of stuff by my bed when the K drama notebook caught my eye. Ugh, why hadn't I destroyed that thing already? I picked it up with the intention of burning it in a ritualistic fashion. Then I remembered one of the steps. I flipped to the list and skimmed it until I stopped at number 23.

23. Take Drastic Measures for Your Happy Ending
Something epically dramatic now has to occur in order to throw you two back together, so that while you are both trying to move on, you realize that you must be together against all odds. You are MEANT TO BE. Prove it. Again, life-threatening is always best. Perhaps an avalanche escape.

Drastic measures.

I thought of holding his hand for the first time and running down the road in a red lace dress. Of Luca putting his beanie on me. Of his arm slamming across me during the car accident. Of his warm hand when it held my neck during our first kiss. His hunched back as he stared into the ocean, feeling sad for me.

I was *literally* having a K drama romance-montage moment.

Then I felt a familiar frenzy take hold of me—the determination that helped me push through all things in life, the thing that never let me take no for an answer. The thing that convinced me as a kid that I had moved a pencil with my mind.

And it was all further impacted by Luca. Luca's hands, his smile when he glanced at me sideways, the way he tugged on his beanie. The way he always came through when I needed him.

I couldn't predict my future with Stanford, but I *could* do something about Luca. All was not lost. Yet. The K drama steps had won me Luca once; I had to try one last time.

I dug my English notebook out from the pile. My fingers grazed over the doodle from the first day we met. Me in that black dress. I picked up my phone and texted Luca's stepmom: **Hi Lillian, do you think I could get a prom dress made in two weeks?**

Instantly: **Hells yes, honey.**

~~CHAPTER~~ STEP 23:
Take Drastic Measures for Your Happy Ending

"If he doesn't go for it, you always have Max the freshman as backup boyfriend," Wes offered helpfully from the other side of Violet. I groaned and leaned back into the leather upholstery of the limo.

Fiona slid away from her date, Leslie, and hobbled across the limo in her heels to crouch down in front of me. "Hey, just be honest, okay? He's going to forgive you." I clutched her hands and stared at them nervously. Her nails spelled out FIONA and LESLI in hot pink.

"Ugh, everyone's in love." I groaned. Fiona shrugged.

"Ew, who said anything about love?" Violet said while edging away from Wes. He grabbed her lightning quick and pulled her into his lap. She slapped him away, but she wasn't kidding anyone.

"Violet, are you *sure* Luca will be there?" I asked for the billionth time.

She rolled her eyes. "How many times are you going to ask me this, Hye-Jin. Cassidy promised." We had convinced Cassidy to ask Luca to prom, even though she felt nervous about the whole thing. While the thought of Luca coming to prom with someone else made me want to jab out my eyeballs, I trusted Cassidy and was grateful for help. Although I couldn't help but suspect that she probably enjoyed it *a little bit.*

We finally pulled up to the hotel where prom was being held—a castle-like building on top of a hill overlooking the ocean, all lit up with fairy lights. Everyone piled out of the limo and I could hear the music before we even stepped onto the property. The dance was on the terraced grounds, a beautifully manicured area complete with gazebos and a giant swimming pool.

We were about to enter the lobby when I stopped. "Wait!" I called out, panicked. Everyone turned around and stared at me.

"How . . . how do I look?" The desperation in my voice was not becoming.

There was a second of everyone assessing me and I felt my stomach drop. Then:

"Hot." Wes.

"Pretty good, for you." Violet.

"Worthy of love." Fiona.

I laughed and covered my face to hide the creeping blush. When I glanced at my reflection in the lobby mirror, I hoped they weren't just being nice.

The dress had come out perfectly. Lillian came through like a millennial fairy godmother—using her fashion networking, she had my dress made in record time. And it fit me like a glove: made up of black lace, it was strapless, and short in the front, then the back was a long bustled skirt covered with black feathers. My hair was insanely blown out like a supermodel's (Fiona had to get a massage after finishing the task, my thick hair was no joke) and was swept to one side, exposing an ear studded with shoulder-length silver earrings (some clip-on, I wasn't willing to get extra piercings, even for Luca). The final touches? Black lace gloves and a killer pair of strappy black heels.

I was Luca's drawing come to life.

And in real life, it was kind of a bonkers outfit.

But I hoped, prayed, that he would recognize it. That was step 1. That he would recognize it and soften, giving me a chance to talk to him. To show him with *action* how much he meant to me. And then if that didn't work . . . well, we would see.

Leslie got swept up in a group of cheerleaders and Fiona made a face and grabbed my elbow. "Let's eat, I'm starving," she said, leading me to the buffet table.

I scanned the landscape for Luca, but no sign. Fi squeezed my arm. "He'll be here."

I relaxed and looked at her, fully registering how beautiful my best friend was that night. Her hair was dyed in a rainbow ombre, her natural black roots turning into shades of indigo, dark blue, turquoise, then sea-foam green at the tips. It fell into waves around her face and down her back. The hair matched her dress—an off-the-shoulder ice-blue concoction that hugged every curve of her bangin' bod. She looked like a badass mermaid.

"Have I told you lately that I love you?" I said, hugging her.

She scowled but hugged me back. "Okay, let's not get carried away."

"*Selfie!*" Wes exclaimed, jumping in with Violet and taking a photo of us with his phone. I made a peace sign with my fingers.

The night started pleasantly—it was great to see everyone so happy and excited. I couldn't believe that this group of people, many of whom I had known for thirteen years of my life, was soon going to scatter. All of us going on our separate journeys. And wherever mine would lead, Stanford or not, I knew that I could be happy there. That is, once I tied up some Luca loose ends.

Everyone was in a mushy, nostalgic mood. People came up to me and made poignant comments and while it was a little overwhelming, I was undeniably touched. Even Helen Carter, the captain of the soccer team and a girl whom I had always referred to as She of One Facial Expression, had started tearing up as we danced to Rihanna.

It was such a nice evening that I almost forgot about Luca. Almost.

Then I spotted him across the dance floor, laughing at something some Art Club guy was saying. I stopped in my tracks. Cassidy was standing next to him and when she spotted me her eyes widened. She mouthed, *Wow*, and looked me up and down. I smiled and made a thumbs-up sign at her.

And then . . . Luca turned his head slightly and our eyes met. In a slim navy suit and crisp white shirt without a tie, he looked so devastating that I almost ran over to him. Standing here, not moving, felt like the most unnatural thing to do.

But I was frozen, because I was watching his face register me. His eyes swept over me—from my feet to the top of my head. His lips pressed together and his eyes filled with a flash of emotion before going blank. I held my breath, waiting.

And then he turned around and walked away.

My legs almost collapsed beneath me. Cassidy threw me a helpless look before running after him. Wes immediately crossed the dance floor and came over to me. "Are you okay?"

I shook my head. "No."

"Stubborn-ass John Stamos," he muttered.

Fiona was right behind him and looked determined. "Don't worry, Des. Just give him some time. He's got to register the dress, your general hotness in that dress, and then—"

"It's okay, you guys." I took a deep breath. "I've got a backup plan."

They exchanged glances. "What do you mean?" Fiona asked, her voice a little strained.

298

What I meant was that I was going to switch up my sassy K drama heroine into a whole other variety. The helpless damsel-in-distress kind. In the footsteps of that most famous of fakers, Jan-Di from *Boys Over Flowers*, with her last desperate move at the party in the very last episode.

"You'll see." I scanned the dance until I spotted him sitting at a table with Cassidy. She was gesturing with her arms wildly while talking to him and he looked *pissed*.

Luca wasn't that far. In the physical sense, at least. I walked over to the deep end of the pool and stared into the water. This was it. I teetered on my heels and let out a little scream.

A little slip, a clumsy plunge, a giant splash—seemed fairly basic.

The lacy folds of my black dress floated around me in the water and I caught a glimpse of my sushi-printed underwear. Damn, didn't think about that when I was getting ready. Oh well, can't be sexy all the time.

I waited a bit, even doing a backflip in the water before I started swimming up to the surface. As I rose higher in the water, my movements grew more erratic; I kicked my legs spastically and waved my arms around, creating a riot of churning waves above me.

Once I broke through the surface, strains of dance music floated through the night air, mixed with the sound of people laughing. When I opened my eyes, water dripping into them, I saw a few people pointing at me—but did *he* see me? I looked over at the table, and there he was, looking in my direction, but I don't think he even knew what he was looking at yet.

It was now or never. Like never-ever never. I threw my arms up in the air and screamed, *"Help!"* There was a beat of silence. If silence could sound dubious, it was the most dubious silence ever to have passed in the world. I let my head dip under the water for a second and took a chlorinated gulp before bobbing up again, spitting the water out to yell a choking, *"Help!* Please!" And as I floundered in the water, I spotted him.

He was pushing through the crowd. Running.

I dipped my head down under the surface to hide my smile, waiting for him to heroically jump into the water. But instead of doing that, he ran toward the wall alongside the pool and grabbed a long-handled leaf skimmer off its peg.

What in the world?

With the skimmer in hand, Luca ran over to the edge of the pool, knelt down, and stuck the skimmer toward me. "Grab it!" he shouted, the end with the net now a few feet away from me.

For crying out loud.

I splashed a bit more, halfheartedly this time, and reached for the net. When I grabbed it, I decided to add a bit of flopping-around flair—tossing my body backward so that my head went underwater again. But in doing that, I pulled extra-hard on the skimmer, and heard a loud splash.

Uh-oh.

I opened my eyes underwater and saw Luca's body sinking.

Well, okay, not exactly what I pictured but great, now he could actually pull me out.

Then I noticed something. Something off, something wrong.

Damn. It. All. To. *HELL*.

Luca couldn't swim.

STEP 24:
Get Your Happy Ending

How the hell did Luca not know how to swim? His dad owned a boat, for God's sake!

He was rapidly sinking to the bottom of the pool and I swam over to him, my arms slicing expertly through the water, my legs perfectly straight despite the weight of my dress tangled up in them.

I reached his thrashing body but when I tried holding him, he pulled us both down. His eyes were wide and I could tell that in his panicked state he was swallowing massive amounts of water.

Shit, shit, *shit*. I needed air, so I swam up to the surface and took a deep breath. For a brief second I could hear people screaming and a couple of people—one of them Wes, I think— jumping into the water. I had ducked down again and grabbed Luca's arms when I realized with alarm that he wasn't moving anymore. His eyes were closed. *No.*

Without his thrashing I was able to drag his body to the shallow end, where we both surfaced. People surrounded us immediately, and hands reached out and pulled Luca out of the water, from my arms. Wes and Fiona splashed to my side.

"Are you okay?" Fiona sputtered with water dripping down her face.

"I'm fine! I need to help Luca!" My dress was like an iron suit dragging me down as I struggled to get out of the pool. Wes and Fiona gave me a giant push so that I whooshed out, dress clinging to me. Violet and Cassidy were waiting on the edge to pull me out.

"He's over there!" Violet pointed to the grassy lawn by the side of the pool. A few people were hovering over Luca's body. I pushed them aside and dropped to my knees beside him.

"Luca!" I cried as I felt for his pulse. I frowned when I felt its weak rhythm beneath my fingers.

Violet ran over and stood by us. "Do you know CPR?" she asked while wringing her hands.

Just since kindergarten. I placed the heel of my left hand over the center of his chest and then placed the right on top of it. Then I pushed down straight onto his chest and repeated the movement every few seconds. He still wasn't waking up, though, and I started to panic. Holy crap, I killed him. I killed my ex-boyfriend.

I was about to tilt his head back to administer mouth-to-mouth when his eyes fluttered open and he started coughing out some water.

A cheer rose in the crowd and he immediately rolled over and heaved water into the grass. The cheering faltered a little. "Ew," someone muttered.

"Are you okay?" I gently pounded his back as he spit out the rest of the water.

After he finished coughing he looked up at me. "What . . . What happened?"

"You almost drowned!" someone yelled.

He looked over at the pool and it seemed to register. Turning around swiftly, he grabbed my arms and scanned my face. "Are you okay? Did someone help get you out?"

There was an awkward silence as everyone started to understand what was going on. I nodded, tears already welling up. "I'm fine. Are you okay?"

"I'm fine . . . I thought . . ." He was still trying to understand everything.

"Desi saved *you*," someone shouted. "She's, like, a trained lifeguard."

Mother—*!* I heard Fiona groan behind me.

"What?" he looked at me, hair matted down, water dripping into his eyes. "You fell in, you were drowning."

I was quiet. His confusion was replaced by pure fury.

"Are you joking? Did you fake that?"

The hollow space where my heart used to be constricted. "I—I didn't know you couldn't swim!"

A murmur went through the crowd. Luca stood up and grabbed his hair with both hands, like a tortured Shakespearean character. *"Are you joking?"* he yelled again. "You freaking faked it!" And there it was. The Rage. In all its glory.

I sprang to my feet, too, and the emotions of the past few weeks seared through me. "Who the hell doesn't know how to swim? You're from *California!*"

"I *hate* the water!"

"Your dad has a boat—"

"Have you ever seen me near the water? Why do you think I hate the stupid Carpe Diem *so much?"*

"I thought it was just part of your Daddy issues!"

He pointed at me. "Shush! *Shush up*, you! What kind of messed-up human does this? Did you not learn *anything*? What is *wrong* with you?"

My breath caught in my throat then and I felt two bodies come defensively to my side. Luca glared at them. "You guys are enablers. What, did you help her with this?"

Wes cleared his throat. "Um, actually we had no idea she would do this. Had we known—"

Fiona interrupted him. *"Had we known*, we would have helped, you little ingrate."

And then I felt true loss. A void that even my friends couldn't fill. I spoke, defeated and weak. "Thanks, but—it's okay, you guys. It was all me—it was always all me."

Luca stilled and looked at me, eyes blazing. "Then, I *repeat*, what kind of demented manipulator does this kind of stuff? *Why?*"

"Because, you stupid idiot! Somehow I can ace a test with my eyes closed but can't speak to a guy without my pants falling off!"

Some giggling erupted around me. I glared at everyone. "Oh shut up, like you guys are all so perfect." I looked back at Luca. "Don't you see that if I didn't follow the steps, if I didn't do absurd shit like this, you wouldn't like me? I just . . . I knew if I could control *how* I got you to like me, I wouldn't mess up!"

He stared at me, his expression incredulous. "Are you serious? You think that I like you because you staged a freaking *car accident*?"

It was then that I grew keenly aware of allllllll the people surrounding us. Oh, God. Not only had I blurted out my soul to Luca, I had done it in front of the entire freaking senior class of Monte Vista High School. I burned from my ears to my toes despite being sopping wet. Suddenly my magical black dress felt like a cheap witch costume. A damp one. The insanity of this latest stunt hit me like a ton of bricks and I wanted to sizzle into a puddle and die.

And then, in the world's worst DJ timing *ever*, the music switched from dancey to a ballad. Apparently bored by Luca and me, the crowd dispersed and slowly made its way back to the dance floor. And there we were, Luca and I, staring at each other while surrounded by dancing couples and Adele crooning her ballad of lover's lament.

His eyes flashed betrayal and hurt one last time before he started running in the other direction.

"Luca!"

But he kept running until he was just a darting figure in the distance. Luca, who never ran.

I slowly sank into the grass, my dress spilling around me like black liquid. The voices of my friends buzzed around me, indecipherable.

What have I done.

I closed my eyes and started to feel the *finality* of it all. Every bone in my body was tired. I was truly ready to give up.

Then I heard the voice that had helped me my entire life. *You can always control how hard you fight.*

My eyes snapped open. I sprang up, grabbed the sodden train of my dress, and ran. Fiona and Wes started to follow me but I yelled, "I got this!" They stood behind as I ran through the immaculate rolling green lawn, the sparkling night ocean within view. I heard Wes shout, *"Hwai-ting!"*

I didn't stop running until I spotted Luca sitting on some craggy black rocks facing the ocean. Trying to catch my breath, I walked up to him slowly.

"Do you want to end up with pneumococcal pneumonia?"

He startled and turned around. "Desi?"

My heart was pounding, the sound drowning out the roar of the ocean. "You heard me, Mr. Delicate Constitution."

He stood up and ran his hand through his wet hair. "Why are you here?"

I put my hands on my hips. Wonder Woman pose. "Because I need to, once and for all, explain myself. Without an audience."

His anger was replaced by exhaustion. Luca looked so tired then. "I just don't think I can believe anything you say, Desi."

My legs shook but I kept my pose. "I know. And I get it. I'm so sorry that I almost killed you tonight. Truly. But here's the thing. I'm not here because having a boyfriend validates something for me, because it checks off another box at being perfect or something."

His expression was hard to read but I powered through. "It's because . . . I *like* you, which is just a part of my *being* now, something beyond my control. But I'm *choosing* to do it despite knowing that you might reject me, that my heart could be broken again. It's something I—I have no control over. And I'm giving it up. Willingly."

Something changed in Luca's expression then—a softness came over him almost immediately. "Why?"

I threw my hands up in the air in frustration, Wonder Woman pose thrown into the ocean. "Because I love you!"

I let the words hang between us—the thing that had driven me to insanity the past few months.

Luca stared at me, only moving to hastily wipe water off his face. Our eyes were going to be locked forever. My legs were shaking so hard I didn't know how much longer I could stand there.

And then.

He strode over, pulled me into his arms, and kissed me. Not a gentle, sweet kiss—but an urgent one. I slumped into him and kissed him back, my hands tangled in his wet hair. I kissed him with the entirety of my remorse and the promise to be better.

And when we finally tore apart, my heart returned home—beating furiously.

He cradled my face in his hands. "I love you, too."

The shitty heartbreak clouds parted and I felt warm again for the first time in weeks. "Really?"

"Why is that so hard to believe? Do you really think it was all those K drama stunts that made me like you?"

I nodded. He shook his head. "To be honest, I found all those incidents really freaking weird. Thought you were just *super-*unlucky."

My laugh mingled with sniffles. "I *was* unlucky. With guys, anyway. And then you came along and I just didn't want to be unlucky anymore." I shook my head. "And I fully know how completely bonkers it all was, and I'm really, *really* sorry. Especially about endangering your life." I paused. "Three times." He laughed, releasing that embarrassing honk I loved so much.

"But Luca, the thing is, I wanted to make it happen no matter how completely bonkers the plan. I wanted to make it happen from the moment you drew this dress."

He raised an eyebrow. "Don't even get me started on this dress."

"Lillian helped me with it, you know."

He sighed. "I'm not surprised." Then he got very serious. "It wasn't the K dramas. It was you. How can you not see that? Your hot brain. Your dedication to everything. Your hilarious snort. How you are with your dad . . . you've made me like *my* dad, somehow."

He brushed aside a strand of my hair. I was incapable of responding, every part of me warming up with every word out of his mouth. "And you're so strong, so determined not to be sad for the sake of your dad. To not hurt *him*. That's . . . beyond. That's special. You don't need Stanford, Des, they need *you*. You're a once-in-a-lifetime deal."

Every part of me from my eyelashes to my toenails tingled. And then I smiled ruefully. "I'm finding out about Stanford next week."

He shook his head. "Speaking of Stanford. Why didn't you tell me you missed your interview? Why didn't you tell me *that day*?"

I startled. "What? Who told you?"

"Your dad. I went to pick up my car this morning."

What the heck! My dad hadn't said a *thing*. But knowing his mushy romantic heart, I wasn't surprised. I looked down. "I didn't want to put that on you. It was my decision."

"I never would have let you do it."

"I know. But *I* wanted to."

The admiration on his face melted away whatever insecurity was left in me, and I felt purified. Reborn. He pulled me into a hug so hard that I lost my own breath. "Let's get out of here," he whispered.

I smiled into his neck. "Okay."

He clutched my hand tightly as we started walking back toward the hotel. But then I stopped and he turned around.

"Luca. I can't face them right now."

He nodded. "Okay, I'll go and bring my car around?"

I nodded and we held hands until the very last second, loath to untangle our fingertips. I watched him walk back toward the hotel and sighed, touching my hand to my chest. That's when I felt something clinging to my strapless bra.

Oh, *right*. I pulled out the K drama list, sopping wet at this point. Pulpy and dripping ink.

I wanted to shred the thing to bits, to shove it in my mouth and eat it if possible. But the more I stared at the list with all its ridiculous rules and steps, the more I began to register why I loved those dramas. Not because they were helpful, or because they were a useful tool for my own purposes.

It was because they were unapologetic love stories.

Yes, all the antics were fun, the clichés exhausting, and the drama *dramatic*. But in the end, they were about people sticking together through thick and thin, not knowing if it would work out. Real love: It was all about risk and having faith. There were no guarantees.

Luca's car pulled up alongside me and my heart warmed at the sight of that Honda Civic, lovingly restored and given a second chance by my dad. I crumpled the list into a ball and shoved it back into my dress.

Then I hopped into the car and looked at this boyfriend of mine. "So where are we going?"

Luca shrugged. "I don't know."

And for the first time in my entire life, I was okay with that.

EPILOGUE

"Move your big head."

"Pardon me?"

A pickle crunched in my dad's mouth before he responded. "You heard me. I can't see TV."

"*I* have a big head?!" I screeched, turning around to glare at my dad from my position on the floor. "I have a perfectly normal-size head, because I got Mom's, not *yours.*" Even so, I readjusted the pillow propping me up against the coffee table, tucking my chin into my chest as I slid down a little lower.

"Luca, tell her. You know the truth." My dad stretched a leg out from his position on his recliner behind us and poked Luca in the back with his white-sock-covered foot.

Next to me, Luca's shoulders started to shake with silent laughter and I squinted up at him. "Don't answer that," I warned.

"Don't let her be bossy!" my dad said.

"Don't be bossy about me being bossy!" I yelled back.

Luca reached over and gave me a K drama finger-flick to my forehead. "Don't yell at your dad."

I clutched my forehead while my dad laughed uproariously in the background. A little yap accompanied his laughing. I turned around and pointed at the brown furball sitting on my dad's lap. "You stay out of this, Popcorn!" My dad's puppy yawned in response, rolling onto her back so that my dad could rub her belly.

"Now can you both stop being annoying so we can finally watch this episode?" I barked as I hit Play on the remote and the credits to *Descendants of the Sun* started.

Luca pulled in closer to me and I nestled into his shoulder. I felt a poke in my back. "Appa!"

The foot poked me this time. "*Ya.* What are you doing in front of your dad?"

Luca instantly released me and scooted away. But under the blanket we were sharing he reached for my hand and we laced our fingers together in the space between us.

He whispered, "Do you think Captain Yoo is going to finally profess his feelings in this episode? Or will another natural disaster interrupt them again? I swear to God I'll murder someone if they don't kiss in this episode."

I shook my head ruefully. "You think he's going to confess already? In your dreams, buddy. We haven't been tortured enough yet."

Luca pulled his beanie over his eyes and dropped his head back. "My *God*. If I have to watch them save another orphan's life instead—"

"Be quiet!" my dad hollered.

"It's just the credits!" I snapped.

My dad bit into another pickle. "So what! Also, no talking back now, Desi. Stanford rejection punishment."

Oof. The rejection letter had come two days after prom and while it was a huge blow, I had been somewhat prepared for it. And now, three months after graduation, it was a fading sting.

When I had stood at the podium at graduation, about to start my valedictorian speech, I looked out into the crowd of tasseled caps and cheap polyester gowns, the sun blinding me. The ocean breeze had whipped through the stage at that moment and I'd lifted my hand to hold on to my cap.

"Unexpected things happen," I said into the microphone. "But it's how we react to them, how we learn and evolve from these things that shapes us into who we are."

Once the rest of my speech was done, caps were thrown, cheers shouted, and I faced my graduating class with a huge grin on my face, knowing my Stanford rejection letter was sitting on my desk, framed to remind me of that message every day. It was what I thought of as I held back tears helping Wes store all his comics in boxes before he left for New Jersey. What I thought of when I ran alongside Penny as Fiona drove off to

Berkeley, boxes filling up every inch of the car. It's what I would think about the first few days settling into my dorm at Boston University.

And it's what I thought of as I spent the last few days of summer with Luca and my dad. The crushing sadness that came over me whenever I thought of leaving my dad was tempered by knowing that I was going to be an hour's train ride away from Luca. (I had created a schedule for the entire school year so that we would see each other at least twice a month.) As for leaving my dad alone—well, Popcorn and her refusal to get potty trained were going to keep him pretty busy. That and the online dating profile I had set up for him (shudder).

The drama started, with boyish Captain Yoo and doll-like beauty Doctor Kang getting drunk together in a kitchen, alone. A love ballad is in full swing; the two are staring at each other, moving closer, inch by inch. They kiss! Then . . . she runs off.

Luca kicked the blanket off us and yelped, "Are you *kidding* me right now?"

My dad and I cackled. We loved torturing Luca with K dramas; this was the third one he was watching with us this summer.

"Don't worry, one of them will get seriously hurt soon, *then* they'll have to admit they like each other. I hope it's another land mine!" I said gleefully.

"I love how there are land mines just hiding in every corner of this army base. So random. Also, I didn't know they needed

South Korean military presence in the Mediterranean," Luca scoffed.

I pushed a lock of hair out of his eyes and adjusted his beanie. "Once you start going down Disbelief Road, you're lost forever, boyfriend," I said. "Just sit back and believe, it's so much more fun that way."

THE ULTIMATE K DRAMA
STARTER GUIDE

Brought to you by Desi and Dramabeans!

For all the newbies who have no idea where to start, fear no more! There's a K drama out there for everyone. The one stipulation for this particular guide is that you must like romance.

Let's begin! First things first: Do you want to watch a **romance romance** or a **rom-com**?

ROMANCE ROMANCE

Okay, **historical** or **contemporary** setting?

Historical!

Check out *Princess's Man*. **Is there historical stuff with *gender***

bending, perhaps? Of course—*Sungkyunkwan Scandal* is what you seek.

How about historical with *fantasy* elements? See *The Moon That Embraces the Sun*. **Specifically *time travel*?** You're looking for *Faith*.

Contemporary!

Oh man, where to begin . . .

How about something with *action*? So many goodies—if you like your heroes undercover, watch *City Hunter* or *Healer*. **Action but with *guns and tanks*?** Get yourself some *Descendants of the Sun*. **But I also want some *alternate-reality* stuff.** That means you want *The King 2 Hearts*.

Let's go back to *high school*. OMG, why, but if you must, then see *Heirs*. **What about *college*?** Check out a classic, *Feeling*.

Something more grown-up—how about an *epic political saga*? There is truly only one, the great *Sandglass*.

What about a *Cinderella* tale? The ultimate classic is *Star in My Heart*.

Friends-to-lovers? Get thee to *Propose* and *The Producers*.

Um, *body swap*? Yup, there's *Secret Garden*.

What about the most romantic of all—*melodramatic terminal-illness* stuff? Look no further than the weepy Four Seasons series: *Autumn in My Heart, Winter Sonata, Summer Scent,* and *Spring Waltz.*

ROM-COM TIME!

Straight up, try *I Need Romance.* **Cool, but I love *K-pop*, too.** Then check out *You're Beautiful* and *Dream High (#1).* **Speaking of *high school* . . .** The most outrageous is *Boys Over Flowers,* but on the other end of the spectrum is the ***slice of life*** *Answer Me, 1997* and its follow-ups *Answer Me, 1994* and *Answer Me, 1988.*

Let's dig into *fantasy*. *So* thrilled to share *I Hear Your Voice, My Girlfriend Is a Gumiho,* and *My Love from Another Star.* **Do any of them have *body possession*?** Of course, *Oh My Ghostess.*

What about something less extreme, like *gender bending*? Prepare to be obsessed with *Coffee Prince (#1).*

Is there such a thing as *trendy* rom-com? In K dramas, yes. And the original is *Jealousy*.

I bet you can't find one about *multiple personalities*! Ha-ha, ye of little faith. Check out *Kill Me, Heal Me*.

What about that old chestnut, *relationship contracts*? It takes fresh new life in *Full House* and *My Name Is Sam-Soon*.

Now, go forth and drama! And if this wasn't enough info for you, be sure to check out dramabeans.com. ☺

xo

Desi, javabeans, and girlfriday

ACKNOWLEDGMENTS

This book's journey was appropriately long and dramatic (alas, short of wrist grabs and car chases). And a whole lot of other people's hours were logged into this fun book of mine.

First, thanks to Judy Hansen, the toughest and bestest of them all.

Thank you to my lovely editor, Margaret Ferguson, for her wisdom, patience, and for making me think much, much harder. And for reminding me to give Appa a dog! To Jasmine Ye for her K drama expertise and thoughtful notes. Many thanks also to Elizabeth Clark (that skirt!), Melissa Warten, Chandra Wohleber, and Andrea Nelkin.

As my dad would say, "Believe it or not . . ." I had to do a lot of rando research for this book. Many thanks to: Chris Ban for the tennis talk (RIP tennis). Toby Cheng for making Desi the most accurate car nerd. Emma Goo for all things art class. Sharon Kim for the police backup. Desi Stewart for her name and for answering questions about grandmas and food. David Zorn for schooling me on boats. Susie Ghahremani for introducing me to the nice folks at RISD—Robert Brinkerhoff, Lucy King, and Bonnie Wojcik.

Thank you to Found, Dinosaur, and the Semi-Tropic for providing me space, caffeine, and good vibes.

고맙습니다, best romance writers in the entire world: K drama writers. To the *Healer* sound track. To Healer. ♥

To my *eonnie*s: Lydia Kang for the Gchats that kept me sane and for being Dr. Lydia; Ellen Oh, for your unwavering support and for everything WNDB.

Thanks to all the wonderful and supportive early readers of this book: Natalie Afshar, Alison Cherry, Maya Elson, Cindy Hu, Nicole McInnes, Kara Thomas, and Amy Tintera. Thanks to the Lucky 13s, who were with me from the very beginning of this entire author thing. To the Bog, 🍸🗡. Thanks to Celeste Pewter and Kaila Waybright for keeping this author going.

Endless thanks to Sarah Chung (javabeans) and Jennifer Chung (girlfriday) of Dramabeans for providing the most expert K drama advice. And thank you for creating the most amazing K drama website and community.

To my LA writing women, who are more essential than caffeine: Robin Benway, Brandy Colbert, Kristen Kittscher, Amy Spalding, and Elissa Sussman. We have written so much, texted so many pet photos, and had so much wine. I ♥ you guys beyond measure, thank you. To Amy Kim Kibuishi—forever my first reader. To my author spouses, Sarah Enni and Kirsten Hubbard, for coming to LA just in time. ♥

To Oliver—you were the best writing buddy. To Poppy, who kept it weird.

To the Appelhans, Appelwats, and Peterhans for being my second family and turning this city girl into someone obsessed with trees. To all the members of the Goo-Lee-Chun and Choi-Hong-Han-Seo-Kim families, for keeping it real and Korean, always.

To Halmoni, who taught me to be an independent woman with good manners and a manicure. You are truly missed.

To my sister, Christine, for all the sister things (like meeting me for Panda Express when needed and enabling online shopping for stress relief). To my parents, for everything, but most importantly, for introducing me to K dramas those many years ago—who knew all those tedious trips to the video store would pay off? Thank you for always laughing at my running commentary.

And finally, to my husband, Chris Appelhans. For the many late-night brainstorming sessions, for insisting on a true love story, for pushing me to always be better, for believing in me the most. Thank you, Original Cute Art Boy.

GOFISH

QUESTIONS FOR THE AUTHOR

MAURENE GOO

What did you want to be when you grew up?
For the longest time I wanted to be a journalist, like my mother. She used to do live broadcasts of American current events from an audio mixer set up in her bedroom in LA, which were then aired in Korea.

When did you realize you wanted to be a writer?
I always loved reading, but didn't write my real first piece of fiction until I was in ninth grade. Our assignment was to make up our own Greek myth and I wrote one that I thought was brilliant at the time. My teacher's impressed feedback was that first high I felt from having someone read my work.

What's your most embarrassing childhood memory?
I have many, many embarrassing childhood memories. One of them was in seventh grade, I was padding my bra with random bits of stuff I found (cotton, socks, etc.) and the cotton pad wriggled out and fell out of my shirt while I was talking to some boy. I don't THINK he noticed??

What's your favorite childhood memory?
One time my family and I went camping and our tiny blue tent flew up in the air and got caught in a pine tree. The camping

trip had been pretty miserable because of the heat and mosquitos but when that happened—it was this moment of hilarity mixed with magic, and my cousins and I still talk about it to this day.

As a young person, who did you look up to most?
On the surface, my parents. I was a Goody Two-Shoes. But deep inside, I was obsessed with celebrities and wanted to be perfect and adult and cool like them.

What was your favorite thing about school?
I loved reading and arts and crafts.

What were your hobbies as a kid? What are your hobbies now?
Honestly, all I did as a kid was read books. I hated sports and spent endless hours in Stoneybrook, Connecticut, with the Baby-Sitters Club.

Did you play sports as a kid?
Not really—I took tennis and swimming lessons but nothing ever stuck. I hated being bad at things. And I was bad at sports.

What was your first job, and what was your worst job?
My first real job was out of college, working as a sales person at the Gap. My worst job was this temp position I had one day in a literal mail room. The people who worked with me were, like, dead inside, and we had to listen to a static-y radio all day long.

What book is on your nightstand now?
I have a huge pile! At the moment I'm reading *A Wrinkle in Time* by Madeleine L'Engle for the first time! Along with

Goodbye, Vitamin by Rachel Khong, and *Love, Hate, & Other Filters* by Samira Ahmed.

How did you celebrate publishing your first book?

So not glam: I was online all day thanking everyone. But I did have a really good dinner out with my husband. I remember all the food: risotto with peas, champagne, and banana pudding for dessert.

Where do you write your books?

During the day, I get all my writing done in coffee shops with friends. In the evening, I'm home in my office.

What sparked your imagination for *I Believe in a Thing Called Love*?

I've watched K dramas all my life and had always joked that I wanted to make my own one day. Back then, it was going to be satirical. But the more K dramas I watched, the more respect and genuine love I had for them. I loved the idea of translating the perfection of K drama storytelling into book form.

What challenges do you face in the writing process, and how do you overcome them?

I get easily distracted. My body knows *exactly* how many seconds I have until a deadline and makes me suffer. So, just getting in the zone and starting is the hardest part. Getting off the Internet is *very* hard for me.

What is your favorite word?

If you ask my editor, it's *toward*. Which is always used incorrectly. But my whimsical answer is *ephemeral*.

If you could live in any fictional world, what would it be?

I know a lot of people want to live in the world of Harry Potter, but Hogwarts is kind of my nightmare. Your life is *always* in danger! So, I'm going to go with the Prince Edward Island of *Anne of Green Gables*. I know it's a real place, but I want to live in *that* version of it. So darn pleasant.

Who is your favorite fictional character?

I will always love Ramona Quimby. What a truly special, real kid she was.

What was your favorite book when you were a kid? Do you have a favorite book now?

A book I read over and over again was *Little Women* by Louisa May Alcott. But I probably read every BSC book about 864,560,987 times. A book that I think of immediately as a favorite now is *Cloud Atlas* by David Mitchell. Oof, what a book.

If you could travel in time, where would you go and what would you do?

This is always hard for me because I love certain periods of American history but know that it was actually disgusting and full of pestilence and racist, violent people. . . . HOWEVER, if I could be isolated from that, I'd love to visit the Wild West or Steinbeck's California.

What's the best advice you have ever received about writing?

The first panel I ever did was with the late and wonderful Ned Vizzini. And he could sense all my insecurities as a debut author and told me afterward, "Just be yourself and honest and your readers will find you." I think about it all the time.

What advice do you wish someone had given you when you were younger?
To keep doing things even if they are hard or you're bad at it. It'll be rewarding in the end, and you're tougher than you think.

Do you ever get writer's block? What do you do to get back on track?
Sure. I am very easy on myself—I take a break for as long as I feel like (even if on deadline!) and let myself "fill the well": I watch TV, read graphic novels, go out with friends, etc. I try to fire off other parts of my brain and I can usually start writing soon after. Forcing myself to write during a block never works.

What do you want readers to remember about your books?
I want them to remember the characters warmly—that's how I felt about my favorite books when I was younger. They were like old friends.

What would you do if you ever stopped writing?
I would probably read a whole lot more and do more design work.

If you were a superhero, what would your superpower be?
Speed. I'm so impatient and wish I had more hours in my day.

Do you have any strange or funny habits? Did you when you were a kid?
I have to wash my feet every night before bed, no matter what. I also do this little morning run toward my cat's scratch post with her every morning. If I don't do it, I feel like my day is going to be unlucky. As a kid I had some compulsive habits, for example I had to count syllables on my hands when people spoke (I could only stop when the sentence was a multiple of five—your entire hand or both hands).

What do you consider to be your greatest accomplishment?
The obvious and honest answer is being a published author. I never even dreamt that this could be my job when I was a kid. The other corny answer is being a good friend. I'm a sap.

What would your readers be most surprised to learn about you?
That I could quote *The Sound of Music* in all its entirety.

When one of **Clara Shin's** trademark pranks goes too far, her father sentences her to a summer working on his food truck—and Clara isn't one for serious work. But will a budding friendship, a cute boy with a literary name, and a growing respect for her father's business change who she is entirely?

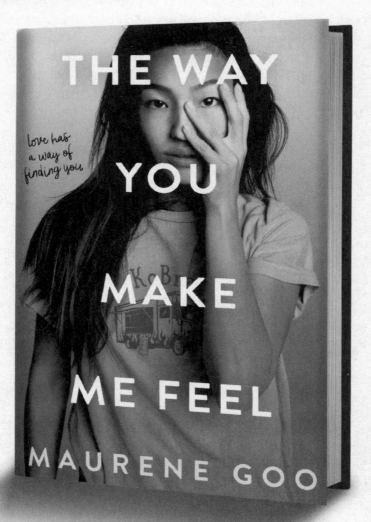

love has a way of finding you

THE WAY YOU MAKE ME FEEL

MAURENE GOO

Keep reading for an excerpt.

CHAPTER 1

THIS PAPER PLANE WAS NEAR PERFECT.

Crisp edges, a pointy nose, and just the right weight. I held it up, closing my left eye to aim it toward the stage. Rose Carver and her short-brimmed black hat were in fine form today, a perfect target, her face lit up beatifically by the stage lights. As she went on about junior prom announcements, I grew more focused.

"Clara, aim it at her face."

My eyes swept over to Patrick Keen sitting next to me. He was slouched so far down in his seat that his chin was touching his chest, his long, pale limbs folded into an impossible position.

"That's not how I roll, jerk," I said.

"Yeah, we're here for the giggles, not tears," Felix Benavides whispered from my other side. He looked at me for approval when he said it, eyebrow arched.

Sometimes these two really knew how to kill a joke. Glancing around the auditorium to make sure no teachers were watching, I lifted the plane into my line of vision . . .

"Clara Shin!"

I startled, the paper plane dropping by my feet with a clatter. The voice had come over the speakers. Why was Rose saying my name up there?

I cupped my hands around my mouth and bellowed, "WHAT?" It reverberated off the wood-paneled walls and high ceilings.

Rose rolled her eyes and exhaled into the microphone, making it squawk. "I just said you're nominated for junior prom queen." She held up a piece of paper and stared at it, in disbelief at the words she was seeing.

Patrick and Felix burst out laughing and then reached over me to high-five each other. *Oh my GOD.* "I'm going to *kill* you guys," I hissed. As people swiveled their heads to look over at me, I started to form an idea.

Rose cleared her throat into the microphone. *"Anyway,* the other nominees are—"

I stood up, making the folded upholstered seat bounce loudly as it closed. "Thanks, Rose!" I hollered. She frowned, then squinted into the audience to see what I was doing. I remained standing, then held up my arms dramatically. "And thank *you,* student body, for this honor." I projected my voice as I looked around. I saw a few teachers get up. *Need to make this quick.*

"Thank you for letting me into your hearts. And now, my promise to you: if I get voted prom queen, there will be some much-needed changes made to Elysian High . . ."

Rose's voice interrupted me from the speakers. "You don't get to *do* anything if you win prom queen. It's not like being class president!" she scoffed into the microphone. She would know; she *was* junior class president.

"Regardless!" My voice boomed. "I will promise you all one thing . . . as Queen Clara." I racked my brain for what, the improvisation making me buzz. Then, an idea struck. I motioned for Patrick to hand me my backpack. He tossed it to me, and I reached into the front zippered pocket. "I promise that us girls will not be prisoners to our bodies! We will have equal rights!" Some girls cheered in the audience.

Rose spoke again. "We *do* have equal—"

"So, in the spirit of feminism and equality—THERE WILL BE FREE TAMPONS FOR ALL!" I yelled, releasing fistfuls of my tampons into the crowd. Good thing I had just bought a new box that morning. Yellow-patterned, regular-flow—they flew into the air and landed on the heads and laps of the people in the rows around me. The laughter came in waves, and girls sprang out of their seats to pick up tampons off the floor, some chasing them as they rolled down the aisles. Boys threw them at one another. More teachers stood up to calm everyone down. Rose Carver stomped offstage in a huff.

The disruption and mayhem fed my soul, and I looked around the auditorium triumphantly.

"Aren't you glad we nominated you?" Felix asked, popping a toothpick into his mouth and grinning. Felix thought chewing on toothpicks made him look like James Dean or something.

I shrugged. "It made things interesting."

"Clara."

I looked down the row of seats toward the voice of my young white homeroom teacher, Mr. Sinclair. I threw him a wide smile. "Hey, Mr. S."

"Hey, yourself. I'm reporting you to the principal, let's go." Because these assemblies were always held during homeroom, Mr. Sinclair was left in charge of me. Lucky him.

Patrick let out a low whistle. "I'll go with you, Mr. S." He winked at him.

Young, handsome Mr. Sinclair, with the chiseled jaw and thick blond hair, rolled his eyes. "Not this time. Clara. Now." He adjusted his tortoiseshell glasses, a nerdy little signature gesture that made everyone in his classes swoon.

I grabbed my backpack and took my sweet time walking by everyone in my row to get to him. The audience was already starting to disperse when I followed Mr. Sinclair down the aisle toward the double doors.

"Nice stunt," Mr. Sinclair said as we wove through the streams of students headed out of the auditorium.

"I live to please."

He shook his head. "Aren't you sick of detention by now?"

"Nope, can't get enough."

"Why can't you channel that smart-mouth into your school-work?"

The May Los Angeles sunshine blinded me the second we stepped outside, and I pulled on my mirrored aviators. "Are you saying I'm *smart*?"

Before he could answer, someone called out my name from behind us. I turned around and made a face. It was Rose Carver.

Tall, graceful, and precise in her movements, Rose walked briskly over to me. Her skinny jeans fit her dancer's legs like a glove, her floral-print blouse was tucked in, and the pixie cut under her hat showed off her delicate features. Rose looked like a long-lost Obama daughter.

When she reached me, I was annoyed that I had to look up at her. "What?" I asked.

Her expression was focused and determined. I could feel the bossiness rolling off her in waves.

I *hated* Rose Carver.

She jabbed a finger into my shoulder. "You need to shut this down."

"Shut *what* down?"

"This whole prom-queen thing. You had your fun. Tampons, *hardy har har*," she said, throwing her head back. Then she focused her laserlike eyes on me again. "Now, drop out of the running and let someone who *actually* cares have a chance to win."

Her condescension was like manna from the gods. I squinted up at her. "You mean, someone like *you*?"

She rolled her eyes. "Yeah, or anyone else, really."

"You're so selfless, always thinking about the greater good," I said with a smile.

Her eyes closed briefly, as if she was harnessing all that impeccable self-control exercised by high-achieving ballerinas everywhere. "I didn't spend *months* as the head of the prom committee only to have you make a joke out of the whole thing." The thought of spending months caring about prom was suffocating.

I stood on my tippy-toes to try and be at eye level with her. "I'm not going to apologize for you wasting your social life on *prom*." Her eyes flashed and I continued, "You know, I was considering dropping out. But you just made me change my mind."

"Clara, Rose. That's enough," Mr. Sinclair said. "Let's go."

I patted Rose's arm before walking away. "See you at prom, Rose."

From behind me, I heard her shout, "You're *such* a child!"

I continued down the familiar path toward the principal's office.

CHAPTER 2

THERE WEREN'T ENOUGH HOT DOGS AND FLAMIN' HOT Cheetos in the world to satiate Patrick and Felix. After my inevitable detention that afternoon, I met up with them at one of the thousands of 7-Elevens in Los Angeles, this one on Echo Park's main drag—Sunset Boulevard, a few blocks away from Elysian High.

Despite what it means to popular culture, Sunset Boulevard isn't a glamorous street littered with movie stars driving around in convertibles or something. For one thing, Sunset runs here all the way from the beach. It's like twenty-two miles long. It starts at the Pacific Coast Highway, passes by mansions near UCLA, gross clubs and comedy bars in West Hollywood, tourist traps in Hollywood, strip malls with Thai food and laundromats in East Hollywood, juice shops and overpriced boho boutiques in Silver Lake, and then lands here in Echo Park, another quickly gentrifying eastside neighborhood full of coffee shops and taquerias.

When I got to the 7-Eleven, the AC hit me with an icy blast as I stepped inside, the electronic bell chiming. Patrick and Felix were picking out change from their wallets to pay for their hot dogs, and Felix's girlfriend, Cynthia Vartanyan, was there, too. She sat in front of the magazine rack, her skinny, crossed legs encased in sheer black tights, her long, thick black hair tucked into a knit beanie, her fingers flipping through the latest issue of *Rolling Stone*. Of course. She was one of those insufferable snobs who pieced together a personality with obscure music facts.

We didn't get along. One, because Felix was my ex-boyfriend from freshman year, and she couldn't hang with that no matter how many years it had been. Two, my favorite thing to do around her was ask if she'd ever heard of *X* band—a band that was always on the radio. The self-control needed on her end not to go off on some pretentious rant about mainstream music was amazing.

"Hey, kids." I dropped my backpack down next to Cynthia, and she looked up at me with a small, tight smile.

"Please keep your belongings on your person!" barked Warren, the gawky and perpetually greasy-haired clerk.

I opened a bag of Cool Ranch Doritos and popped one in my mouth. "Only if you ask nicely, babe." He flushed but let it go. Warren secretly loved having us hang out here. Once, we ran off a potential robber by throwing candy bars at him and screaming until the guy dropped his switchblade and bolted. There was an unspoken rule from that day on that we were allowed to loiter for as long as we wanted. And that's literally all we did. Hang out at 7-Eleven. My adolescence would end up being represented by a variety of Frito-Lay products.

"What's up, future prom queen?" Patrick asked before taking a huge bite out of his hot dog. Patrick probably ate more calories in a day than Michael Phelps, but he still looked like a Goth scarecrow.

I tossed a chip at his head. "Thanks for *that*."

Felix grinned, his teeth straight, white, and slightly vampiric. "It was a last-minute stroke of genius." Like me, Felix lived for pranks and disruption. Compact and graceful, he was basically a male, Mexican American me, but with much better personal grooming habits. And that's what ultimately killed our relationship—turns out when both people in a couple are stubborn and easily bored, things get tiresome, fast.

And if there was one thing that bonded the three of us, it was the ease of our friendship. There was never any drama or conflict. We existed in a carefully balanced ecosystem of chill—while making sure we kept things interesting, always.

And normally something like running for prom queen would be considered too much work. I looked at Patrick and Felix, who had gotten me into this mess. "You know, this backfired on you guys. I was going to drop out, but then freaking Rose Carver confronted me after the assembly," I said, swinging myself up on the counter by the coffee machine.

"Clara!"

I blew Warren a kiss. "Just keepin' it warm." He harrumphed but continued to organize cigarettes.

Patrick frowned. "What did Overlord Carver have to say?"

"I should drop out since I don't *really* care about winning."

Felix plopped down next to Cynthia and tossed an arm across her shoulders. "Who *does*?"

Cynthia snorted as she snuggled into Felix. "Dorks."

Felix and Patrick laughed, and I let out a brief guffaw. Something about Cynthia's jokes never flew with me, but I knew if I didn't laugh I'd hear it from Felix later. He was always asking me to be *nicer* to her, as if we should naturally be friends by our gender alone. Or by the fact that we've both had his tongue down our throats.

"So, are we gonna do this? Really?" Felix asked.

I nodded. "Yup, good job, bozos. We're in this now."

"All right. I guess we've gotta up our campaign game," Patrick said, tossing the foil hot dog wrapper into the trash. "Signs, slogan, the whole eight yards."

My eyelid twitched. "Nine yards."

He shrugged. Precision was not Patrick's strong suit. He was funny, though—quick to abuse his slim body to make us laugh, and a pitch-perfect impersonator who once made me pee my pants during a school play by imitating the lead's nasal voice, which had vibrated with phlegm on every vowel. I was never bored with Patrick.